Heroes Are Hard to Find

Sebastian Beaumont was born in Scotland in 1960. He gained a degree in Visual Art and Creative Writing at Alsager College before moving to Brighton in 1987, where he now lives with his boyfriend, the actor Simon Lovat. Beaumont has worked variously as a graphic designer, photographer, care assistant and model, and is currently a fiction reviewer for *Gay Times*. His first novel, *On the Edge*, was published by Millivres Books in 1991.

Heroes Are Hard to Find

Sebastian Beaumont

Millivres Books
Brighton

First published in 1993 by Millivres Books (Publishers)
33 Bristol Gardens, Brighton BN2 5JR, East Sussex, England

Copyright (C) Sebastian Beaumont 1993
The moral rights of the author have been asserted

ISBN 1 873741 08 1

Typeset by Hailsham Typesetting Services, 4-5 Wentworth House, George Street, Hailsham, East Sussex BN27 1AD

Printed and bound in Great Britain

Distributed in the United States of America by InBook, 140 Commerce Street, East Haven, Connecticut 06512, USA

Acknowledgements
To Simon Lovat, Lynda Del Sasso, Keith Elliot, Tim Craven and Judy Upton for their help with my manuscript; to Wolfe Aylward for his friendship and for giving me the opportunity to learn about quadriplegia.

for
Rob Cochrane
and
in memory
of Hong

ONE

It was curious how, after eight years together, my feelings about Andreas' departure were so contradictory. Whilst I would never have chosen it, there's no doubt that part of me had wanted him to go to Thessalonika – to see if I would miss him, really, to see if he could settle his blighted career by moving back home to Greece, to see if he would still want me to follow him out there after six months (as we'd promised each other every day for more days than I could remember). But there was anger too, that he should have left me behind. Anger, maybe, because it was my choice to stay.

I moved into the new, rented flat single-handed. We'd previously been living down on the seafront and now it was sad to move so few blocks away from that uncluttered view. Andreas had seen the place briefly when we'd answered the advertisement, but now I stood in the living room surrounded by boxes; surrounded by the solitary prospect of unpacking all this alone.

My flat was in an old building, part of a mid-Victorian terrace, bow fronted and decorously shabby – the sort of house that people will tell you is lowering the tone of the area. There was a stretch of grass to the front, verdant and dotted with dog shit. Beyond, a Regency crescent curved in peeling splendour.

I stood there that day, March 3rd, and looked around the expansive, dilapidated living room. Ill-fitting windows and worn carpet made it feel like the venue of some bizarre beginning. I could do anything here. I could have eccentric parties, bang nails into the walls to hang my pictures; I could redecorate in whatever crazy colour-scheme I chose. Or I could leave it exactly as it was, dirty-pale, expressive.

Part of me was anticipating doing those things I never

got round to with Andreas. I could spend hours in the bath, eat fresh coriander sauce with paprika, keep absurdly irregular hours. I could gate-crash parties, dash out for a junk food blow-out, go for a late night booze-up or a heavy, all-night political debate at the Wednesday Direct Action meetings. But still, I knew his absence was going to be difficult and disorientating. It is always hard to put words under wraps – words like *we* and *our* and *us*. I had never done it before and didn't feel inclined to start learning to do it now.

I was standing in the living room holding the magazine, the one containing the advertisement that would change everything. People like to think that they are given some inkling when life is going to change, but that hardly ever happens because change grabs us unaware, by the scruff of our over-extended necks, and shakes us good and hard.

The magazine was *Gay Times*. My advert, inconspicuously placed in the Employment Wanted column, read: *Brighton. 29. Smart, numerate graduate, seeks part-time work*. It was followed by the telephone number of the new flat. The magazine had only come out that day. The phone had yet to ring.

I needed money. Friends said to me that it was stupid placing an ad in a gay magazine; that people would think I was advertising for sex. But I had a horror of being caught up in the treadmill of the ordinary. I didn't want to get an obsequious job working with people who were dead inside, largely because I wasn't confident that I wouldn't die too. Besides, I didn't want full-time work. I had my career, despite occasional financial crises.

At that time I was working as a model. I say that with some defiance, because I know what people think. They think that I must have been arrogant, that I'd reckon I was ludicrously handsome, that I'd have demanded a glamorous lifestyle, that I was shallow, or materialistic, or promiscuous, or all of these things. But I wasn't. I met some shallow types in the business, true, boys who lived for superficial sex and material trappings. But for each person like that, there is always an exception.

I have what my agent used to call a `particular kind of look' – which is to say, not to evade the issue, odd. But odd in a certain photogenic way. I have dark hair, full (thick) lips and angular cheekbones. When wearing a layer of photographic make-up, I looked plastic, false, like a perfect wax dummy. I have largish dark eyes and long, long lashes (not always an advantage for a man – I have been known to trim them). I have what might be described as a strident nose – not too long, but prominent, which results in a classical full-face shot, but an almost comic profile.

Work came and went. Sometimes I'd get a whole string of jobs, to the point of turning some down. When Andreas was here that meant eating out, going to the theatre, buying clothes, upgrading the car, subsidising him for a while – taking a holiday when it was all over. But conversely, I'd regularly go a fortnight, a month . . . six weeks without work. Then we'd rely on the money from his physiotherapy to get by for a while. We'd run up debts, too, which was our style. It was difficult not to, with the mortgage and all that boring financial stuff that you get caught up in these days. But it suited us. At least when we had money we enjoyed it.

That's why I wanted part-time work – I was in another of my occasional fallow periods and I no longer had Andreas to help me out financially. All our capital was wound up in his venture – setting up a physiotherapy clinic in Thessalonika with his business partner, Cosmas. We'd sold the flat to raise money, I'd sold my car, pumped my Visa card dry. I had the last of a series of seasonal tv ads for a building society to shoot over the summer, against which I had taken out a personal loan. Though lucrative, the ads were holding me back in the UK – I would otherwise have gone down to Greece with Andreas from the start.

Andreas' absence was a palpable thing – tangible in the form of unruffled sheets on his side of the bed, smaller piles of washing, the lack of upturned novels left half-read.

Once, whilst unpacking, I came across a faint blood stain on a sheet – the result of one of Andreas' nosebleeds – and felt overwhelmingly separate from him. I realised then that this separation, despite being unwanted by both of us, was going to be a chance, for me at least, to learn some new kind of inner strength.

Either that or I'd fall apart.

I say that with a certain insincerity. Of course, I knew I wouldn't fall apart, but there was a portion of me that saw being apart as something tragic and I wanted to live up to that image of what was happening to me.

TWO

There was one flat on each of the five floors of the house I was living in. I had the second floor. In the basement was Gary, another gay man – not that he'd introduced himself as such, but it was easy to tell. He had a familiar dress-code of wide-belted jeans, baggy sweatshirt, Doc Marten's and white socks. His slick gelled short hair was as light as his smile. We'd said hello, but no more. I think I may have seen him in the bars, but can't be sure.

That's how casual these things can be. How chancy, the way two people meet. We said hello one day when a letter arrived for him in our hall. He had a separate entrance, so I took it down to his door and we met, over tea, and talked for some time.

Gary was lonely, that much was obvious, but he wasn't looking for a lover. He said we'd have to go out for a drink sometime, and I agreed.

And then the phone rang.

It would be wrong of me to say that I only had this one reply to my advertisement. But it was the only one that mattered. There were one or two unusual sexual offers, but I wasn't interested.

It was Max who called. A friend of his had seen the ad and had passed on the magazine. I'd been ready for almost anything, but I was surprised all the same.

`How much do you know about cripples?' he'd asked.

`Why?'

`Because I'm one. I'm looking for a helper, part-time.'

And that was it.

I agreed to go over a couple of times before deciding whether to make a regular commitment – taking into account that I'd have to fit it round my modelling.

He's a thirty-seven year old quadriplegic (I wrote to Andreas), *but not completely paralysed. He does have some slight movement in his shoulders, so he can use his elbow to press buttons set into a panel by his bed. That first day was weird, I can't tell you how weird. I turned up and he said, did I want to do some work with him, and I said I'd give it a go, so he said, right, empty my urine bag. Just like that. No introductions, no chit-chat, no ruminations about life and the prospect of employment. We got on with it – and then I opened a bottle of wine, which we drank. Really good French red, served with olives.*

I was ready, as I've said, for the unusual. But this was something else – a quadriplegic hedonist.

Max and I were suited to each other. We had several things in common; a love of food, theatre and conversation – plus our sexuality. Most of his nurses and helpers were heterosexual, which meant that a side of his life was always marginalised. He could talk about it to these people, but they approached it from their own angle. No matter how acceptant they were of homosexuality, it was still different. I was the only person he could talk to about sex, and I think it helped him to do so occasionally. People so often think of disabled people as neuter.

It is difficult now to remember my exact feelings when I first saw Max because, physically, I came to see him as so ordinary, so unremarkable, that to think of him as disabled was to miss the point. But I was shocked the first time we met. I mean, really shocked to walk into his room and find him inert on that gadget-ridden bed. He was so dependent – on his nurses to get him up and feed him breakfast, to clear his bowels; dependent on the drugs that he took in profusion to keep him alive and relatively free of pain, on helpers like myself who got him out of bed from time to time; who wrote his letters and cooked his food. Even in that first moment it struck me how utterly dependent he was.

Once, I asked him what he would choose if he was given one wish – any wish. 'To be alone,' he replied without hesitation.

When he asked me on that first day to empty his urine bag and reposition his legs, I didn't know what to do. But he talked me through it; something he'd been doing for twenty years – telling new people how to empty his urine bag. He lay facing the ceiling and said: 'There's a bag dangling from the right side of the bed as you look at me. Turn on the white tap at the bottom of it and let it drain into the yellow jug . . . '

When I turned back the covers to move his legs and saw the catheter, it made me wince. A fat, pale blue rubber tube stuffed up his dick – far too large to look comfortable. (But then, he assured me, no one can feel them once they're in.) His legs were withered, with strangely compressed toe nails and odd swellings from where people had bashed, crushed or mishandled him in the past. And when I moved his knees they quivered in spasm as though I was causing him pain.

'Don't be distressed,' he told me. 'They do that. It's normal. Why don't you find a bottle of wine from the rack behind the door? I think we could both do with a drink.'

How can he be so cheerful? I sat there by the bed trying to list my own problems: you going away; settling into the new flat; worries about money. And it felt like I was some creepy privileged shit complaining about nothing. Even being a volunteer with the Helpline never made me feel like that; but then maybe that's because we have come to EXPECT our lives to be punctuated by Aids in one way or another. I sat beside the bed and fed Max some wine through a straw and felt like a fraud – feeling sorry for myself about you. (Does that sound awful? I do miss you and that IS something real and difficult. But being with Max gives it some kind of perspective. Doesn't it?)

I've got the pictures up at last. Thanks for the view of the White Tower, I've got it by the bed. Write and tell me how it goes with your first customer.

love Rick

PS *I've decided to stop missing you. It's not constructive.*

Gary and I did go for a drink, on Wednesday night, to The Dolphin, a bar down by the Palace Pier.

'A drink to the winter season,' said Gary. 'A drink to this uncrowded pub. How long will it last? Another month?'

'Less, maybe,' I said, thinking of the summer influx of

gay visitors that would start in earnest around Easter.

I saw David across the room and he stared a little too obviously at Gary, then came across. David was a friend from my first days in Brighton; someone who had recognised my homosexuality as something separate from my relationship with Andreas; as something that needed further expression through friendship.

'Hello love,' he said, kissing me briefly and looking mischievous. 'You've been quick off the mark. Your lover's only been gone four days. Hello Gary.'

Gary dipped his head by way of greeting.

'So,' I said, 'no need for introductions.'

Gary shrugged.

'I'd be careful of that one,' David whispered in my ear after he'd ordered another drink.

I elbowed him gently and he smiled. He was always reading innuendo into everything. He hadn't tired of it, although Andreas and I had never given him cause to speculate.

'But don't let me stop you from getting to know one another,' he said, moving off. 'I've got business of my own.'

He picked up his pint and wandered back to a well-built young man with a tumescent belly who was leaning against the juke box trying to look . . . what? Aggressively alienated?

'You know David?' I asked.

'No, not really,' Gary replied. 'I think he introduced me to his dick once. But that was a long time ago.'

'He has a tendency to do that,' I said.

I looked closely at Gary as he sat and fiddled with a thick gold ring. A long time ago, he'd said. I tried to guess how old he was. It was difficult because he had such smooth, taut skin, and the lines – of which there were a number – were so finely etched as to be invisible from a distance. Thirty perhaps? Or maybe older. Thirty-five? I don't even know why I was curious. But perhaps we're all curious about these things.

David was thirty-nine. I knew this because, of late, he'd

started lamenting the approach of his fortieth birthday.

'Who gives a toss?' I'd asked.

'I didn't when I was twenty-nine,' he'd told me. 'Just you wait.'

He had thick, dark hair like my own. It was thinning slightly but gracefully and made him look his age with its sparks of grey.

'David's paranoid about his age,' I said to Gary. 'It's something I can't understand. It's such a waste of time.'

'For you, perhaps,' said Gary, 'though as a model I'd have thought you'd be more prone to that anxiety than most.'

'I'll just get different work as I get older,' I said. 'And anyway, as a character model I've never been exactly mainstream. My kind of work isn't dependent on looking late-adolescent. There's only a point in worrying about things that we know we can change.'

'True,' said Gary, turning the ring on his finger. 'So,' he sighed, sipping his drink, 'how do you know David?'

'Met him on the beach. He tried to pick me up.'

'Did he succeed?'

'No.'

'Because you had a boyfriend?'

'I was with Andreas at the time. He tried to pick us both up.'

'For a threesome?'

'Uh-huh.'

'Life slips by so very fast, you've got to go for things,' said Gary. 'I admire him, really. If that's what he wants. And why shouldn't he want it? Our horizons change so fast and so completely – and age is such an unknown quantity. And love is such an uncertainty, and sex is . . . sex is sex. Sex is good wholesome fun.'

He said this with an anguish that made him shift on his seat. He pulled at his ring as he spoke, turning it on his finger once more with unconscious determination. It was chunky, with four gems set in it – a sapphire, a ruby, an emerald and a diamond. He didn't look the sort to wear fake. I'd noticed the ring when we'd first met, because it looked so out of character.

'No, that's wrong, I'm sorry,' he said. 'I hate talk about how wonderful sex always is. Sex can be good, is often good, but it can be shit-awful too. It can be absurd and pointless and divisive and unhappy.'

Later, we walked back along the seafront. It was dark and breezy and cool. The lights on the Palace Pier dazzled as usual with their superficial glitz, but further out the sea was dimly turbulent. The West Pier, crumbling slowly, seemed calm; its indistinct bulk more beautiful than its noisy counterpart behind us.

When we got back, Gary smiled.

'Care for a midnight cup of tea?'

I accepted, of course, and we descended the steep steps to the basement.

'Damp,' he said, running his finger along the wall in the hallway where the paper was beginning to sag.

'How long have you been here?' I asked.

'Since I lost my job. And don't ask about when or why,' he added quickly. 'Not yet, anyway.'

But I found out sooner than I might have imagined, an hour or so later. I recognised the bleeper at once. Of course I recognised it – how many gay men of my age wouldn't? Gary looked at me hoodedly to see if I was surprised, then took his pill-box out and swallowed his AZT with some tea.

He smiled at me gently.

'Should I have told you before?' he asked.

'It's none of my business,' I replied.

He shrugged at this, a shrug of resignation that was to become familiar.

'Are you asymptomatic, or what?' I asked, then: 'You don't have to answer that.'

'No,' he said. 'I'm not asymptomatic. I have Aids.'

He told me he'd gone down with PCP eighteen months before, and then again a year later. He'd been on aerosol Pentamidine fortnightly since, without recurrence.

'I feel well at the moment,' he told me, 'though I've lost nearly two stone.'

He'd been on AZT for over two years, but was having trouble with anaemia.

`And they're thinking of switching me to something else. There are alternatives these days, so perhaps I'll be lucky.'

THREE

'You knew, didn't you?' I said to David the next day when he phoned.

'About Gary? Yes. Why, you didn't do anything unsafe did you?'

'No.'

'Good. I'd have told you he had Aids then and there if I thought you might.'

'Don't pretend it was even a possibility,' I said.

'I trust you, Rick. Did you do anything safe with him?'

'Yes. I had a cup of tea with him. That's safe.'

'Ha ha. Come and see me in town.'

We met in Browns Bar and had muffins and espresso. David, never a man to remain silent when he had something to say, got straight to the point.

'I know you miss Andreas,' he said. 'After eight years you'll have grown together. It'll be hard without him. Expect it to be hard, especially at first.'

'I hate all this,' I told him. 'I hate the fact that I miss him. I hate the fact that I find it difficult to sleep alone in our bed. I hate the fact that when I'm alone in the flat it feels as though I'm waiting. It seems so stupid and petty and dependent. I want to get on with my life without being debilitated by someone's absence.'

'Time,' David whispered. 'That's all it takes. I know, I've had so many men leave me. At least yours is coming back.'

I took his hand and we sat for a moment in silence.

'You looked so sad last night in The Dolphin,' he said, 'I had to come over to say hello.'

'I wasn't sad.'

'You looked it. It's a right, you know. It's allowed. Do you fancy him?'

'Gary?'

'Yes.'

'No,' I said. 'I don't know. Maybe a little.'

'Be careful, that's all.'

'David,' I sighed, 'I don't know why you're so interested in the possibility of me sleeping with Gary. I've already got a lover. I have no desire to alter the situation – or the lover. You know that, and it's typical of you to goad me. Actually, I don't think he's looking for a lover. And I don't think he fancies me.'

'Easy to say, but the fact is that Andreas is away. And don't look like that, you know I'm right about this. How long has Andreas been gone – five days? How randy are you? Go on, tell me.'

'I've been wanking, don't worry.'

'And how satisfying is that?'

'It's not too bad, actually.'

'And that's after five days. Not too bad. How's it going to be after four months?'

'What are you trying to say?'

'I'm telling you to be realistic about your needs. It's a matter of survival.'

'Now you know why so many men leave you,' I said. 'No, scrub that remark, it was unforgivable.'

I unlinked our fingers and finished my espresso.

'As a matter of fact,' I said, 'I haven't even thought about the subject of fidelity. I don't want to. I still haven't properly forgiven Andreas for going. If I slept with someone, it would only be out of spite.'

'What are you talking about?' David asked. 'What do you mean, spite? You were the one who encouraged him to go in the first place.'

'No,' I said. 'Once Andreas was set on going, I was supportive. It doesn't mean I didn't try and persuade him to stay.'

'You never told me this.'

'No. I still haven't worked through what I feel about it. Haven't you ever thought that he might have set up a clinic here, in Brighton?'

'It did cross my mind. But Andreas explained that property, wages and the cost of living are much cheaper out there. The initial investment would go much further. I can understand that. Besides, it's a newer field in Greece – there are opportunities to build a practice out there that just don't exist here.'

`If I didn't have this contract with Profile Two until the end of August, I could have gone down there with him. If only he'd left it for six months . . . '

`Business opportunities don't wait,' David assured me. `Andreas would probably never get an offer like that again. Besides, six months isn't all that long in terms of the rest of your lives.'

`Don't act like it's a huge problem, then.'

`I'm only teasing, love. You know me. Andreas has always put you first, you must know that. He wouldn't have gone if he hadn't been sure that you were happy to follow him.'

`There's happy and there's happy. I still feel I'm being forced into following him down there when what I really want to do is stay here.'

It was difficult to put into words my precise feelings about Andreas. David, I knew, thought Andreas the nearest thing to perfection. For myself, I still felt a residual anger at being put in the position of giving up my career in order to follow him down to Greece if his venture was a success. I know I was cynical about modelling, but it was still my job. Perhaps I was angry with circumstances, rather than Andreas, but I did feel that he could have tried to make things work in Brighton before leaving the country so readily at Cosmas' suggestion. It was a decision that I couldn't help feeling he'd made for himself alone, rather than for us. And the fact that I had backed him to the tune of £15,000 made me feel even more rueful, given my present penury.

`So why aren't you at work?' I asked David.

`As you know, that's the beauty of being self-employed,' he said, `you can take an afternoon off to spend time with a friend. I didn't set up in business with Keith because it was the best way for a builder to make money. I did it because I wanted to manage my own time.'

He rattled a teaspoon in his empty cup.

'Oh,' he added, 'I've sent Toby and Sue round with the long ladders to clean your windows. I know they don't open from the inside.'

FOUR

The third time I went to see Max, I met his neighbour.

`Do you mind?' he said as I D-locked my rusty bike to his railing.

`Pardon?'

`Do you mind not locking your bike to my railing.'

`It's not in your way is it?' I asked.

`If one more person chains their bloody bike here . . . ' he choked, then slammed his front door.

Max's house didn't have railings, so I locked it to the disabled parking sign, causing an obstruction on the pavement.

`He's a git,' said Max. `He's called Eddie Tavistock and he hates living next door to a cripple. When I applied for a disabled parking space outside the house, they came and painted the space in the wrong place – in front of his house. He's complained several times to the council, but they won't change it. They say, quite rightly, that it's near enough. But the ambulance is too tall for him – it blocks out some of the light to his basement. Serves him right, the bad tempered shit. My helpers often lock their bikes to his railings because it's the only practical place to do so. But he comes round to complain all the same. I tell him to fuck off.'

I smiled at the thought of Max's aggression – he was so sure of himself, in spite of his physical immobility. As I smiled, the door opened and his mother glanced round the door.

`Hello Max,' she said, `everything okay?'

`Yup, thanks,' he replied.

`Need anything from the shops whilst I'm out?'

`No.'

With a nod to me she left.

I'd been surprised to find that Max was living with his mother. It was such a cliché – to still be living at home. But in reality his mother lived a completely separate life in the maisonette upstairs, keeping in touch daily by intercom. It got round the legal need for night supervision. Max's emergency buzzer was connected to the upstairs floors and his mother was paid some kind of pittance to be always available to attend him in the night – infrequent but essential cover.

One evening I took Max to the Cross-Keys, a gay bar over towards Hove. There were a couple of people there that I knew from the Helpline. I smiled and helloed from a distance. Malcolm from the Homecare Team came over and I briefly introduced him to Max. We talked for a minute or two, and I was impressed that he didn't stare, unlike most other people there.

Max looked extraordinary, I know, strapped into his wheelchair, wearing a thick leather jacket. Still, people stared more than necessary. Max, it seemed, was oblivious to this as I lifted wine to his lips; but as the weeks passed, I realised that he got more stares here than anywhere else, and I wondered why.

`It's curiosity,' he said.

`No, it's worse than that,' I reckoned. `It's the fact that you're an outsider here. Everyone has to be a norm – their norm. Look around. How many people are different here? They're all the same. Jeans, casual shirts, T-shirts, Docs. I thought that being gay meant not having to conform. It's stupid.'

`Everyone wants to belong,' Max said with a profundity that choked me for a moment as I looked at him, sitting there so cut off as-it-were.

`But here you can only belong if you look the same as everyone else, or if you're ready to at least give the impression that you're available for a fuck.'

`Sounds okay to me,' he smiled. `I wish I was available for a fuck.'

`Oh I'm sorry, Max,' I said. `I didn't mean it to sound like that.'

Despite my dislike of Max being stared at here, it was at

least somewhere to go where you could hold hands with your lover without being knifed, even if the people were a bit samey. But, of course, it wasn't the only gay bar. There were other more eclectic places. I find I have this thing about conformity. Perhaps that's my problem – conforming to the fact that I mustn't conform.

I mentioned the responses I'd got to my advertisement in *Gay Times*.

'Tell me all,' he said with a smile.

So I told him about the man who wanted to massage me. The one who wanted to cook dinner for me and for me to eat it in the nude. The one who wanted to rim me until I came . . .

'He said he'd pay me seventy quid for that one,' I said.

'You should have done it.'

'Firstly, I'm with Andreas, secondly, I should think it's impossible and thirdly, he sounded the greasy type.'

'Wonderful,' said Max. 'Perhaps I should put an advert in myself. I'm sure there must be someone, somewhere, who wants to pay to fuck a cripple.'

I laughed at this, but felt uncomfortable. Max did have a certain edge to his humour – and a kind of sad optimism that made me want to cry.

We ended up talking about the Helpline.

'I do the telephones,' I said, 'as well as a little fund-raising. I also join in at demonstrations. I love having a public shout-in at people and institutions I despise.'

'But it's not all fun, I assume.'

'No,' I shrugged. 'I didn't join for the fun. That was a pleasant surprise. I guess I joined because I was fed up with seeing the authorities doing sod-all for people with Aids. There was no point me sitting back and criticising them for not doing big things, when I wasn't prepared help with little things.'

For my thirtieth birthday on March 19th, Gary bought me a butterscotch and pecan tart to celebrate, which I shared with him in my flat. I phoned down to invite him up after the woman in the flat below me had found the tart on the doorstep.

'I'm with a friend,' he said.

'Both of you come up, then.'

They appeared; Gary laughing with pleasure at his gift.

'This is Paul,' he told me, 'my volunteer helper from the Centre.'

'We know each other,' I said. 'We're sitting in on the phones together next week. How's things?'

'Great,' said Paul. 'Gary's made life so easy for me these days. I hardly ever see him, he's so well. This is just a social visit.'

Gary smiled.

'There was a time when I thought I'd never be able to wish anyone happy birthday again. But here I am. My birthday is on June 1st, by the way. Put it in your diary. It's going to be huge.'

Again he twisted the ring on his finger. When he noticed me looking at it, he smiled and held it up.

'It's a bit conspicuous isn't it?' he said. 'But it's my protector.'

Paul touched his shoulder by way of affirmation.

'When I was first diagnosed as having PCP,' Gary told me, 'I couldn't think of the future at all. I had a friend, now sadly dead, who was into symbolism as therapy, and he encouraged me to buy this ring. It was far more expensive than I could afford, so I took out a loan – and that was the start. It was the first thing I'd done which had a future commitment attached. I wanted to live long enough to pay off the loan. Which I did, two months ago. As long as I've got the ring, I've got something to remind me of the power of hope.'

Our conversation was interrupted when the phone rang. It was Fotofit, a character model agency in London.

'Hi, Rick,' a woman said. 'This is Marti from Fotofit. You sent your card in to us last week to see if we had any room on our books. Look, I know it's short notice, but are you free this coming Tuesday? We need fifty people for a communications ad and there's a space for you if you want to do it. It's £400 for the day, plus expenses. Oh, and bring your book in for us to see.'

The call was so unexpected and so reassuring that it lifted my day. After Gary and Paul had gone, David phoned me from London.

'Look,' he said, 'I've realised it's your birthday. Sorry I forgot, but it's your fault for not reminding me. It's only just gone six, so why don't you grab a train and come up here. It's going to be pretty wild this evening. I'm staying with Ali. You remember Ali? He's got some of his extreme friends coming round tonight, so anything could happen.'

I had no recollection of an Ali, but then that's not surprising given how many people David knew; given how many people he'd introduced to me and I'd forgotten, and how many he thought he'd introduced to me when he hadn't.

'Thanks,' I told him, 'but I'm entertaining myself this evening.'

'You've hit middle-age with a bang,' he said. 'Don't go staid on me.'

'I haven't changed just because I'm thirty.'

'Don't you believe it. Being thirty does the strangest things to people. Especially when they don't expect it.'

I stayed in, cooked an elaborate meal, and slowly drank my way through a bottle of Chateau de Nages. I ate spinach and coriander soup, flageolet beans in yoghurt with paprika, sesame blinis with olive and caper paste – and fresh strawberries and cream.

My birthday meals in the past had always been great festive occasions – elaborate affairs with four or five courses, several different wines; all eaten and drunk by a select group of friends. Andreas had a real talent for that, and a way of mix-and-matching guests to perfection. I looked at my food this evening and yearned suddenly for his company.

Andreas always said that good food should be shared with others. But, apart from missing him, I felt calm sitting there by candlelight, listening to music. I'd rather have sat on my own that night than be surrounded by our regular dinner guests – people who by their presence would accentuate Andreas' absence.

After the meal I took my time over coffee, but I felt that the sacramental part of the evening had past. I had dedicated the meal to Andreas, thought of him, remembered him as best I could. But David was right in a way. I was playing the occasion down, trying to make it seem like nothing. If I wasn't going to celebrate my birthday, I could at least celebrate being taken on by a new agency.

Andreas phoned at ten.

`Hi, birthday boy,' he said.

`Hi.'

`Did you get my present?'

`No.'

`The post takes so fucking long from Greece.'

`We decided not to send presents,' I said. `We also decided not to phone each other.'

`Fuck it,' said Andreas. `Anyway it's not my phone. How are you?'

`Okay. Wondering why your usually impeccable English has degenerated into swearing.'

`I miss that so much,' he said. `I don't swear very often, but it's so difficult having to be polite to everyone all the time. I miss being able to swear.'

He took a deep breath.

`Fuck, fuck, fuck, fuck, fuck!'

`So, you phoned up just to say fuck to me?'

`And happy birthday.'

`Thanks.'

`Look, Rick, I'm drunk. It's the first time I've let my hair down since I got here. I'm round at Ria's. She sends her love, by the way, and wants you to come down soon. Oh, God, it's so good to be with someone who knows I'm gay. Oh, God! Fuck, fuck, fuck, fuck, FUCK!'

`Okay,' I laughed. `Thanks for phoning, now go away and swear at someone else. And by the way, I've got work.'

`Good work?'

`It's money, at least.'

`Shit,' he said, `I love you. This is agony and it's only been eight days.'

I went clubbing. On my own. It was something I hadn't

done for several years, not since my favourite club, Trollopes, closed down in the Eighties. I sometimes used to go and dance by myself, or with friends, when Andreas went drinking with colleagues from his practice. David and I had occasionally dressed up together, David in full drag – a habit he still succumbed to from time to time – me in something exotic and skin-tight.

Tonight I went down to a place just off the sea front. A place where they play good music; somewhere not particularly cruisy. I wanted to celebrate the fact that my aloneness was fine right now. That I felt good. I'd been a number of times with Andreas, but he had to be in a certain kind of mood to want to go clubbing. He had to be feeling reckless before even stepping onto a dance floor.

This time I danced for myself; I danced to celebrate cracking my worklessness at last – the building society ad didn't count because I'd already spent the money. Being out of work is somehow self-perpetuating, don't ask me why. But now that I'd got one job, I knew others would follow.

I saw a number of people I recognised. People I said hello to as I passed – ex-lovers of my close friends, people I'd met through my modelling, actors, businessmen, my dentist . . . That's the thing about Brighton, you can't go out for the night without your movements being noticed. I knew this evening would be remarked upon. "Only eight days and he's cruising already . . . " I knew that certain acquaintances would say this, in the shabby way that people have when their lives are so empty they have to fabricate gossip about others.

Sod it, I thought. Who cares?

I went home that night, calmly alone. I briskly walked down to the sea and listened to its soothing motion. By the pier two bedraggled men approached me, weather-cracked hands extended, a dog slinking behind, and asked for money. I gave them a fiver, shivered at the thought of their predicament, then returned, at last, to an empty, but not desolate, bed.

It's a question of will-power, I thought. David's got it wrong. I can last six months. Easy.

FIVE

29th March

Dear Rick,

Cosmas may be a good physiotherapist, he may have plenty of money, but he's got no business sense at all. We'd initially decided to open on April 1st. That's a joke! May 1st is a possibility. Just. And we had all the advertising lined up and so on. The premises are fine, as premises, or they will be – once we've knocked a few walls down.

My father is still enthusiastic, though I haven't seen him for a week or two – my mother doesn't like travelling in from Kavala and he doesn't like to come without her. Still, he's been spreading the word about me among his hospital and doctor friends.

I can't believe how rusty my Greek has become after nine years in England. I forgot the word for demolition the other day. And people joke that I speak Greek with an accent like Prince Charles. My mother is enjoying talking to me in English, and she says she still misses English breakfasts after all these years.

I told her, by the way, that you'd be coming to live with me after six months or so. Of course, she thought it a little odd. But then, friendships between men have always seemed odd to her. I'm quite convinced by the way that, at least for now, it's absolutely the WRONG thing to tell her about us. Maybe things will change, but I need their support – especially my father's connections in the medical world – and there's no way that finding out their son is homosexual would help in that respect. I know you'll say it's typical of me to be so reticent, but it's a different culture, Rick. Things can be achieved here, but only slowly, in time. I've got to build something for myself before I can thrust you onto an unsuspecting Thessalonika. I'm sounding defensive, I know, which I don't mean to be. You were such a help when I left the practice in Brighton, I'm sure you'll be just as good here.

By the way, have you seen my old employer at all? I hope he's gone bankrupt, or worse. I thought of making a wax effigy of him and fucking it with a red-hot knitting needle, but then I decided against it on the grounds that it would probably give him pleasure, the hypocrite.

If you do see him, spit in his face from me.
Andreas

PS I hate not having money. It has become so expensive here!

PPS I was reminiscing with Ria the other day. Do you remember when she came to Brighton and we went for a drunken swim in the middle of the night? You were so cute I couldn't believe it. I get sad when I'm drunk, but you get so loving. It's incredible. I miss that already.

SIX

At the beginning of April I took Max out along the seafront. We started at the marina, where the waves fluted up the breakwater under the force of a steep swell. There was a strong breeze which, for the first time that year, was fresh rather than cold. I wheeled Max down the long esplanade of Madeira Drive and on past the Palace and West Piers. We were caught in a light sunshine rich with a growing warmth. It made me want to dive into the sea and swim. But the sea was shitty brown, where in the old days it used to be - at least occasionally – quite clear.

When we reached one of the open air cafés out by Hove, we stopped for tea. Max's breath was beginning to go and I had to pump his legs vigorously from side to side to activate his lungs again – a curious ritual that looked almost barbaric to others, but which had to be done on an hourly basis to stop him from asphyxiating. If left too long, he would acquire a slightly strangled, blue-lipped look that made him seem macabrely vulnerable. He called the leg-pumping `wanking' and would often confound strangers by asking for `a quick wank please, Rick'. I gave his legs an extra shove and then looked around.

`I need a rest,' I said.

`I don't,' smirked Max. `That's one of the advantages of being wheeled everywhere.'

`I need tea,' I told him, pushing his wheelchair up to one of the tables. I left him, briefly, looking other-worldly in a peaked Andean hat and thick cashmere sweater. I brought us tea and cake and we sat, the nearby sea rushing and sucking at pebbles, giving an endless, clattering background to our talk. After a while we drifted into silence.

`Hi,' came a voice from behind me.

I turned. It was Gary, carrying a mug of tea. He sat down

beside us and squinted out to sea.

'Sunshine,' he sighed. 'Hello summertime . . . I presume you're Max. I'm Gary, Rick's downstairs neighbour. It's nice to see him working so hard.' He looked at me with a smile, then glanced around as if it was the first time he'd ever seen this place – as if he was a first-time visitor struck suddenly by déjà vu.

'This is one of those stranded moments,' he said. 'Here we are, suddenly, drinking tea in the sun and the breeze. Can't you feel the summer approaching?'

He sipped his tea. I held Max's mug whilst he drank from a straw. Gary smiled and leaned towards Max.

'How long have you been like that?' He asked.

'Quadriplegic? Twenty years,' Max said. 'I was in a car crash when I was seventeen.'

'You're the same age as me, then,' said Gary. 'Thirty-seven. When's your birthday?'

'10th of July.'

'Three days after mine. What's it like to have a broken neck?'

'Inconvenient.'

Gary laughed.

'So what's new? Life always fucks things up one way or another.'

'I think,' said Max, 'if it's a question of one way or another, I'd rather have the other.'

'Don't be so sure,' Gary said with feeling.

'Let's not start discussing who gets the better deal from life,' I suggested, 'it could get nasty.'

'So what's wrong with a bit of heavy post-modernist nihilism, Rick?' Gary asked. 'No stomach for a bit of tragedy, huh?'

'That's the problem with the young, these days,' said Max, 'they've got no sense of chaos.'

'Hear, hear,' Gary agreed.

'I don't know why I've suddenly become young,' I said.

'Young-er, then,' smiled Gary. 'You've got a late-adolescent age-fixation.'

'Oh, thanks,' I grimaced, 'I'll break out in pimples next.'

'Don't be so sensitive,' Gary told me. 'Age is only important to those who worry about it. You said so yourself. And you were feigning such indifference at the time.'

We sat for a while in silence. It was sheltered where we were, and the eddying breeze was warm enough to be soporific. I was about to start drifting off when Gary abruptly sat up.

'What a wave!'

I turned to see the last powdering of spray drifting across the end of the jetty to our left.

'It's great when that happens,' Gary said. 'It's so elemental. Want to come and look?'

'Yes,' Max nodded.

'In a minute,' I said, 'I haven't finished my tea.'

'Who says we need you?' said Gary, getting up. 'Come on, Max, I'm brilliant with a wheelchair.'

I sat and watched Gary stride off with Max. He pushed the wheelchair with reckless abandon, talking briskly whilst Max nodded in agreement. The fine salt spray that was being carried across the esplanade had settled as a mist on my glasses, which I took off now to clean. Slightly blurred, my bright surroundings seemed more than ever like a stage set, conceived for exactly this moment – to be experienced once, briefly, and then struck forever.

I was impressed by how Gary could arrive, meet Max, and suddenly be okay with him. I'm much more of a circumnavigator and find myself slipping too often into small talk. Gary was awesome, really. And his talk of nihilism was laughable. Neither Gary nor Max had any dragging weight of pessimism about them, though I could understand why they'd been so jokey about my untragic situation.

Gary and Max went right out to the end of the jetty and watched as the swell caused a jet of spray to leap in front of them, catching them once with a twisting spurt that Gary was too slow to avoid. They came back a minute or two later, dripping; laughing.

'We've made a decision,' Gary informed me. 'We're having a joint birthday party, and you're our first invitee.'

I did the phones at the Helpline that night, with Paul. He was talkative about Gary, having never said much about him before for the sake of confidentiality.

'He's so well,' he told me, 'especially in comparison to when we first met. Then, he was in hospital with PCP and he really thought it was the end. He has incredible will-power. I can't help admiring people when they drag themselves back to health like that.'

I was agreeing when the phone rang. It was the evening's first call – a heterosexual man who'd had sex with a prostitute in Mombasa eighteen months before. The condom had split. Now he had a sore throat: was it Aids? I dealt with his question point by point, then returned to our conversation.

'How long have you known Gary?' I asked.

'Eighteen months, I reckon. You?'

'A few weeks. Since I moved into my new flat.'

There was another call. Paul took it. A safer sex advice conversation ensued in which a sub-theme of guilt over infidelity became obvious. Paul talked it through.

'So,' he said as he hung up, 'how's it going with Andreas and Greece? We already miss him in the phone group.'

'He's got to get his premises sorted out before he can start business. But I have a feeling the practice will flourish.'

'You sound like you're not bothered if it doesn't.'

'Part of me hopes that it'll fail so that he can come back to Brighton.'

'It'd be great to see him back, but surely it'll be as good to go down there and set yourself up in some way. The challenge is amazing! I'd go.'

I took another call. A young man had been sacked from his job when they'd found out he'd got Aids. The landlady had seen and read the letter of dismissal. She'd emptied the contents of his room into the communal hallway and changed the lock on his door. He was phoning from a payphone on the street. He had no friends that could put him up; he was short of money; he felt sick.

As I talked to the guy, I wrote a note to Paul: "Is Piers in the building?"

He left the room to go and look. Piers was one of the resident HIV counsellors.

'This is my last 10p,' the man said.

'Give me your number and I'll phone you back,' I said.

'I can't,' he told me, 'there's someone waiting.'

'Give me the number anyway,' I said. 'I'll phone as soon as the line's clear.'

He got as far as the first three digits, then the line clicked and went dead. Piers came through – it was the Wednesday night open evening, so he was still at the Centre. I explained that I didn't know who the guy was, where he was, or how to get in touch with him.

'A hoax?' Piers suggested.

I shook my head. You can tell real panic when you hear it.

'Nothing you can do,' he said. 'Wait and see if he rings back, then find out where he is. I'll make sure I'm in the building until you knock off. Tell him I can come straight over, wherever he is.'

But the guy didn't phone. I left later, worrying, with Paul and dropped into The Dolphin for a drink. On the way we were begged at by a smiling woman. I'd seen her before and it always amazed me that she could smile so much when her life was so hard – she'd aged ten years in the two seasons I'd seen her on the streets. I gave her a pound.

'You worry too much,' Paul told me.

Perhaps he was right. Thoughts kept on flashing through my mind; images of young men with Aids dying on the street. Life was so hard sometimes and it hurt to see people who had come loose, somehow; people who had hit some impasse, were reeling, unstuck and unable to right themselves.

Max took me out for a significant meal a month or so later. I'd gone round early to start on the long, laborious process of getting him up and found that he wasn't there.

I went into his room and saw his empty bed, its bulk

commanding the middle of the room. Standing for a few moments, I surveyed the numerous paintings that hung from his walls. Strange and caustic simplicity jostled with meticulous etchings and bright designs. Even the ceiling – especially the ceiling – was hung with paintings so that Max could lie there and look up at them. The whole room seemed sinister without his presence.

There came a movement from outside the room, and Gary looked in.

`Oh, hi Rick. We're out here on the patio. Come and join us.'

I had seen the patio from the kitchen window, but now, when I stepped out onto it, I found it had been transformed. Where previously it had been merely a small concrete expanse surrounded by a wildly overgrown border, it now looked neat. The borders were dug, the patio was clear of its overgrowth of grass, and a mound of severed greenery took up the corner by the bins.

`Well,' Gary demanded, `are you surprised to see me here?'

`No,' I replied – though I was.

`How about my gardening?'

`What can I say?' I shrugged.

Gary laughed.

`Max's mother came down personally to thank me.'

`I tell you what,' said Max. `Seeing as I'm already up, and seeing as it's gone six, why don't we all go out for dinner?'

I phoned a nearby French restaurant and booked a table, then we went for a drink at The Exeter.

`Straight, unfortunately,' said Max, `but with easy access. I haven't been since the change of management at Christmas.'

Gary held the door open whilst I pulled Max in backwards over the small step. Inside it was brightly lit, with red plush and sparkling brass. There were a number of people there, all younger than us. A juke box played some kind of electro-rap.

I wheeled Max up to the bar.

`What do you want?' I asked, fishing for his wallet in the bag that dangled from the back of his chair.

'Red wine,' he replied.
'Gary?'
'Whisky.'
I ordered the drinks, but the barman – a rather glamorous-looking young man with sideburns and hair gummy with hair-product – stared at Max without hearing me.
'Excuse me,' I said. 'We'd like to buy some drinks.'
'Huh?' the man said, turning from Max. 'Right, what can I do for you?'
'For a start, you can stop staring at my friend,' I told him, 'and then you can get me a red wine, a white wine and a whisky.'
The barman hate-stared me briefly, then turned to get my order.
'You'd have thought he'd never seen a person in a wheelchair before,' I said.
'Actually,' said Max, 'I thought he might have been admiring my looks.'
'No,' Gary disagreed, turning Max's wheelchair round and moving off to find a seat. 'He was after your biker's jacket. Look at him, he's a budding SM freak if ever I saw one. One look at you and he started dreaming of being run over by your great fat tyres.'
The barman returned with the drinks and as I was paying he leaned towards me.
'D'you have to bring him in here?' he asked.
'What do you mean?'
'Look,' he whispered, 'it's a young-people place, this. And we're not equipped to deal with wheelchairs.'
'You don't need to deal with wheelchairs,' I told him. 'That's what I'm here for. I deal with the wheelchair.'
'You know what I mean,' the man said.
'Yes,' I said. 'I know exactly what you mean.'
I turned to Max and Gary.
'Hey,' I shouted across at them, 'this gentleman here wants us to leave. He says he doesn't want a cripple in his establishment.'
The man grabbed my arm.

`That's not what I said,' he hissed.

`It's what you meant though, wasn't it?'

`No, no,' he said, looking around embarrassedly. `Look, let me help you over with your drinks.'

I walked over, carrying Gary's whisky and my wine; the barman followed with Max's. I sat down, and the young man leaned over to place Max's glass in front of him.

`Sorry mate,' he said. `No offence.'

Max without a sound contracted his shoulders suddenly and managed to whip his hand up to neatly knock the glass from the barman's hand. It traversed the space between us and the bar and shattered against the foot-rail. There was a momentary silence. Nobody moved for several seconds, then Max looked up.

`I didn't tell you,' he said with absolute calm, `not only am I disabled, I also suffer from spasms.'

The barman didn't know how to take this. He bent down to clear up the glass.

`Um,' he said uncertainly from the carpet, `what brings them on?'

`Bigotry mostly,' Max told him.

Max and I laughed all the way to the restaurant. Gary wasn't so pleased.

`You've hardened his prejudices, that's all,' he told Max. `If you'd acted in a civil way, you might have shown him that you were okay. Now he'll be convinced that all disabled people are trouble.'

`I see,' I said. `This guy was prejudiced to start off with, so what are we supposed to do, shirk the issue? Sit quietly in the corner in case we offend him? Come on, Gary, his prejudice is his problem. It's good that he got it thrown back in his face.'

He walked on, wheeling Max.

`We've all got to stand up for ourselves,' I went on. `We've got to be what we are without compromise. I hate this "don't rub it in their faces and they'll leave you alone" philosophy. Too many people do that about too many things. It gets you nowhere.'

'People don't change their attitudes because people like us sit back and shut up,' said Max. 'People only change when they're forced to think.'

'Still,' Gary said. 'I think it causes unnecessary trouble.'

'No one's denying that,' I agreed, 'but the barman's attitude was unnecessary too. Remember that.'

We arrived at the restaurant twenty minutes late. There were three steep steps down into the eating area.

'Leave me here,' said Max, 'you go in and get them to let me in through the fire exit.'

The waiter looked troubled.

'You're late,' he complained. 'I'm afraid we can't let you take your table this late. You won't be finished by nine thirty, which is when our next party is due.'

I looked at my watch.

'An hour and a quarter,' I said. 'We can eat a meal in that time. Unless the service is slow.'

The waiter looked dubious.

'I've got a disabled friend waiting outside,' I said. 'Do you mean to say you're thinking of turning him away?'

'Okay, okay,' said the man. 'Come in, but please, quickly.'

'Can't,' I told him. 'You'll have to open the fire exit first...'

When we were eating, some time later, the waiters hovered anxiously, looking at their watches. They hadn't been happy when I'd rearranged my seat so that I could feed Max. It had caused some obstruction at the adjacent table, but the couple there hadn't minded – it was only the waiters that disapproved.

'Actually,' said Max, 'I don't blame them for being anxious. I was thrown out last time I came in here.'

'Why?' Gary wanted to know.

'I was kissing a friend of mine. Douglas.'

'What's so terrible about that?' Gary huffed, blowing out his cheeks in indignation.

'The kiss in question was what Douglas describes as a tongue-in-gob-job.'

'Oh, well...' said Gary.

'He's a heroin addict,' Max continued. 'A lovely man. I think he was on speed at the time.'

SEVEN

7th April

Dear Andreas,

I did the communications shoot yesterday and EARNED my money. They had me sitting around for seventeen hours for only forty minutes' filming. I had to carry a wedding cake across the set. That's all. It was incredibly impersonal – the director called me `Mr Wedding-Cake'. He sat there shouting, `would Mr Wedding-Cake please walk FASTER!' I felt like asking him to demonstrate exactly how to walk extremely fast whilst carrying a three tier wedding cake. But we have to be such sycophantic non-entities in this profession . . .

I'm glad Ria is back in Salonika. Say hello and tell her to visit me. If you can't come over, then she should try. I haven't seen her for nearly two years. (Is she still living with that fabulous woman from Sienna? You haven't said.)

Lots of things have been happening here, and nothing. It's difficult to say what I mean by that. I seem to spend a lot of time with Max and Gary (the guy in the basement I told you about) – and David, of course, who seems stuck in his perpetual-youth groove at the moment. Seducing plump fifteen-year-olds by the looks of them.

Have you thought of coming clean with Cosmas by the way? I haven't met him, but maybe HE's a closet case and is waiting for you to say something before confessing all . . . Stranger things have happened, as you know. And, anyway, if we're ever going to make a life out there then we'll have to tell people eventually. I've got another shoot lined up for Thursday of this week, courtesy of Fotofit, so you never know, I might be too famous and too busy to come to Salonika at all. (It's going to be such a wrench to leave here.)

love Rick

PS It's a BAKERY commercial and I'm the man stoking the Victorian ovens. Oh, the GLAMOUR!

EIGHT

'Of course,' said Gary, 'I can't have sex with him. That's the beauty of it, really. I don't even have to think about sex.'

We were at a drinks party at David's house. I'd invited Gary along as my *and friend*. David had camped it up and was wearing some kind of effete Regency costume, borrowed from a BBC costumier – complete with powdered wig and silver-buckled shoes. He was the only one who had dressed up. I was sitting with the two of them in the corner, discussing Max. Gary was obviously taken with him. It was strange to have witnessed what might be referred to as love at first sight – but that's what it had been that day when Max and I had bumped into Gary at the open-air café (though deep-interest at first sight may be more accurate).

'Apart from his sense of humour,' Gary went on, 'Max makes me feel that I'm not so badly off. Everyone I talk to goes tragic when they find out I've got Aids. I don't blame them – *I* go tragic when I think about it. But Max . . . look at all the things I can do that he can't. I can get out and about, I can do whatever I want by getting up and doing it. Okay, my energy levels are depleted, but I can still get around. I have that independence at least. I can cook for myself, feed myself – go to the toilet by myself.'

'You can have sex,' said David.

'Oh,' he shrugged. 'I don't know about that.'

'You don't have to stop,' David persisted.

'At the moment I feel that sex has got me into a lot of trouble,' said Gary. 'I can't break my association of sex with death. And that, I can tell you, is definitely not erotic.'

'Let me get you another drink,' I said.

The kitchen, as usual, was even more full than the rest of the house. People stood there, avoiding the music, talking.

I poured myself some wine and a whisky for Gary. As I reached for the ice, I was embraced from behind.

'Rick,' David whispered into my ear.

I doubled up as he tickled me gently. I hate being ticklish, but what can I do?

'Leave off,' I told him. 'Drunkenness is no excuse for tickling your guests.'

'We'll see about that. Do you know everyone here?' David asked.

I looked around, but didn't recognise anyone.

'Here we go then.' David took my hand.

'Okay everyone,' he said loudly, 'this is Rick. Rick this is Dee, Neil, Christian, Jonathan, Graham, Cha Cha, Calvin and Desmond.'

'Hi,' I said, waving slightly, knowing this was an unsuitable gesture but feeling at a loss for the correct way to greet eight strangers.

'Actually,' David went on, still addressing the general company, 'do you want to know something interesting?'

We all looked at him expectantly.

'I,' he said with a slight smile, 'have had sex with every single person in this room.'

There was a pause as people tried to decide whether this was funny, indiscreet, rude or just tacky. I raised my hand.

'Please sir,' I said, 'may I be excused?'

'Okay,' he conceded, 'everyone, that is, except Rick here. Not that I haven't tried.'

He put his arm round my shoulder and squeezed.

For a moment, I felt profoundly depressed. Why was it so important to David that he had slept with all these people? Why? And why was I so opposed to being his four hundredth lover, or eight hundredth, or three thousandth... Maybe it was because I suspected that numbers make us all anonymous in the end.

I turned away from David's soft embrace and went back to Gary. He was talking to a man I'd played tennis with a few times – Jerry, an actor. They looked as though they'd become closed off, so I handed Gary his whisky and, leaving them to it, wandered into the garden. David followed me out.

'Cheer up, love,' he said.

'Why do you say that?' I asked. 'I'm okay.'

David shrugged. 'I know I'm drunk,' he said, 'as you observantly pointed out in the kitchen. But whilst I'm in the mood, I might as well say it.'

'Say what?'

'You know, Rick. The night is young etcetera etcetera. You don't have to be alone if you don't want to be.' He looked at me in the gloom and twisted a silver lock of hair between his thumb and index finger. He looked suddenly stuck in a time warp, peering at me from a centuries-old gloom.

'I see,' I told him, 'you're making a pass at me.'

'Not exactly a pass,' he whispered. 'More of a verbalised wishful thinking. You know I'd always comfort you if you were lonely.'

I nodded. 'I know.'

'And not just with my body.'

'Yes, I know that too.'

He tugged my elbow and we walked over to a couple of garden chairs, deeply shadowed and sheltered by the west side of the house.

'God,' he sighed as he sank into one of the chairs. I sat beside him and we looked up at the starless sky; at the orange tinge on the billowing clouds.

'I'm so lonely,' he said with a touch of anger, a touch of panic. 'Why is that Rick? Am I really that much of a shit that people don't want me? I've given so much out, so much loving, and got so little in return.'

What could I say? I was in the smug position of having a lover, albeit absent, but nevertheless a long-term stability. I refused to become holier-than-thou about it. I also refused to assume that my monogamy was any better than David's choice for himself. Would he be happy with monogamy? Maybe. Maybe not. Would I have been happy with promiscuity? Maybe. A part of me was curious at the thought of it – curious when I thought of all those bodies I might have explored if only circumstances had been different. This thought was followed by the realisation that circumstances were different, now; that I was no longer bound by Andreas' physical presence. It was a thought tinged with deceit and underhandedness – it was scary.

I left the party alone. Gary was still talking to Jerry, so I put on my jacket and slipped out, blowing a silent kiss to David who was talking intently to a dark-haired young man. The poor boy was leaning precariously over the telephone table and looked set to have an accident – of one kind or another.

I left and walked the two blocks to the seafront. There, the breeze was stronger and the waves looked dimly blurred in the distant street-lighting. The tide was low, so the waves broke some way out and rolled in, conferring a secretive hiss as I leaned over the railing of the esplanade.

It's 2 a.m. I thought. I'm out here on the esplanade . . .

That's the way it is sometimes: you say, this is it, here I am – and it means something. Standing there, being there.

I turned and began strolling home. The long Regency façade of Brunswick Terrace to my left glowed across the wind-burnt grass of Hove Lawns. I felt the slight, pleasant disorientation of being in a familiar place at an unfamiliar time; of being mildly drunk and walking in the fresh air.

As I walked, I saw a shadowy figure by the first shelter I passed; one figure and then one more. The night cloaked the anticipation between these figures, and yet, despite the darkness, the sexual tension was obvious, in the way the figures moved; in the way they paused as I went by.

I walked past a middle-aged man in a dark leather jacket, who looked meaningfully at me, but whom I ignored. I then passed a younger man wearing what looked like a rugby shirt. David had told me about this late-night cruising, but I'd never experienced it myself. It made me smile, made me curious – made me hope that people were here for fun rather than out of desperation. At the next shelter, I took the single step up to the benches and leaned against the wall.

Once there, it was incredible how what had seemed to be darkness out on the esplanade now looked relatively well lit. I also realised that I could not be seen from the main esplanade – I could stand here and watch. I did this for a minute or so before realising that there were other men near me, within arms reach in fact, and I hadn't seen them. A shadow slipped before me, a hand grasped my crotch.

I smiled again. I couldn't help it and knew that if I could see them, these people would be set with intent faces – that almost cringing sneer of lust – and my smile would be taken as a smile of condescending hauteur. Which maybe it was, because there was something funny about all this; something absurd about the rich external overlay of silence. I was being a voyeur, I realised, and a prick-tease, which made me feel suddenly self-conscious. I turned away as fingers found my fly.

My eyes were becoming used to the dark and I saw that there were maybe six men here, none of whom had a silhouette that invited me to explore their bodies further. Here was the ultimate in dim lighting; the acme of pot-luck.

I quickly walked out onto the esplanade and bumped – literally – into a tall figure, taller than me, who staggered, stumbled and fell to the tarmac. He seemed disorientated, so I took his arm and helped him up. He smiled at my embarrassment and moved aside so that the distant lighting would reveal my face. He turned so that I could see his profile, then slumped against me.

He was younger than me, perhaps, and as thin – and maybe handsome, though it was difficult to tell. He wobbled briefly, stopped, leaned forward so that his face loomed inches from mine.

`You don't mind giving me a hand back to my apartment?' he asked, smiling in a lost sort of way.

I shrugged and helped him for a few paces.

`It's not far,' he whispered to my feet.

Not far turned out to be Brunswick Terrace, two hundred metres or so away. He was staying in a south-facing flat at the top of three laborious flights of stairs. When he unlocked his door, he gestured inside then sagged against the doorframe so that I had to squeeze past.

`Hi,' he drawled, `my name's Brian.'

The flat was pale and bare. There was a rucksack in the corner by the sofa; a magazine on the coffee table was the only sign, apart from the rucksack, that anyone was living here.

`Uh, I'm only staying a couple of days. I guess you've guessed I'm from the States.'

`Yes,' I told him with a smile, `I'd guessed.'

He walked over to me in slow-motion and took hold of each lapel of my jacket, pulling me forward, and briefly kissed me on the lips.

`So who are you?'

`Rick,' I told him, pulling away slightly.

`Okay, Rick, pleased to meet. Jesus, it's great here isn't it, by the sea . . . '

His smile seem stuck in place, as though he had difficulty stretching his lips down over his teeth.

`Jesus,' he said, `Jesus.'

I was beginning to realise that he wasn't just drunk. There was something wrong with him – something illicitly chemical wrong with him. He had a glazed look to his eyes, and a kind of tight good humour that was uncomfortable because it was so mysterious. He stood there, holding my lapels, looking into my eyes and smiling his creepy smile.

`Stay?' he suggested.

`No,' I told him, `I can't. I was just helping you back here. Now I'll go.'

`Stay for coffee at least,' he said, `and no messing. I'm a good boy. Please.'

I hesitated and looked around. He took my elbow with boyish insistence and tugged it slightly. I shrugged.

`Okay,' I replied.

He disappeared into the kitchenette. I turned and looked out over the Lawns to the sea, and the esplanade where we had just met. So this is how it's done, I thought. I could fuck him senseless, literally probably, if I wanted to. And he is handsome. He is also peculiar. But he's sexy. Yes.

The kettle boiled. I heard it boil, but I didn't hear the

sound of coffee being made – the clink of cups and so on. When Brian didn't appear, I crossed the room to see where he was. The kitchen area was little more than an alcove, and Brian stood in that small space and stared at the kettle. His smile had gone and in its place there was stark emptiness.

`It's okay,' I said, `I'll make the coffee.'

`Milk?' I asked.

No answer.

`Sugar?'

Silence.

I took the mugs into the sitting room and then went back to Brian. Taking his elbow, I lead him out into the room. He followed me without resistance.

`Look,' I said, `coffee.'

`Hey,' he said, `thanks.'

I sat and looked at him as he raised the coffee to his lips, took a great gulp (presumably burning his mouth), then replaced the mug on the table. It was an impressive display of weird behaviour. I watched his pale eyes to see if he would blink, and he did – eventually – in a fluttering movement, accompanied by a shiver.

`Gee,' he said, `I kinda freaked.'

He leaned back against the sofa and began to breath gently. I sipped at my coffee, wondering if I should say something – wondering what was appropriate to say to a spaced-out American. When I did talk, I mentioned the weather, trying unsuccessfully to be humorous and sarcastic. When he didn't reply I noticed that he'd fallen asleep. I finished my coffee without haste, smiling at the strangeness of the situation, then left.

NINE

April 25th

Dear Rick,

I know you were hostile to this suggestion when we talked about it before, but teaching conversational English really seems to be a possibility. English is the language that everyone wants to be fluent in – especially in the medical profession. I'm meeting loads of people who would pay good money for private tuition. I know it doesn't sound glamorous, but it would be a start. A degree in English from a good British university is worth a hell of a lot to people who keep being ripped off by bad teachers.

Dad's going to let me have the lease on the Thessalonika apartment that he's currently letting. It should be vacant around August – so there'll be somewhere for us to live when you come down. I'll be living with Cosmas and his wife until then. Not the best arrangement, but they have a big flat and we can avoid each other when necessary.

Tell David I got his wonderful letter and will reply when I've got the time. You didn't tell me, by the way, that this Gary person has Aids. Be careful there, that's all. I don't mean from the point of view of illness and infection; I mean don't get too friendly. We both know how tragic you get when people die . . .

I'm glad you got some more modelling work at last. It's good not to have to worry about you on that score. (I do worry. I can't help remembering things like the KETTLE INCIDENT. Please don't burn the house down, electrocute yourself, get run over because you're in a dream. I keep fearing all these things. I'm sorry, but I can't help it.) Meanwhile, here in Thessalonika, everything has been slowed up by the lackadaisical builders who think that knocking down a wall or two is a mammoth operation that should take weeks, if not months. God knows when we'll be in business. At least I'm not paying Cosmas board and lodging. He, by the way, is basking in having such a cosmopolitan business partner. My years in England have given me a certain

CACHET *here which is rather sick-making, tho' useful.*

I try not to see this as an in-between time – a time of waiting. I'm trying to feel that days without you are still real and meaningful. I wish now that we had come down here together and, yes, I know we've been through all that stuff; about your contract with Profile Two. But I can still wish, can't I?

There's plainly plenty of business to be done here, and the Greeks like nothing better than expensive treatment from abroad. So we'll try to deliver.

love Andreas

PS Please write more often. It does help.

PPS Do you remember our midnight swims down by the pier? The sea here is so polluted I'm sure it would be fatal to swim in – even to have in contact with your skin, probably. I can't help reminiscing about the past now I'm here. Is that bad? Do you remember that party when David knocked himself out falling down the stairs in those six-inch stilettoes that he never got the hang of? You revived him with champagne, I think. I'll get some in for when you come down.

TEN

It made me smile that Andreas had mentioned the kettle incident. It had happened early in our relationship and I don't think he ever came to understand it.

I'd had a habit of washing the electric kettle by complete immersion in soapy water. I know it was an electrical appliance, but the wiring was simple, and I always rinsed and dried it thoroughly before using it again. It was one of those white plastic jug kettles with medium-grey trimmings. Being by the cooker it would get badly soiled with spots of oil and grease. As time passed, it became more and more difficult to get clean, so one day I decided to put it in with the handwashing when I did the laundry. I reasoned that if it fused the kettle, then that would be an excuse to buy a stainless steel one. If it didn't fuse, then we'd finally have a clean one.

Andreas never noticed, and never mentioned it, because it was one of those chores I did as a matter of routine. But one day he came into the bathroom to find the kettle immersed in the sink along with two of our wool sweaters.

He wasn't annoyed. He was astonished.

`How could you do it?' he'd asked.

`But I always clean it this way,' I told him, `always.'

On this one occasion – perhaps because I didn't dry it out properly – when I plugged it in it exploded dramatically in Andreas' face. It was an occasion of sod's law I guess, but Andreas spent days afterwards sighing in the way people do when they want to show that they still haven't forgotten. His sighs always ended in laughter though, because humour and exasperation for Andreas were inextricably linked.

It became a comic and, I hope, endearing symbol of my ineptitude when coping on my own. Not that Andreas went away very often – except once in a while to see his parents, and latterly I went with him even then – but when he did go away, he always reminded me about the kettle incident, as though I might do something else that was, for him, utterly inconceivable and, because he couldn't imagine what it might be, ultimately devastating.

The next time I went to see Max, I was tired. I hadn't slept well for a couple of nights because of nausea – the result of some kind of bug, I think, or mild food poisoning. I D-locked my bike to Eddie Tavistock's railings.

Fuck it, I thought.

Max was unbearably cheerful, lying in bed listening to opera on his CD player.

`Figs,' he said, `I had fresh figs for lunch, with honey. I haven't had figs for years. They make me puke if I'm not careful, but they're worth it.'

`How nice,' I said. `Maybe we can puke together?'

He hummed for a moment.

`And convulsions,' he said, `I've had convulsions from eating too many figs.'

It was one of those days when your mind slips, when you loose your concentration at disconcerting moments. I was getting Max out of bed (he had a sling that I put underneath him and then attached to a winch that was set in the ceiling. I could haul him up and down this way without difficulty), but that day I wasn't with it. I stood there staring out of the window, the winch switched to it's slow upward haul.

`Hey,' Max wailed after thirty seconds, `Hey! Rick!'

I was startled to turn and see that Max had been winched right up. He was dangling by the light, face pressed against the ceiling.

`Is this absolutely necessary?' he asked. `I'm not enjoying myself.'

`Oh God, I'm sorry Max,' I said, releasing the winch mechanism and gently lowering him into his wheelchair.

`You're ill,' he said. `Why don't you go home?'

`I can't. I'm looking after you this evening.'

`If you call being squashed against the ceiling being

looked after, then I'd rather be left on my own.'

'Okay,' I said, 'point taken.'

'Cheer up,' he told me.

'If someone says that to me once more,' I said, 'I'm going to kick something.'

The evening didn't improve for me. We went out for a drink, but wine only made me feel worse. When we got back, Max persuaded me to take one of his sleeping tablets.

'Have it later,' he said. 'You need a good night's sleep.'

I took it with water in the kitchen. When I left, I discovered that Eddie Tavistock had used his own chain to lock my bike to his railings. There was no way I could release it. I looked at the dark, flaking paint, the rusting wheels, the worn tyres. It didn't seem worth saving, but I went to Eddie's door anyway.

'No,' he said when I asked to remove the bike. 'Serves you bloody well right. If you leave your bike there after you've been warned, then you'll get what you deserve.'

Mrs Tavistock edged back the curtain in the bay window to have a look at what was going on. I smiled and waved.

'Keep it,' I said, 'why don't you? Have it as a gift from me.'

I turned from his door, walked round to the stranded bicycle and kicked it as hard as I could. The back wheel buckled slightly as I trod on the spokes.

'Two can play at this,' I said. 'You'll never get that D-lock off.'

But walking home was more difficult than I'd thought. Max had warned me that the tablets were real zonkers and I soon realised what he meant. My co-ordination began to go. Although I didn't feel disorientated, or particularly sleepy, it was as though my mind was gradually shutting down. I remember reeling along the pavement towards the flat, feeling peculiarly lucid and peculiarly detached as my body became less and less capable of motion. I fumbled for long, panicky moments trying to get the front door open. I literally crawled up the stairs. I must have managed to get to the bedroom, because that's where I woke at five-thirty, fully dressed, cold, aching, with a pile of vomit on the carpet dangerously close to my cheek.

Avoiding the sick, I crawled into bed, pulled the covers over my head, and went back to sleep.

I woke again at nine-thirty to find Gary shaking me.

'Rick?' he was hissing, 'Rick, are you alright?'

I blearily looked up.

'What are you doing here?' I managed to whisper.

'Max phoned to make sure you were okay. He was worried because you looked so ill last night. When you didn't answer, he phoned me.'

I had no recollection of the phone ringing.

'You left your front door unlocked, so I let myself in.'

I turned over in bed and winced. My stomach cramped and my head buzzed.

'Don't get too close,' I groaned. 'I don't want to give you this bug.'

'Never mind about that,' he said. 'Get your clothes off and get back into bed. I'll clear up this lot.' He indicated the sick.

I didn't have the energy to do anything but comply whilst Gary found a bucket and a sponge. He stuck an electronic thermometer in my mouth.

'All this gadgetry of mine . . .'

After rinsing the sponge, he came back.

'Thirty-nine,' he informed me. 'You'll live. I'll get you something easy to eat for lunch, and lots of fluid. I've got some soluble paracetamol downstairs that I'm not allowed to take whilst I'm on AZT, so you can have that.'

I lay and listened, comforted by his concern.

'God, this is ridiculous,' I groaned. 'You shouldn't be looking after people.'

'Why not?' he asked. 'It makes a great change.'

I fell asleep again, waking at noon to find Gary in the room once more, carrying a tray with some creamy soup of which I only managed a few mouthfuls. I drank and drank, at his instigation, until I felt sick. But I sweated too, profusely, drenching my sheets – needing to drink more and more.

Gary changed my sheets, got David over to give me

dinner, and stepped in to look after Max in my place. My brain felt too big to fit my skull. It reverberated and began to press in on me with muffling intensity.

David gave me some herbal preparation that burned my throat and made me sweat even more.

'Chili pepper cough linctus,' he said as I gasped and reached for the water. 'Get better, Rick.'

'I'm trying,' I whispered.

The following day, along with visits from various friends and acquaintances, I received a small parcel from Andreas. It contained a candle in the shape of the god Pan – a faun with goat legs, curly hair, horns and an enormous hard-on. Unfortunately, in spite of careful packaging, the penis had broken off. It had also arrived seven weeks late. In the bottom of the box was a bright card which said HAPPY BIRTHDAY. Inside was scrawled: *hope this gets to you on time. Pretty obvious choice of gift, I know, but some clichés have a certain beauty nevertheless. Love. Andreas.*

David came round in the afternoon. When he saw the emasculated Pan, he laughed, picking up the disembodied penis.

'Not very good is it?' he said. 'Hardly big enough to be a micro-dildo. I suppose you could use it to ravish a nostril.'

'Don't talk about it,' I said. 'I can't even contemplate sex at the moment.'

'Anything I can do whilst I'm here?' he asked.

'No, Gary's done it all. You could get me some iced lemonade, maybe.'

When David came back, he looked serious.

'I'm sorry I implied those things about Gary the other day in The Dolphin,' he told me. 'He's been brilliant to you.'

I nodded and lay back, feeling suddenly exhausted by the intensity with which I hated being ill.

ELEVEN

The Den of Sickness
4th May

Dear Andreas,
　Good job you aren't here to see me languishing. I look terrible. Greasy hair, four days' stubble – THREE spots. I'm bound to get the best casting of my life tomorrow. "Oh, I'm sorry, we weren't looking for a hideous grease-ball with sweat-slicks under his arms. Actually we quite wanted a presentable thirty year old . . . "
　I'm exaggerating. I only have two spots.
　I've been in intensive care. That is to say David, and especially Gary, have been caring for me intensively. Even Max came round. It took both David and Gary to get his wheelchair up to the second floor, but it was good to see him.
　You must have opened for business by now. How's it going? I bet your sexuality will be found out as soon as you start manipulating all those beautiful young sportsmen. Your fingers are so homosexual. (Like every other part of you.)
　Say hello to your dick for me when you're next in touch. I've almost forgotten what it looks like – nothing like the wax effigy you sent to replace it, I know that. At least your dick isn't detachable. Mine's out of order at present, though whether that's good or bad news I don't know. It's the only part of me not missing you. Which makes a change.
　love Rick
　PS Max and I are going out boozing soon, if I'm up to it. I'm walking him down to The Crayford to see how it goes. I won't be driving, so who knows what might happen?

TWELVE

I woke up the next morning feeling revived, suddenly, and happy – which came as a shock, considering I'd fallen asleep the previous night feeling feverish and exhausted. I got up, cooked myself some eggs, toast and coffee; ate and drank slowly, at the window, looking out over the crescent.

Afterwards I tidied the flat, changed the bedding, watered the plants, scrubbed the kitchen floor, the oven, all the windowsills. At eleven I bathed, changed and shaved, then went to the florist on the corner to buy a bouquet of carnations and roses for Gary.

He seemed restless, somehow, as though caged. He accepted the flowers with a smile.

`Let's do something,' he said.

`Such as?'

`Something meaningful.'

`What? Something energetic? Intellectual? Arty?'

`Something political.'

`I've got some posters upstairs that I've got to put up around town,' I told him, `they're from the Brighton branch of GAF.'

`GAF?'

`Gays Against Fascism,' I told him. `It's a direct-action group that I'm a member of. We're thinking of changing the name now that more lesbians are getting involved; someone suggested GLAF but it doesn't have quite the same ring about it.'

`What are the posters advertising?'

`A demonstration against the Family Conference. It's one of those self-congratulatory fundamentalist Christian events and it's being held here the week after next.'

`And what's specifically wrong with these Christians – apart from being so extreme?'

`Oh, you know, lesbian mothers are evil, single parents

are evil, gays are evil, people with Aids have brought it on themselves and deserve everything they get.'

'Right,' said Gary, 'that's good enough for me. I'll help you put them up. When shall we do it?'

'Tonight,' I said, 'when there's no one around. After 2.30, when the last people have gone home from the clubs.'

We went out together and pasted the posters up with flour and water. For Gary, I guessed, it was a way of venting some of his anger at people who wished him harm. At 3.00 o'clock we went unobserved and easily found space to put up our fifty posters – on boarded up shop-fronts, building site perimeters, telecom connection points.

We saw last year's graffiti, faded from a summer's sun, but no less true for that: *Our Silence is Our Collusion.*

'We have all colluded at one time or another,' I said, later, as we drank tea back at his place, feeling displaced and dazed with tiredness. 'That's what helps us see what it is we are doing, and gives us strength, in the end, to fight.'

I got a casting the following afternoon, as feared. A good casting – arranged by Profile Two, my main agency – to advertise a celebrated sherry. I had my hair cut, shaved carefully, steamed five days of grime from my face, covered my two spots with spot-stick and powder, then went up to London.

'Look executive Rick,' Jane said.

'Oh, so you are still trying to get me work these days?'

'Sarcasm isn't helpful here. We haven't forgotten you. Things are quiet at the moment.'

'Quiet for me anyway,' I told her.

I had to sit on a stool for a profile shot. The stool was too tall.

'Can't you sit a bit lower?' the photographer asked me.

'Can't you lower the stool?' I replied, looking down at the complicated adjuster on the central pivot.

'I don't know how.'

'Then raise the light-screen, maybe?'

'Look,' he told me, 'I'm not the photographer. She's

gone out for a few minutes. I don't think I ought to fiddle with anything. I was told that everything was set up and I should just shoot the film.'

He looked back through the camera.

'You are too tall for this,' he conceded.

I slumped.

'Nearly,' he said.

I slumped some more.

'Great.'

He snapped a polaroid. I got up and went over to watch the image appearing.

'Great,' I said, 'so long as you want a hunchback. What are all the other people up for this casting – midgets?'

The assistant laughed.

'Don't worry,' he assured me, 'I'll explain.'

The train to Brighton was late and I went straight to Max's place from the station, angrily sighing to myself about the casting. How could anyone get a model to hunch like that? It was absurd.

When I got to Max's I noticed that my bike was still locked to Eddie Tavistock's railings. I could see that he'd been having a go at the D-lock with a hack-saw – without any luck. I laughed as I passed and trod on a few more spokes.

'Don't they realise that it costs money to go to a casting?' I complained to Max as I organised his wheelchair and outdoor clothes.

Max smiled and said nothing. I hate getting angry about these things, about the unnecessary disrespect with which models are often treated. But that's the way it is.

I chained Max to his sling and winched him up. Of all the things I ever did for him, this was the one that made him seem the most helpless; being hauled out of bed like so much meat. As the sling became taught, his fingers would flutter as though some elusive current was passing through his hands.

When he was in his chair, I wheeled him down to The Crayford, which was a notorious live-music dive in the town centre. I'd been there once or twice several years before to see some of the more outrageous new bands playing. It had a reputation as a lively but dangerous place – precisely what had attracted Max. He smiled at me as I wheeled him through the door.

'This looks more like it,' he shouted. A couple of weeks before he'd complained that most pubs were lifeless.

'What would you like to drink?' I asked.

'Whatever's the thing to drink in a place like this.'

I bought us each a bottle of Pils, without glasses, and wheeled Max over to one of the stained tables towards the back. Unclassifiable music was reverberating round us from an awesome PA; the band appearing later was *Urban Nightmare*, with *Two Lies For Tomorrow* as the support. A DJ was filling the intervening time with a blanket of noise. I liked it. Max was mesmerised. It must have been years since he'd employed a helper who was prepared to take him somewhere like this.

At the table beside us there was a group of five tattooed youngsters. Three boys and two girls. Both girls sported heavily accoutremented hair – braids, shaved sections, dyed streaks . . . the boys had mohicans. A dog lazed at their feet. They nodded hello to Max, who beamed back.

'Maybe I should get my nose pierced,' he said as I gave him a swig of his beer. 'What do you think?'

'If you want,' I replied, 'though I have a friend with a small but noticeable scar from having had a sceptic nostril. Not pleasant.'

Max gave the closest he could get to a shrug and looked around the venue. Bare floorboards were scuffed and marked, wood panelled walls were splintered here and there from various forms of abuse. It was coming on for ten-thirty and the place was getting crowded. There was a mix of students, punks, new-wave hippies and heavy metal enthusiasts.

'Eclectic or what,' Max observed. He finished his drink and looked around. 'Let's have something else to drink.'

'Such as?'

'Ask them at the next table what they're drinking, then

buy us all a round.'

'Okay.'

I leaned over to the youth sitting closest to us.

'Excuse me,' I shouted, 'my friend wants to buy you all a drink.'

The boy looked at me for a few seconds then smiled.

'Right,' he said.

'What are you drinking?'

'Sam Smith's.'

I went to the bar and ordered seven pints. As I paid, the boy and one of the girls came up.

'Give me a couple,' said the girl. 'I'll carry.'

'Your mate,' said the boy, 'is he loony or what?'

'Curious,' I replied.

'A rich bastard?'

'No, poor but slightly weird,' I said.

The boy crowed with delight.

'Great,' he laughed, 'poor but slightly weird. Describes the lot of us.'

I returned with our pints. Those on the next table raised their glasses to Max as *Two Lies For Tomorrow* came on. The band fiddled with their instruments for some time, to alternate shrieks of feedback and dead silence from the microphones; but when they eventually started playing, they were engaging. With pop keyboards and a violinist, they wailed their way through a couple of songs to general enthusiasm and widespread dancing.

'Let's get closer,' Max shouted.

It didn't seem a practical idea, but I was prepared to give it a go. Usually people are willing to give way to a wheelchair – but not here. I was jostled and once nearly fell when someone bashed against me.

We ended up on the right hand side of the small stage, people dancing around us. Max was obviously enraptured by it all until, during the third song, a heavy youth in a tattered greatcoat bashed Max's head with his elbow, then stumbled heavily against him. The wheelchair, in spite having its brakes applied, heaved over to one side, teetered briefly, then crashed to the floor.

Fortunately, Max was well strapped in and didn't fall out, but it was difficult to pull him up with so many people surrounding us. Luckily, the teenagers Max had plied with Sam Smith's were close by and, elbowing the coated youth aside, righted Max's wheelchair with ease.

The elbowed youth, furious, punched me in the back.

`Get out of the way next time,' he shouted at us.

`Get out of the way yourself,' countered Max, shaken, but if anything exhilarated by what had happened.

`Sod off,' the youth yelled.

The boy whom I'd talked to earlier took this opportunity to heave himself at the youth with the coat, shouldering him in the chest and pushing him back towards the bar. Several of The Coat's friends joined in at this point and fighting started in earnest. I tried to move Max's chair back, but I tripped when someone fell across me, and I found myself sprawling on the floor. There came a searing blow to my ear from a boot and I somehow became separated from Max. I tried to feel my way out of the mêlée, but before I'd extricated myself, the rough hands of two bouncers had grabbed me. I was dragged, struggling, across to the entrance and then dumped unceremoniously on the pavement.

I put my hand to my neck and felt the warmth of my own blood, and worse, I could hear a high pitched wail, like a distant electronic scream, in my injured ear.

Still dazed, I stood slowly and leant against the wall as Max, his eye already swelling and discoloured, emerged, wheeled by the youth for whom he'd bought a drink.

`Here mate,' he said, stopping the wheelchair beside me, `don't bring your friend here again, eh? It wouldn't be appreciated, not after what was said in there. G'd luck, right,' he murmured to Max, patting him briefly on the shoulder.

I nodded, still disorientated, as the youth disappeared back into The Crayford.

`Are you alright?' Max asked.

`Are you alright?' I countered, looking at the darkening bruise on his cheek and round his eye.

`Never better,' he smiled. `Now, let's go home and get you cleaned up.'

Back at Max's I discovered that my ear was bashed and swollen, but the blood had come from a small gash by my temple, just above the hairline. I washed the cut and put antiseptic on it, still disorientated by the wailing in my ear. Max was high from the encounter, even after I'd put him to bed and given him a sedative.

`Thanks for the evening,' he said as I prepared to leave. `I'm sorry you got hurt.'

When I got home, there was a message on my answer machine.

"Hi Rick, Jane here from Profile Two. Great news, you've got the sherry job. Friday or Saturday next week. Could you phone back as soon as possible and confirm that? Okay, well done, byeee!'

Why did they always trill like that at the end of their messages? All of them did it at Profile Two. It made me feel like a four year-old who'd won a class prize. I rang back straight away and talked to their answer machine.

`Hi, Jane. Rick. Just getting back to you about the job next week. That's great. I'll do it. What do I wear?'

THIRTEEN

The following Thursday I went down to meet Gary at the Cross-Keys. We'd decided to go on to The Arches afterwards to dance. It had a great reputation for atmosphere and music, though I'd only ever been there once. Gary was coming down to the pub from Max's, where he'd spent the day yet again.

I sat, ruminating about recent events. My ear had healed okay, though the cut on my head was crusted and caught every time I combed my hair. The tinnitus had subsided, but had yet to disappear completely.

I am ambivalent about having to wait on my own in pubs. I always feel that other people think I'm on the prowl. Sometimes it makes me feel good; sometimes – like tonight – it makes me feel uncomfortable. This evening I'd arrived ten minutes early for a nine o'clock meeting. At half past, the phone on the bar rang.

'Rick?' one of the barmen called. 'Is there a Rick here?'

'Hi,' Gary said, 'sorry about this, I've only just got back with Max. We've been out to Littlehampton today in the ambulance, discovering what a dive it is. I'm putting him to bed, then I'll be down. I might as well meet you at The Arches. Max wants to come too, but there's no way we'd get him down those spiral steps . . . '

Even worse. Turning up to a pub, waiting all evening, and then leaving alone. What a waste of time. It was too late to go back home, and too early for the club.

'Been stood up, huh?' the barman asked.

'Change of plans,' I said.

'Well,' he said with a philosophical shrug. 'It's not so bad then. Was he your boyfriend?'

'No,' I said. 'A friend.'

The barman nodded.

'I've seen you before. You come in with that man in the wheelchair.'

'Yes,' I said.

'Sometimes it's you and sometimes it's another guy – so high, light hair. Big eyes. Fancy ring.'

'That's Gary,' I said, 'the one who phoned.'

'Ah,' he smiled. 'He's okay, Gary. He laughs a lot with your friend. They make us all laugh.'

'We look after him. His name is Max. We take him out for drinks or to the theatre.'

'Good. Now, listen, let me buy you a drink.'

'No, thanks,' I told him, 'I've got to go.'

'No,' he smiled, 'you don't have to go. You were waiting here for a friend to come and have a drink, so there's nothing else you have to do.'

'Okay,' I said, shrugging slightly.

The man nodded, turned to serve another customer; poured me a glass of wine.

'White wine,' he said, 'as usual.'

I raised the glass to him.

'Good,' he said, 'cheers . . . ?'

'Rick.'

'Oliver.'

We shook hands formally over the bar. I felt ridiculous. I also couldn't think of anything to say. I couldn't use my small-talk opener and ask him what he did for a living . . .

'Your ear,' he said, reaching out and touching it, 'what happened?'

'A bar brawl,' I replied. 'It's not something I do regularly. I was with Max down at the Crayford.'

'Well,' he said, 'if you go there . . . '

'You're always here when I come in with Max,' I said. 'Do you work here every day?'

'Six days a week,' he said, 'it's very boring.'

We talked for a while about Brighton, but by now the bar was getting crowded. Oliver turned away every few moments to serve. I watched as he did so; as he joked with his customers, with the other two barstaff; as he turned back to smile at me. His eyes were slightly slanting, giving his face a streamlined look. His casually elongated face looked relaxed. When he came back to me, he placed his hands wide apart, palms down on the bar.

'Mr Rick. Another drink?'

'Okay,' I said.

He tilted his head to one side as he nodded.

'Good.'

'That man,' I said, 'beside the cigarette machine . . . '

'Yes?' Oliver glanced across.

'Do you know him?'

'No, why?'

'He seems interested in you.'

'Oh well, he made a pass at me when he bought his drink.'

'And that happens a lot?'

'Sometimes,' Oliver confided, leaning close and smiling, 'I'm the one that makes the pass.'

'Ah.'

'Mmm,' he nodded and smiled again.

I glanced at the man by the cigarette machine. He looked at me for a moment then left, leaving a half drunk pint on the top of the machine.

'So, what are you doing tonight, then?' Oliver asked me.

'Actually,' I said, 'I'm meeting Gary down at The Arches.'

'Coincidences,' he smiled, 'aren't they strange . . . I'm going there too. We can walk down together.'

At eleven, Oliver went round gathering the glasses and stacking them on the bar. After he'd done this, he crossed to talk to one of his colleagues. They spoke for a short while, glancing at me once or twice, then Oliver came over.

'That's Bob, my boss,' he said. 'He's letting me off early – seeing as I have a date.'

Well, I thought. Well . . .

We left together and Oliver put his arm through mine. We walked like that to the club. There was a queue when we got there, but rather than join the end, Oliver pulled me up to the door.

'Oliver!' the doorman yelled, embracing him,

enveloping him in his long arms. `Come on in. Who's this? Mmm-mmm.'

`Rick, meet Gus. Gus, this is Rick.'

`Hi, sweetheart,' he plucked my cheek, then pushed me through the door.

`Let me get you a drink,' Oliver said.

`You've bought me drinks all evening,' I told him. `It's my turn.'

`I didn't pay for your drinks at the Cross-Keys,' he said. `I won't pay now.'

He went to the bar.

`Angel!' the barman yelled, this time so as to be heard over the music, which reverberated through my internal organs with pronounced, though distinctly agreeable, vibration. The barman was leaning over to kiss Oliver, thrusting a can of lager into his hand.

`Two,' Oliver screamed. `Two. One for my very good friend Rick.'

`Very good friend,' the barman yelled back, `or *very* good friend?'

`I don't know yet,' he laughed, taking the second can and steering me to one side out of the crush.

`Lager,' he said. `If you want wine, you'll have to buy it yourself. It's nasty here, I must warn you.'

`Lager it is, then.'

Oliver ripped back the ring-pull and drank. As he did so, someone bumped into him.

`Ooh la la,' the young man said.

`Lulu!' Oliver shouted, falling into his arms. `Lulu, meet Rick. Rick, this is my French friend Guillaume.'

Lulu held out his hand.

`Enchanté,' he whispered so I could read his lips.

I was looking round, trying to see if Gary had arrived, but the club was so recessed and multi-levelled that I couldn't tell.

`I'm going to look for Gary,' I said. `I'll be back.'

Oliver took my face in both hands and, leaning forward, he kissed me on the lips.

`Don't be long,' he said.

I wandered round the club, trying to work out what kind of sexual agenda had been set. I realised, now, that I'd flirted with Oliver at the Cross-Keys – not just this evening, but each time I'd seen him. He was so watchable, that was the thing, and I'd never stopped myself from looking. I'd flirted, and he'd flirted back. Well, it felt okay. It felt natural. It felt close, which was something I'd missed since Andreas' departure.

Gary wasn't there, so I wandered back to Oliver. When I came up to him, he turned and took my hands.

`Dance?' he said, and began to gyrate slowly without moving his feet. I followed suit and he gently pulled me to him, so that we were swaying in a loose embrace. He rested his chin on my shoulder and sang pum pum-pum pum pum in my ear to the beat of the music. Then he bit my earlobe.

I looked out across the floor, now crowded and colourful, and saw David, leaning against the far wall, smiling broadly and watching me. He'd decided to come butch this evening and was wearing ripped jeans, a heavily studded belt plus leather cap and braces. I wondered if I should pretend I hadn't seen him, but decided it wouldn't help, so I shrugged and smiled back. Oliver noticed my shrug and turned.

`Gary?' he asked as David began to weave his way towards us.

`No,' I said. `Another friend.'

At either side of the dance floor there were tiny stages, and on each there was a go-go dancer. Oliver edged nearer to one of them and began to imitate the ducking, half-flailing movements. The dancer, noticing him, smiled and blew a kiss.

`Alright,' said David, arriving at my side, `what's going on? I saw you two.'

I looked at David. I couldn't even smile, I was so caught up in it all. Oliver beckoned me, so I pulled David over.

`Oliver, this is David.'

`Hello.'

Oliver stopped dancing.

`Beginnings,' he said. `I love beginnings.'

He began dancing again, and we both joined in, David with a half smile and a look of concentration that said: "I'm remembering every detail of this, storing it all away for future reference". I could tell and I wondered how he would be seeing it – what he would be assuming.

`More?' Oliver asked, up-ending his can to show that it was empty.

`Please.'

He meandered off, leaving me with David.

`Jesus,' said David, `this is serious. The way you followed the boy with your eyes, Rick, it's obscene.'

`Is it?'

David smiled and kissed me.

`Are you okay?' he asked.

`Yes.'

`Don't do anything you might regret.'

`What does that mean?'

`It means, if you're going to do it, do it – don't regret it.' He squeezed my hand. `I won't tell.'

`Actually,' I shouted, `Andreas and I didn't discuss this. We didn't decide that we shouldn't do it.'

`Of course you didn't discuss it. Andreas is the most devoted monogamist I've ever met. You didn't need to discuss it to know what he'd say. But that doesn't mean you are the same as he is. Do you know him, by the way?'

`Oliver? Not before this evening,' I said. `Why, do you?'

`No, not really. I've seen him serving drinks at the Cross-Keys. He's also one of the regular go-go boys here.'

`Ah,' I sighed. That explained why he knew everyone.

Oliver came back with three cans. He handed one to David, then one to me. I saw David watching him carefully, then he looked at me with an appreciative nod.

`Well done,' he shouted in my ear. `I'm pleased for you.'

`I don't know what I am,' I shouted back. `Confused, I think – and drunk.'

`What's confusing about this?' David wanted to know. `You fancy the man and he fancies you. What's confusing about that?'

'Don't be simplistic.'

'Don't be so fucking cerebral, Rick,' he yelled back, 'listen to your dick, for once. Now go and dance with him. Go on.'

'Okay. Keep an eye out for Gary, will you? I'm meeting him here.'

I crossed to Oliver again and he put his hands on my shoulders, swaying me from side to side. He began to sway with me, then executed a complicated set of arm movements which I didn't try to imitate. He laughed and put his arms up in the air. I danced round him, slowly. The swaying had made me feel disorientated and I tried to count how many drinks I'd had. I couldn't, which always means I've had too much – too much to make rational judgements anyway. Oliver went and got us a couple more cans and we continued to dance.

'You move well,' Oliver told me.

'So do you, of course,' I said.

'Why of course?'

'Because you dance here, don't you?'

'Oh, you know?'

'I've never seen you. David told me just now.'

'This week,' he said, 'I'm doing Saturday.'

Gary did turn up. I saw him talking to, then dancing with David. He didn't come over to say hello, but waved to me once. He had never met Andreas, so didn't understand what was going on here. I refused to think about it. At the end of the evening, when the lights went up, Oliver looked at me.

'Well,' he said.

'Well?'

'Well, well, well, what now?'

'Look,' I said, 'this is stupid. I feel awful. I have to tell you; I have a boyfriend.'

Oliver nodded briefly.

'Uh-huh,' he said. 'Where is he?'

'Thessalonika,' I said.

'This is a problem?'

'Probably.'

'Are you going to invite me back for coffee, then, or are you going to go home alone?'

I looked at him standing there, a slight smile; a possibility.

'Would you like to come back for coffee?' I asked.

'I'd be delighted.'

Gary was at the door as we were leaving.

'Gary,' I said, 'this is Oliver.'

'Hi,' said Oliver.

'Are you going to walk up with us?' I asked.

'Okay,' Gary replied, 'if I'm not intruding.'

'No, no,' Oliver assured him.

We set off.

'Did you have a good time?' I asked Gary.

'Mmm,' he said. 'I had a talk with David. He's all right. He's devoted to you,' he added with a smile.

At the flat I made coffee, feeling drunk. I wanted to be slick, experienced, but I wasn't and I knew it would show. I went for a piss, although I didn't need to go. I washed my dick.

Right, I decided. This is stupid. I am not an adolescent. I know what I want to do. I am going to do it.

I took the coffees upstairs, put them down on the mantelpiece, walked over to Oliver who was standing in the window, put my arms round his waist from behind and leaned my cheek against his neck. He leaned back against me, reached behind with his arms and pulled my head forward slightly.

'Hi,' he said.

'Hi.'

I noticed that he had a mole at the back of his neck on the raised part where the central tendon stretches. I placed the tip of my tongue there for a moment, then pulled away slightly to look at his hair; dark but with an astonishing variation of shade from mid-brown to black. Just the arch of his cranium turned me on, and the way it fitted neatly into the curve of my palm.

So this was it. All this talk of the cheapness of infidelity –

even the word infidelity itself, with its judgmental overtones. All the talk of seediness. The crude jokes at parties. All that I had observed of others as they took lovers – the superficial way it would later be discussed. A good fuck. A big dick . . . People don't talk about what they really feel. Maybe our memories are too short. Maybe we have never learned a language to express our sexual feelings. All I was aware of was a vast momentum, an energy that eclipsed all discretion.

Oliver was not perfect, physically, but his imperfections were startlingly beautiful – the prominence of his collarbone; the fleshless earlobes; the eager protrusion of his upper lip. I couldn't stop touching him, experiencing him. I had suspended all rationale for the sake of physical pleasure, and it's intensity was a reward in itself. The time of sharing; those moments of orgasm; the hours that elapse between meeting, sensing a possibility and then discovering the reality of the possibility – it defies all prurient labelling.

So, was Oliver a good lay? Was I a good lay? How many times did we do it? I knew I would be asked these questions by David. I knew I would answer him with a shrug. I would say: I didn't measure it, David. I didn't count.

FOURTEEN

In spite of a nagging, unexamined feeling of guilt, it felt good to wake up with someone beside me; it felt good to wake up and make love, to get up and eat breakfast with a man whose body I had searched, echoed, opened, and tasted.

Oliver had been peculiarly recessive, physically. At first I'd taken it as shyness, but I gradually realised that he was simply lying there waiting for his body to be appreciated. To have his body made love to. I could do this as far as it went, but I am not without feelings of my own and I wanted some kind of reciprocation. He sensed this, I think, and panicked at the thought of rejection. Oliver wanted adoration, but would grovel before being subjected to rejection. It was naive of him, I thought, and insecure, and caused me to feel paternal – ridiculously, as he was twenty-six, a mere four years my junior.

But there was something breathtaking about him. I don't mean his beauty – though he was beautiful – I mean the significant points, for me at least, of his physical geography. He had a prominent vein on the inside of his forearms which, on close examination, pulsed visibly beneath a discreet nap of hairs. His earlobes were thin and pierced; once in the left lobe and six times in the right, though he wore no earrings; they were fine punctures that made his skin look embellished – ritualised. He had a freckle at the point on his nostril where the flesh went pale when he flared it, causing it to appear and disappear at will. His nipples protruded, permanently erect, ready for the attention of nipping teeth. I could see that they too had been pierced in the past – in some previous incarnation, perhaps, when he had wanted a different kind of attention from his lovers.

We smiled a great deal that morning, as we made an

effort to be polite, to forget our hangovers. We ended up at the seafront café sitting in the cool air.

'Let me ask you something,' Oliver said. 'I want to ask how come you're so honest.'

I laughed.

'Considering I've just cheated on my boyfriend,' I replied, 'the last thing I feel is honest.'

'That's not the point,' he said. 'I should tell you that you're the only person who has ever told me that they have a boyfriend *before* getting into bed with me. You know, that's attractive, honesty like that. Also, you didn't say any of those things that people say to me. You know, "I love you, I love you" and all that. And "you're the most beautiful creature I have ever seen". I hate that. I hate it. It's so unnecessary. They don't say it to me, anyway, but to themselves, so that afterwards – when I am safely out of the way – they can say "I slept with someone unimaginably beautiful".'

'You are good looking,' I said. 'I'm not surprised if people go on about it.'

'No, you've missed the point. People get love and sex mixed up. They make generalisations during a particular moment of infatuation. It's no surprise that disappointment always follows.'

'That's cynical,' I said.

'I see things in that kind of way right now. Alas.' He put his hand to his forehead and struck a mock-tragic pose, then smiled.

'Are things as bad as that?'

'They were,' he said. 'But now I'd say they're looking up.'

We went to the Palace Pier and watched the waves and gulls. We ate donuts; went down to sit in the sun on the shingle of the beach. Last week had been actually hot. Now, it was too cold to sun-bathe. It was nearly June and I felt the long, dragging feeling of a summer ahead.

'Look,' he said, 'I know this is going to sound a bit forward, but I'd like to ask you to give me something.'

'What?'

`Your yin and yang ear-stud.'

This was the first time I'd been asked to part with a material possession in this way. I didn't know anyone who would have asked such a thing and, whilst it seemed presumptuous, it was also intriguing. I hesitated for a moment before deciding.

`Yes, of course you can have it. I had to buy a pair anyway, so I have a spare one at home.'

I took the stud out and passed it to him.

`Thanks,' he said, `will you put it in?'

I did so, thinking that I would never have asked a virtual stranger to give me an item of jewellery like that, despite the fact that it had cost so little. It amused me that Oliver had the nerve.

`I want something of yours as a memento,' he said. `You know, these things mean a lot – to have something material to remember important happenings. I've always been like this. It helps.'

`It's pleasant to find someone so easily pleased.'

`I have to work at three,' he said. `Am I going to see you again?'

`Um,' I said pausing to throw a pebble into the gently shushing water.

`Okay,' he said. `You know where to find me, so there's no need to answer now.'

`No, it's okay,' I said, `I can tell you now. I do want to see you again.'

`But you feel uncomfortable because of your boyfriend?'

`I'm trying not to think about it.'

`Okay,' he said, `this is difficult. But am I putting any pressure on you? Am I making any demands?'

`Not yet,' I said.

Oliver laughed. `Now who's being cynical . . . Look, kick me out; tell me to fuck off if you think I'm going too far. Agree that you'll do that, and then you'll be all right.'

`Okay.'

`Right,' he said, getting up. `I'll come round to your place. Half-eleven okay?'

I nodded and he crunched his way across the pebbles to

the esplanade, leaving me to look out to sea. The deft imprint of his buttocks in the gravel beside me felt slightly warm as I pressed my palm downwards.

I wandered home, suddenly purposeless. What had I done during all those weeks when I was alone? Why was I so totally at a loose end, so in danger of boredom? I phoned David at four and got his machine.

'Call me,' I said.

I busied myself in the kitchen making soup, a leek and cream cheese pie, feta and avocado samosas and a green bean casserole. I did what I did, I thought. That's all. I just did it. But the problem was, I did it in public. That was what might cause trouble. I knew so many people in Brighton – it was unlikely that I would have gone unseen.

I read a book for all of seven minutes; watched television for about as long. Did my tiny pile of laundry. Phoned my agent.

'Good,' Jane said. 'I'm glad you called. We've got the details through. It's tomorrow, Saturday, in Fulham. Ten-thirty call. They want to try several things, so it could be a long day. All clothes provided, but take the usual extras – I don't think they've got a make-up person. Well done, Rick. It's two hundred an hour. Phone through first thing Monday with your hours . . . '

David phoned at six-thirty.

'Come over, for God's sake,' I told him. 'I've cooked enough for six.'

'Well?' he asked when he arrived.

I took a breath.

'Yes, I'm going to see him again. Tonight, after the pub closes. Yes, I like him. No, I don't think it's serious. Is that satisfactory, or do you want to know more?'

'What's he like in bed?'

I sighed in annoyance.

'I thought that would get you,' he laughed. 'I only said it because I knew you'd expect me to say it. I'm not interested, actually.'

He leaned down and pulled a bottle of wine from the

carrier bag he'd been holding.

'That's not true,' he went on. 'But I know you're not the sort who'd discuss it.' He handed me the bottle. 'It's a Nuits St George evening, yes?'

'I'm not drinking,' I told him. 'I'm working tomorrow. I'll have a sip of yours.'

David followed me to the kitchen, sitting at the decaying yellow formica table as I stirred the casserole.

'What's it like?' he asked.

'What?'

'His dick?'

'David . . . '

David jumped up and kissed me, holding me for some time whilst he laughed.

'Rick, Rick. Why are you so serious, love? I was only joking. A bit. Sex isn't so serious. Not the sex you had, anyway.'

'Okay,' I conceded, 'maybe it isn't serious. But nor is it a joke.'

'I presume you kept it safe. Because you never know, I mean, even if he wasn't a dancer and that.' He released me and sat down again as I served the soup. 'Can I ask a question?'

'Of course.'

'If you'd wanted to have a go at sex – you know, in a casually interested way, whilst Andreas was in Thessalonika – why didn't you say so to me?'

'I couldn't have sex with you, David. It would change our friendship too much.'

'How do you know?'

'I just do.'

'I have a number of friends that I have sex with,' he told me. 'It's made our friendship better, if anything.'

'Then I'm happy for you,' I said. 'And, for what it may be worth, you might like to know that if I was single and looking for a lover, I can't think of anyone I'd rather have a relationship with.'

'That doesn't make sense. You're embarking on a relationship at the moment.'

'I don't know what I'm embarking on,' I told him. 'An affair at best. You know that. Maybe I'm having what I should have had more often when I was younger – an adolescent fling.'

'How quaint,' he said, with a hint of sarcasm. 'But don't forget the eight years you've been with Andreas. Don't let this young man jeopardise that.'

'That sounds ominous,' I said, 'coming from you.'

'I know I was flippant in the club last night, encouraging you and so on. But I only did it – have only ever done it – out of mischief, and because I know you never succumb to that sort of temptation. Now, of course, you have and things are different. Andreas is the person you should be thinking about right now. You've slept with Oliver, so don't regret it; it would be a waste of energy. But he isn't for you. Just look at his lifestyle, his personality. He's like a macho man with heels and a handbag.'

'I know,' I said. 'That's why it's okay. I know it could never work, so that stops him being a threat.'

'Be careful anyway,' David warned me. 'He may not be right for you, but he is beautiful – and that makes him dangerous.'

Talking like this made me think of Andreas.

'Actually,' I said, 'I have a sort of suspicion about Andreas.'

'Oh?'

'If suspicion is the right word.'

'Tell me.'

'I don't think I'm the first to sleep with someone else.'

'Come off it,' David snorted, 'Andreas just wouldn't. He's so sure he wants monogamy it's frightening.'

'I know. But I think he had a fling a couple of years ago when I was in Ireland doing that The Grass is Always Greener ad.'

'You're just saying that to make you feel better about Oliver.'

'No. I know it must sound like that. The thing is he was so sheepish when I came back, which I know doesn't prove anything, but I always wondered.'

'It's just your imagination,' said David.

'Maybe. But didn't you notice that Andreas had never been outspoken about monogamy until then?'

'As far as I remember, Andreas has always been outspoken about monogamy.'

'Yes,' I sighed, 'I suppose you're right.'

So much for discussing Oliver. I knew David would dismiss any speculation about Andreas having been unfaithful. It didn't fit his image of Andreas as the perfect gentleman/lover/friend. I had also known, in spite of the fact that he'd encouraged me with Oliver, that David would be concerned about any possible disruption between Andreas and me.

His perspective on relationships was so different from mine – he'd never had any kind of long-term stability with another person. He sometimes made me ache; sometimes I wanted to lean into his life and try to stop him from being lonely.

FIFTEEN

Oliver arrived at eleven thirty, carrying a bottle of wine.

`To celebrate ourselves,' he said. `Come on, get some glasses.'

`I can't drink,' I said, `I'm working tomorrow.'

`So what, so am I.' He thrust the bottle at me. `This is symbolic, don't you see. It's *important*.'

`Okay,' I said, `one glass.'

There was a time when I would have bathed, gone to bed at nine, risen early to get ready for a job. But my complexion settled down over the years and I lost the paranoia I used to have about waking with spots. All I needed was to be up early enough for the slight puffiness under my eyes to subside before I got to my shoot.

Oliver sat, or rather reclined, with his arm along the back of the sofa.

`Look,' I said, `about last night . . . '

`You regret it?'

`No,' I said, `that's not what I was going to say.'

`You want to stop seeing me?'

`I want to stop seeing you in public,' I said. `You understand why. If that's too much of a problem for you, then that's fine. I have no right to make demands.'

`You mean you want to stop seeing me at all in public, or stop being intimate in public.'

`I don't want to be seen to be intimate. That sounds calculating, I know, and it is really. But there we are.'

`Okay,' Oliver said slowly. `I can accept that.'

`We don't even know where this is going,' I said.

`So why make it dangerous?'

`Does that make me sound like an absolute shit?'

`It makes you sound honest,' he said. `I've never been someone's secret before. It sounds mysterious at least.'

He leaned back and looked up at the ceiling, his adam's

apple prominent, the sinews in his neck taut. As he stretched, the hair follicles of his upper neck became stippled, standing proud like goose-pimples. The dark bloom of his beard gave him an obsessive, shadowy look that made me tremble. He took a deep breath and let it out slowly, then raised his arm so that the fine gold band round his wrist clinked against his watch. I took his wrist in my hand and examined the plain gold.

`Yes,' he said, `it's another of my acquisitions.'

`And who does this one remind you of?'

`It's none of your business,' he said with a smile.

`It looks as if I got off lightly,' I said. `My ear studs only cost a fiver. This gold must have been expensive.'

`So?' Oliver shrugged. `It's not the financial value of these things that's significant – it's the emotional value. Anyway, the man who gave me this was rich. And on the subject of finance,' he added, `you've never told me what it is you do for a living.'

`Haven't I?' I said, knowing full well that I hadn't. I hate to mention my profession, for reasons already mentioned. I sometimes lie and say I'm a driver, or a gardener or something.

`I'm a model,' I said.

Oliver sat up.

`Is that true?'

`No,' I said, `of course it isn't. I'm a shop assistant really, at Woolworths.'

`No, be honest. Tell me.'

`I'm a model,' I told him.

`A real model? You've got a card and a book and all that?'

`Yes,' I said.

`Let me see.'

`I'd rather we left this for now,' I said. `I've got to be up at seven.'

`For a job?'

`Yes.'

`A modelling job?'

`Yes, a modelling job. And here,' I added, picking up

and passing him a spare set of keys, `the front door has a Chubb lock, so you'll need these to let yourself out in the morning.'

I could see him looking me up and down in that "wow, I hadn't realised" sort of way, and I could see a shimmer in his eyes that told me he was impressed. I have learned from experience not to start on the "actually, it's not half as glamorous as you'd think" routine. People who don't know the profession never believe you.

`Come on,' he said, `let me see your book.'

I sighed and went to the cupboard in the alcove.

`Here.' I handed it to him and he began to flick through.

`Did you do that!' he exclaimed, pointing at me as I posed beside a railway bridge to advertise an aftershave. `I've seen that one. I remember it.'

My days in this ludicrous profession are numbered, I thought. I'm no longer thrilled by this.

There was a time when it was important that people should know that I was a model; important that they should be impressed. But as time passed, I began to realise that this kind of admiration is meaningless, and anyway, people were not admiring me at all – they were admiring the photographs; the image. And that, in the end, had nothing to do with me. It had nothing to do with how I wanted to be seen. And never had this been clearer than here, with Oliver. I could see what was going on in his head – the exact thing that he had complained about at lunch. I could see him falling for that image, the lie – the "you'll never guess who I slept with last night" syndrome.

`Why didn't you tell me?' he asked when he put the folio down. `This is . . . this is fabulous. How did you do it? I've always wanted to be a model myself.'

`I got into modelling by chance,' I told him. `A friend of mine at university wanted to get into fashion photography, and I was the only person who would let him practice on them. That's how I got my first few shots together. Enough to get an agent at least. It's not so easy nowadays. I'm not the one to ask if you want to get into modelling, I'm afraid.'

`Is your friend still taking photos?'

`No,' I said. `He's dead. Suicide. That's this business for you, huh?'

`So what's your job tomorrow?'

`I'll be trying to glamorize a particular brand of sherry. Trying to make men believe that it is a gentlemanly thing to drink – that they are somehow gentlemen by implication if they drink it. Of course, I'm not a gentleman, they are not gentlemen, and the pursuit of gentlemanliness is ridiculous at best, if not utterly sick.'

`Hey,' said Oliver, `your enthusiasm is taking my breath away.'

`You're right,' I said, `I'm not enthusiastic. I think I'm trying to find fault with the whole business, to make it easier for me to give it up.'

`Give up? Why?'

`I want to go down to Greece to be with Andreas, but I'm contracted to my agency until the end of August. I'm shooting a seasonal ad for them. Winter, Spring and Harvest. The weather is so tricky that they've availability checked me for the whole of August. It means I'll have to be at their beck and call at twenty-four hours notice.'

`And you're giving up your whole career. For one person . . . '

`Let's not go into that,' I said. `Right now I want to put my book away and say hello to you.'

`Listen. Is it okay if I have a bath? I'm foul. It's been a long day and I haven't had a chance to get home.'

`I'll run one for you.'

`You don't have a washing machine do you?'

`No. But I've got a spin dryer for hand washing.'

`Right, I can get this lot cleaned then,' he said, looking down at his clothes; jeans and white sweatshirt over a mauve T-shirt. `Do you think I can get it dry by lunch tomorrow?'

`Maybe,' I said. `But borrow some of my things if you need to.'

`No, I don't want to do that.'

I smiled. He had that kind of youthful dress-sensibility

that made him unable to wear anything that wasn't exactly to his taste.

'It's incredible how little we know of each other,' I said, suddenly struck by unfamiliarity. 'You haven't even told me where you live.'

'Near St James Street. I'm not happy there. I don't want to talk about it.'

'Do you live on your own?'

'I said I don't want to talk about it.'

'Fine,' I said defensively, 'fine.'

I went to run a bath, and filled the basin with suds for Oliver's clothes. I got two glasses and took them upstairs.

'Wine,' I said. 'I'm not being very attentive. I should have done this when you came in.'

'You're great,' Oliver said, getting up and taking his wine. 'You're my saviour, Rick.'

And he kissed me with a conviction that made me feel important. I took his hands and kissed his fingers thinking how amazing his nails were, with conspicuous pale half-moon cuticles and a surface minutely ridged and squared at the ends. The skin of his fingers was ruffled at the joints like the roof of a mouth or sand after the tide has receded.

God, I thought, I'm in trouble. He's too intriguing for me to be anything but fascinated.

In the bathroom Oliver took his clothes off, dunking each garment in the suds. Sweatshirt, T-shirt – pulled in a peeling movement of deliberate slowness – jeans, socks, undershorts. I felt like an audience; an audience of one, but nevertheless someone to whom Oliver could perform. He smiled and stepped into the clear water.

'Join me,' he said.

I took my clothes off also, aware that bathing together had always been one of my special times with Andreas; aware that it was entirely different with Oliver. We embraced in the water and the eroticism was heightened by the heat; by the sleep inducing lateness. All this gathered around me as a wrap against my solitude.

I leaned forward to examine his penis. The shaft was oval in cross-section with a slightly raised central ridge on the underside. His foreskin half covered the glans when he had an erection; the loose skin receding as though an offering was being made. The head itself was a tan-mauve, darker than my own which had a strangely vulnerable hue. Together, as we lay stomach to stomach, they pressed with a significant, though uninterpretable, insistence.

`Sex,' said Oliver. `Love. Lust. When it happens it is one thing, and only later can you see what it was that you experienced. Why is that?'

`I don't know,' I told him. `I'll tell you later what I think this was.'

He laughed and leaned forward to give me his full attention, taking my penis in his mouth as though it was a part of some eccentric communion. Oliver always managed to make his actions heavy with significance. Sex was significant anyway, but with Oliver it was momentous. His incredible seriousness in this respect made me feel inclined to laugh, but I always ended up submerged in his peculiar myth-making. His orgasm tonight seemed like the eruption of some terrible inner pain – a fruitful catharsis that left him calm and slightly surprised at the physical result of his climax. It was as if his experience had been so internal that he couldn't imagine any external evidence.

In bed he asked me about Andreas. Maybe I should have been prepared for his questions, but I wasn't. They made me feel clandestine and aware of Andreas as a physical being rather than as a concept.

`How did you meet?' Oliver wanted to know.

`He treated me for an injured knee,' I told him. `I fell whilst running and damaged the coronary ligament in my right knee. I went to Andreas on the recommendation of a friend. It was fun. I had to go twice a week for eight weeks and have my knee wired up and then massaged. I couldn't hide the fact that I fancied him – I've got far too expressive a face for that. The massages got pretty erotic towards the end. It's amazing how much of a turn on strong fingers can be.'

`Mmm,' murmured Oliver. `So who propositioned whom?'

'I asked Andreas if he wanted to go for a run when my knee was better as a kind of celebration of being cured. He agreed and we ended up doing quite a lot of training together – you know, intervals along the sea front and all that. It was amazing how long it took us to get into bed. He'd had an unhappy love affair, and I was shy. But we got round to it eventually, when I pulled a muscle in my back and he gave me a massage back at my place.'

'Love always seems so coincidental,' Oliver whispered as we subsided into silence.

I lay back and thought of Andreas as Oliver's breathing became more even beside me. The facts as described concerning how we became lovers were so clinical, lifeless, that as I was telling them to Oliver, they'd seemed to apply to a different couple.

In reality Andreas and I had been smiling at each other long before I'd sensed anything sexual between us. Friendship had happened first, and though I'd thought him attractive, our friendship had been so immediate, so gratifying, that sensuality cropped up as a surprise, or an afterthought, in the end.

Sex with Andreas had always been a confirmation of friendship. I had never experienced that with anyone else – I certainly didn't feel that with Oliver, whose body electrified me but seemed unconnected to his personality. Sex with Oliver was a kind of triple experience – first there was Oliver, then there was Oliver's body, then there was Oliver again. The middle part of the experience was distinct because I couldn't help disliking the demanding quality of Oliver's self-obsession, whilst at the same time being unable to be anything but lost in an experience bordering on the priapic. It was curious and impersonal, yet as powerful as any sexual experience of my life.

SIXTEEN

May 27th

Dear Rick,

Thanks for your delightful notion that I might be manipulating the lean and healthy. Reality is dishearteningly far from the mark. Two slipped discs, a long-term ankle injury, an elbow and a braced neck. All belonging to the wealthy, weighty bourgeoisie. But why complain? Business has begun. Our doors are not exactly jammed with massive queues. Our bank balance hasn't swollen like a handsomely dislocated joint. But it has started . . .

I still hope that by August we'll be solvent enough for you to come down permanently, though it'll take time to get a clientele established. Cosmas runs hot and cold by turns on the subject of money. One day he sees himself driving a huge Mercedes within a year – the next, he's tottering on the verge of bankruptcy. I try not to think or worry. Why bother? You know how I feel about that.

Ria and her beautiful Italian femme fatale, by the way, lasted all of four months – a brief, intense consummation that could never be sustained. On our last visit we bathed in the brilliance and excess of their passion. This can't be a surprise to you, surely? Ria is philosophical – and alone. We spend a lot of time together. Cosmas probably thinks we're having an affair, though he's heard dark Sapphic rumours concerning her. Who hasn't? My friendship with her is, I hope, making some small space in his consciousness – a gap that I can try to enlarge in time until it is big enough to accommodate you.

There is a crazy porn mag here called LOOK, full of dreadful stories and very few pictures. I'd send you a copy, but you wouldn't understand the Greek. I'll translate it for you when you come down and we can laugh together. At least it's good for a few wanks. That, my dear, is how far I've fallen. *ΤΗΝ «ΕΒΡΙΣΚΕ»*

NA NTYNETIA ΓΥΝΑΙΚΑ, as it says. I'll translate that little story when I see you.

Give my love to David.

love Andreas

PS The more I talk to people, the more I realise this English teaching idea could really work. What do you think?

PPS Do you remember how we first met David on the beach? I was thinking the other day how strange life's coincidences are. How we end up doing things we never thought we would do – and living in places we thought we'd left forever.

SEVENTEEN

I read Andreas' letter on the train, surrounded by commuters. It was a luxury for me to see this daily grind and know that I was not a regular part of it. I'd forced myself out of bed at 7.00, bathed, cleansed my skin, eaten a healthy breakfast, trimmed my nails, carefully styled my hair, absorbed in a self-obsession that seemed utterly trivial. I'd arranged what I was going to wear; ironed a pleated white shirt – then changed my mind. Ironed another, darker shirt. I'd re-moisturised a patch of dry skin at one side of my mouth, cleaned and flossed my teeth, trimmed a few stray hairs by my left ear.

Curiously, when I'd come to put my ring on, I couldn't find it. It wasn't in its usual place by the bath. When I tried to remember taking it off the previous evening, I couldn't – it was so automatic that I usually did it without thinking. But it was gone. I'm a forgetful enough person to be caught out by this kind of disappearance on a regular basis, and I hate it because it is so irritating and mysterious.

Andreas had lost his ring too, a year or two before, and had gone all tragic about it as though there was some kind of omen attached to its disappearance. But nothing adverse had happened as a result, of course.

Rings, I thought, why do people find them so significant when they're just bits of metal?

It was a long day for me. Take a warm morning, a large studio with two real palm trees uprooted and brought in for the occasion, an expanse of scrunched up aluminium foil to masquerade as sea; put me in a stiff wing-collar circa 1916, tuxedo, bow tie – then bathe the whole lot in 60,000 watts of light – and you get the kind of environment that fast becomes a model's nightmare.

I was dining *á-deux* with a pale, late-Victorian blonde, on a tropical veranda, in tropical heat. The famous bottle – star of the shoot – sat on the table between us. The sherry never touched our lips – but long, iced glasses of water were needed after every shot. Because of constant sweating, my colleague had to re-apply her make-up several times. I had to use a light powder, re-applied between shots. And there were many shots. Some for home, some for abroad. We had to shoot the same scene with a British label, a European export label, a Christmas label. It took nine hours in all, which was hell, but suitably illuminated the model's dilemma. One can say to each other over the table "God this is awful. It's so hot. It's so tedious. It's so this and that." But you never say, "I wish they'd get a move on" or "I wish this was over", because every second that ticks, ticks you closer to another hour for which they have to pay you. And you need the money. Always. That's one of the great truisms of working life.

But nine hours at two hundred an hour, less twenty per cent commission for Profile Two – it didn't take much of a mathematician to work out that it wasn't bad pay for a long day's work.

I took an evening train back to Brighton and virtually passed out in my carriage. I was tired and, even after constant drinking, de-hydrated. Being in temperatures well over a hundred degrees for so long does strange things to one's body. It induces an exhaustion that feels terminal and, once outside, even if it's cool, it becomes all the more easy to sweat.

In Brighton I took a taxi to the Cross-Keys. If I had to drink, I might as well do it there.

`Two pints of lemonade and lime,' I ordered from Oliver. `And don't ask me about it. I'm shattered.'

He poured my drinks. This time the other bar staff took more interest in me, saying hi and so on. Oliver had obviously said something about me – about our relationship; my profession. I wondered how Oliver had described me. As his boyfriend? His affair? His `whilst there's no one better to fuck with' companion?

It was only much later I discovered what he had actually

been saying – that we were going to live together. That we were hitched. That we'd sworn affection – love even, though that strangely destructive four letter word hadn't yet been used between us.

If I thought I was in for an evening of quiet conversation, I was wrong. Half-an-hour after I came in, a man walked into the bar. I didn't notice him at first, but soon became aware that things had changed when I saw Oliver stiffen and the other two behind the bar glance at me. I turned.

He was maybe fifty, well dressed, wearing cufflinks and a pearl tie-pin. His receding hair was cropped short and he wore large horn-rimmed glasses. He looked like a man of authority – a man perhaps in the arts; an impresario, an entrepreneur. He hesitated, then came to the bar.

`Well?' he said to Oliver.

Oliver pretended not to hear. One of the other two, Bob, approached him as Oliver busied himself with washing glasses.

`Hi,' Bob said. `Can I help?'

`Yes,' the man said, `you can leave me alone to talk with Oliver.'

`I don't think he's got anything to say to you.'

`He damn well has,' the man said, leaning over the bar and grabbing Oliver's elbow. `What the hell do you think you're doing?' he hissed. `You haven't been home for two nights, and now you've pissed-off altogether.'

`Don't, Duncan,' Oliver whispered.

`Don't what?' he asked. `Don't come here looking for an explanation? When someone disappears, you want to know why, Oliver.'

`You know why,' he said, turning his back slightly to me, out of embarrassment I presumed.

I watched as Duncan's face, flushed and angry, became pale. I remembered saying the previous night how little I knew about Oliver . . .

`I don't know why you left, actually,' he said with a touch of belligerence. `Tell me, why don't you?'

`Not here,' said Oliver, `I'm at work.'

`Where else, then? You didn't leave a forwarding address.'

'If you don't know why I left,' Oliver said, leaning slightly closer to him and lowering his voice, 'then I feel sorry for you. You haven't exactly been Mr Philanthropy have you? You preyed on me Duncan. Okay, I was stupid to believe that you might keep your word about there being no strings, but that doesn't mean you didn't take advantage of me. You may have expected me to live at your expense and for your pleasure, but I'm afraid you got me wrong. I'm not a tart.'

'Yes you are,' he choked. 'After all I've given you . . . '

He leaned over and picked up my half finished pint of lemonade and flung it in Oliver's face. Whether or not he'd intended to let go of the glass, I don't know, but the rim caught the bridge of Oliver's nose and he staggered back a couple of steps, hit the drinks cooler, slipped, and sat down heavily on the lino floor, stunned. The glass smashed beside him. Duncan looked at his hand, briefly, shocked by what had happened. As Oliver tried to stand up he put one finger to his nose. A flush of blood streamed from his nostrils and mingled with the lemonade that was running down his face.

'What have you ever, ever given me?' he gasped, 'except a few sodding quid now and again.'

'I gave more money than that,' Duncan told him, unrepentant. 'And I gave you that watch. Or rather, you stole it.'

Bob lifted the hinged edge of the bar and, walking round, took Duncan's elbow.

'Out,' he said firmly. 'Now.'

Hans, the second barman, followed, obviously prepared for a scuffle. But Duncan shrugged Bob off and walked to the door. As he reached for the handle, the watch that Oliver had been wearing smashed against the doorframe. Duncan stared at it for a moment, leaned down and picked it up then, putting it in his pocket, left. I turned to Oliver.

He stood, hands on the bar, head bowed, shaking.

'It's okay,' Hans said, putting his arm around Oliver. The bar was full and we were conspicuously centre-stage.

'You'd better go,' Bob told him. 'Go home and clean

yourself up. We'll be okay.'

Oliver nodded, wiping his face with a dish cloth. We left together. It didn't seem the right moment to ask for an explanation.

Fortunately, I had some cotton wool in my extras bag and he held this to his nose to absorb the blood that came now in a slow but steady trickle from each nostril. The sweatshirt that we'd washed the previous evening was blood-spattered. His nose was swelling. The slight prominence at the bridge of his nose had enlarged, making him look like a boxer.

Oliver didn't say a word all the way home. I unlocked the outside door and we went up to the flat. In the sitting room were all Oliver's belongings. Not a great deal – two shabby suitcases and a cardboard box against the wall. Oliver looked at them, then at me. He stared at the blood on his sweatshirt then dropped the sodden cotton wool onto the mantlepiece. He pulled the sweatshirt off, followed by his T-shirt, shoes, socks, trousers . . . he kept on until he was completely naked. It didn't make me feel sexual – it made me feel sorry for him. He flung back his head and looked at the ceiling and began to sob, quietly at first, but then so violently that he curled up on himself, crouching as he shook.

I crouched beside him and took him in my arms and let him cry himself out.

'Come on,' I said, 'let's have a bath.'

Later, I realised he'd startled me with this display of emotion. I'd stood there and watched as he'd cried, so openly and so painfully, and I'd said to myself: he's acting. He's acting. And it shocked me when I realised he wasn't. It shocked me because so much of life is merely artifice, and it shamed me that I couldn't tell the difference between the genuine and the false. And that is so important – to have a feel for the genuine. I'd always thought I had it; I always thought I'd see in a person that intrinsic point of his existence. But I'd missed the point with Oliver. I'd missed it when I'd believed that we could simply have an elaborate blow-job and then leave it.

Maybe Oliver had genuinely wanted to be that impermanent fling in the moment he'd laughed so lightly at the mention of my boyfriend. Perhaps he'd thought I was a body he wanted to gratify – and in gratifying, so gratify some part of himself. But here he was, bathing in my bath. Staying in my flat. How had this happened? Maybe he had seen in me the chance to exit from a bad relationship with his previous lover.

`Sorry about that,' he whispered, `I've broken our agreement about discretion, haven't I?'

I shrugged.

`I suppose you want to know who this Duncan is?' he asked when I lay beside him in the water of the bath.

`I'll have to know eventually,' I said carefully. `But more importantly, I want to know what you want from me. Why have you brought your things round here?'

`I'm sorry,' he said, `please don't feel any obligation towards me. I didn't know what to do; it isn't some kind of veiled proposal. I can stay elsewhere if you want, but please look after my things for a while, okay?'

`I'm not asking you to leave straight away,' I told him, `I'm asking you to help me understand what's happening.'

`Oh, Rick,' he said hugging me, water moving restlessly between us, `why are you doing this? You don't know anything about me.'

`Don't accuse me of altruism,' I sighed. `I did what I did for other reasons than that. Altruism doesn't come into it. You give me pleasure, and you know how I stand with Andreas. You're not looking for a relationship – or not with me at least. We both know this, and that makes me feel that I'm doing something that has some purpose – or if not that, then at least something without risk of disaster.'

EIGHTEEN

The first night you sleep with someone without making love to them is always a landmark in a relationship. I can remember the first time it happened between myself and Andreas. I remember thinking *this is it* about us as we lay miserably in bed one evening after he'd been needlessly demoted at work. That, perhaps, is the mark of a successful relationship – the ability to be miserable together.

Oliver was miserable that evening. But I wasn't with him. I was outside, looking in through the window of his distress. And though it distressed me to see him like this, I couldn't share it with him. I still didn't know him well enough to be able to share it. He lay outside my sphere, outside all but the most superficial of intimacies.

In the morning when I woke, I was oppressed by a rough emptiness. I looked over at Oliver, his sleek shoulder raised against me, his dark hair awry – his breath sighing a rhythm for our separateness. I lay and watched him, and felt an insistent loneliness far greater than when I'd been on my own.

He sighed in his dream and rolled over to face me. He had a light pallor to his cheeks, a plush chin; a rich smoothness, despite a prickling of stubble. The reddened swelling of his nose was shiny and taut. It reminded me of sweetness – of things about to burst with final ripeness. I looked at him; reached out and touched the swelling. He lay inert, slight and inviting. Here, I thought, is some kind of mooring for him. My bed is his next stop en-route. Was sex something he had offered up to me – an offering at some obscure alter – or merely a payment for bed and breakfast? I struggled against my cynicism, but couldn't bring myself either to condemn him or release him from suspicion. We'll see, I thought. We'll see.

Over breakfast Oliver seemed unscathed and unembarrassed by the previous evening's weeping.

'You want to know about Duncan,' he said. It was not a question.

I nodded my head in assent.

He took a sip of coffee whilst I cleaned my glasses. It was such a domestic scene that it was a touch bizarre. How long had I known him? And here we were with a kind of domestic intimacy.

'Duncan,' said Oliver, 'is the kind of man who should have a warning printed on his forehead. "I mean well, but I'm a user." And he does mean well, too, I still believe that of him. But he's one of those people that has never really had to work for his money. He's always been comfortable, you know. He has always been a disciple of self-indulgence – has always been accustomed to getting what he wants.'

He smiled at me, and rolled his eyes in mock embarrassment.

'I met him at one of Bob's parties. I was in a bad way at the time – homeless – I was sleeping on a friend's floor. When Duncan invited me back I'd got to the stage of thinking that anything was better than another night on floorboards. He took me home, bathed me – like you did only not so carefully – and took me to bed. It was sheer luxury.

'We had sex, of course, but it was gratitude on my part more or less. And then he offered me the spare room. I took it. I moved in thinking I would have some kind of independence, given that my working hours are so different.

'But it didn't work that way. Duncan wanted to wine me, dine me, show me off and so forth. I hated it. I feel a shit dropping him like this, because if only I'd had the guts to let him know what I wanted – and what I didn't want – right from the start, things would never have got so heavy. Okay, he would have chucked me onto the street, but I would never have developed a revulsion to him, to his house, to his body – or his peculiar short, thick, demanding prick.'

He sat and nibbled a Weetabix, his face swollen and flushed but not otherwise discoloured. He looked in need of protection and I responded by feeling that it was presumptuous of him to invade my privacy like this. It was an unsatisfactory situation, but I decided to let him be for the present. I think my acquiescence was some kind of empathetic reaction – a result of being so adrift myself.

The morning had a late-Sunday feel to it. We sat around for an hour or so whilst Oliver sorted through his belongings. I was empty of emotion, and wary of Oliver now that he seemed so at home in my flat.

`Here,' he said, handing me a small wooden box. `Have a look at this.'

I lifted the brass-inlaid lid. Inside there was a mass of hair; dark, lustrous.

`What's this?'

`A beard,' he told me.

`Another memento?'

`Yes. I was with someone once who had a beard. I persuaded him to shave it off and give it to me. I know you'll think I'm grotesque, but it was the right thing to do at the time. Things have always got to be right.'

`And what other strange goodies have you got?' I asked.

`Here,' he said, handing me a small perspex box containing nail pairings, `I'm not so sure about these. Maybe I'll throw them out. They never came to represent what I thought they might.'

We had another coffee whilst Oliver showed me some more of his items: a contact lens, a square of denim cut from a pair of jeans, a St Christopher medallion, a shoe lace, a champagne cork, an empty bottle of poppers, a nipple clamp – all of which embodied particular memories of particular lovers.

At eleven I had to go off and do some preparatory work for GAF. I asked Oliver if he wanted to help.

`What is it for?' he asked.

`You must have heard about the Family Conference that's taking place this week at the Brighton Centre.'

`Yes, of course,' he told me. `A pompous Christian thing.'

'There's a lesbian and gay solidarity demonstration there today. It starts at two.'

'I wish I could come,' he said, 'but I've got to get to work soon.'

The GAF people were meeting at the house of the group convenor. There was a large front room which, today, was strewn with paper, hardboard, glue, sellotape and lengths of wood. There were already several people there making up placards.

'Hi,' said Tim, the convenor, when I arrived. 'There's plenty to do. Marge has just arrived with the printed posters, so we need someone to glue them to the placards.'

I'm not the neatest craftsperson, but I did pretty well in the end. There were three different slogans: LESBIANS AND GAY MEN HAVE FAMILIES TOO; HAVING AIDS IS NOT A CRIME and LESBIANS MAKE GREAT MOTHERS. We made up fifteen of each, and when they were done I left to meet Gary.

At one o'clock, I rang his bell.

'Ready?' I asked.

'Ready for what?'

'The demonstration,' I said.

'What demonstration?'

His confusion made me laugh.

'The GAF demonstration,' I said.

'Oh, God, is that today? I forgot. I'm looking after Max this afternoon.'

'Bring him along too.'

And that's how the three of us ended up down there. I went round with Gary to help get Max up, and we drove over to the conference centre in his ambulance.

'Some people from the London branch of GAF are coming,' I told Gary. 'It should be fun.'

'Fun?' he said.

'Oh, I forgot,' I smiled, 'you're not into confrontation. But I thought you were getting a taste for it when we went out and put those posters up.'

'There's confrontation and then there's confrontation,'

he said. `I hope you're not intending to brawl.'

`Of course not,' I smiled.

He was, of course, referring to the fight at The Crayford. The ringing in my ear had finally subsided, though Max's face had taken longer to recover. I'd taken him for an X-ray the previous week which, fortunately, had shown no damage to his bones.

If anything, brawling had refreshed Max. He had been so cheerful lately. He sat there with his wheelchair tightly clamped to the floor and said: `Let's make a fuss.'

When we got to the conference centre there were already a number of GAF people gathered, standing some distance from the entrance, placards on the pavement beside them as they waited for others to arrive.

We walked over to Marge, jauntily tartan-clad and with luminous blonde hair. She handed us a couple of placards. Max had a makeshift sign wired to his wheelchair which read: GAYS IN WHEELCHAIRS DEMAND THE RIGHT TO BE PISSED OFF IN PUBLIC. Seeing Gary holding an AIDS IS NOT A CRIME placard made me feel that this protest was awesomely important.

`We're waiting for the London contingent,' Marge told us. `They should have been here half an hour ago. Delegates are already beginning to arrive and we haven't had a chance to get organised.'

But the GAF bus arrived almost immediately, stopping for the couple of minutes that it took forty-five vigorous people to disembark before it drove off, leaving the pool of fresh arrivals milling on the pavement. There had been about thirty of us to start with, which had seemed too few to mount a meaningful protest. Now, however, there were enough. Immediately we were being organised.

`Hey,' a smartly dressed man shouted at us, `what are you doing hanging round like this? You're supposed to be demonstrating at the bigots, not at each other. Come over here by the door and shout. I mean SHOUT!'

There was enthusiastic agreement from around him and, fired by his energy, we surged round the entrance and began to yell our various slogans. People shouted for lesbian rights to motherhood, for gay rights, for the dignity of people with Aids – out of sheer anger at the petty bigotry of those who'd come here to call us dirt.

Several of the demonstrators had acquired passes to the conference and went inside to see whether they would be able to make their views known, in one way or another. They were ejected soon enough, carried out – bleeding in one case – by the white T-shirted Christian `Angels' as the special doormen were called. All this time we were having the resolutions of The Family Conference read out over a megaphone. They wanted lesbians banned from artificial insemination, they wanted single mothers to be deprived of benefits, they wanted people with Aids to be quarantined – they wanted homosexuality to be publicly decried as abomination.

It didn't take long to get us angry – I mean really angry. And it was a passionate experience. People shouted various things, but I stuck to shouting SHAME! SHAME! as these upstanding people passed by with averted eyes and embarrassed glances. Others among us were not so polite, shouting `woman beaters', referring to the demonstrator who'd had her earrings bloodily ripped from her ears with Christian love by fundamentalist bouncers. And there were even heart-felt cries of `fucking bastards'. It was here, before us, that people whose doctrine specifically decreed that they should never pass judgement on others, were calling us abominations from their platforms.

There was a lot of laughter, too, amongst the anger. When so much hate is directed at you from so many people, if you just get angry, how can you ever remain sane? No, we had to laugh at them too – for their hypocrisy in calling us unworthy parents and unworthy family members; for their absurd and dangerous hate – for their peculiar insistence that there is only one correct way to live one's life. Oh yes, it was so appallingly, pathetically stupid that we had to laugh. What else was there to do? Except shout out to them as they passed by, `shame on you, yes you!'

But it came as a shock to me to realise how much anger I felt. I'd lived my life with Andreas for all these years and never once come face to face with a large group of people who really hated us. Oh, sure, I've met endless petty individuals who have wished me ill. But here were people who wielded real media power of social condemnation – people who wanted to use that power to repress us more than right-wing politicians already had. They were here, and we had a chance to make our feelings known. And boy, did I let them know! I didn't realise I could shout so loud – or for so long.

And the only violence perpetrated that day was theirs. How typical, I thought, and how ironic.

For Gary, I know, it was a trauma to face people who believed that his condition was God-sent, people who were glad that he was going to die – glad that there would be one less abomination to threaten their brittle existence... I felt anger for myself, of course I did, but I felt anger on Gary's behalf too – a breathless anger of blinding intensity.

Afterwards we settled for tea at the Grand. We put our placards in the ambulance and went from one extreme to another. First we'd been vocally unrestrained and abusive. Now we sat with hushed voices whilst tea and cakes were brought.

`Do you know one thing that makes me angry,' I said, hoarse from my shouting, `apart from all the other stuff?'

`No,' Max said round a mouthful of scone that I'd just fed him.

`Where was David, and all his friends? Where were all the comfortable gays? How many gays are there in Brighton? Twenty, thirty thousand? How many were there today – a hundred? And half of them came down from London. So long as they've got their pubs and clubs, they couldn't give a toss. It doesn't matter if gay people and people with Aids are being shat on. As long as the shit doesn't fall on them, then it's all right. So long as they can go home and fuck some stranger senseless.'

`Come,' said Max, `you're being unkind. Our real enemies are the people who held the conference, not those who didn't come to demonstrate.'

'But don't you see what power we've got?' I said, 'if only we'd dare use it. If a thousand gays had come today – if five thousand had come – just imagine what we could have achieved . . . '

'It's difficult to motivate people when they're comfortable,' said Max. 'It may be sad, but it's true. Of everyone, not just gays. I don't think we should be so damning.'

Gary shrugged and looked at me.

'I can't lie down and let people trample on my rights any more,' he said. 'I've got too much self respect.'

NINETEEN

I went to The Arches that night to watch Oliver dance. It was disconcerting to see him standing up there – untouchable on his tiny stage – posturing. It felt curious to be on my own in the club, with no one to talk to. Instead I steadily wallowed in the atmosphere; became bloated with rhythms, danced in a vague sort of way and watched as Oliver gradually stripped to a designer jock.

Up there, his body became intensely sexual. At the flat, in bed, in the bath, it had been pleasing in a personal-to-me way. Now, he was to be publicly desired. And that did have an effect. It made me want to take him home and ravish him in some splendid setting. I wasn't sure that I liked feeling this way, but at the same time, part of me felt smug.

It is so easy to generalise about hating this and hating that, and I know I've said some angry things about superficiality in connection with physical attraction. I know this. I know why I said these things, and in the morning – or next week, or whenever Oliver departed – I'd be happy to say them again. But right then, there, in the club, I was electrified to know that I was connected with this sleekly gleaming figure.

We all have this paradox of feeling, I know, and though it is intensely trivial, I'm only trying to be honest about what I felt. Like a man famed for his cuisine being found gorging himself on junk food, I wallowed in my infatuation.

Oliver didn't acknowledge my presence. He seemed to have sunk into a core of shadow – not looking at anything or anyone, but wandering some internal landscape. I realised, then, that I'd placed him in my own emotional landscape, like an ornament positioned carefully; turned this way and that to best catch the light.

I was being shallow. But it was fun, and worse, it was particularly compelling. I could see Lulu, who waved, and Hans from the Cross-Keys, and it made me think of myself as being `with' Oliver in some way. Not because I had made this connection myself, but because others had called it into being by believing that it existed. Even in the knowledge that I was going to let this relationship run its course; even as I was telling myself that it was simple, uncomplicated; even as I laughed and said that it wasn't, I knew it was dangerous.

And there was David, who had encouraged me with Oliver, realising from the start how difficult it could be. David, in his role as concerned friend, would be just as happy to laugh at a happily concluded love affair as he would be to mop up the sorry mess of some disaster.

I am letting this happen, I thought, because I am adrift. Besides, I've been too safe, perhaps, too secure. I can't bear the thought of going on without event in my life except the sheer numbness of waiting to follow Andreas down to Greece.

That was it. I was waiting – and waiting can be the most terrible thing of all. We survive, of course we survive, but inactivity – tedium in fact – can leave us strangely scarred. It left me wondering how this had all happened in the first place. Was it because I was randy? (Yes, but that wasn't something unusual.) Was it because I wanted to explore the cavernous taboos which I had avoided by wrapping my relationship with Andreas round me like insulation?

When we walked home, Oliver was high.

`That's me,' he said, `that's really me, up there, when I dance. Nobody realises. They think I'm some distant being. But that's when I'm most truly myself. That's when I'm most alive – when people are watching me dance.'

We wandered up past the clock-tower and the Regency pallor of Clifton Terrace. I looked down across the town and the dark jitter of the sea and felt possessed by an impermanent perfection. A tired streetperson was walking towards us. Oliver stopped him and gave him a couple of quid. A block later we walked past a group of young men and women making their way home from one of the clubs. As they passed, one of them stopped.

'Poofs,' he said.

'Breeders!' Oliver retorted.

At the flat, we bathed – a ritual that seemed by now indispensable – and later, towel-wrapped and clean, Oliver put on a dance record in the front room and, taking me by each shoulder, he danced slowly, smiling, pulling my towel away; pulling me closer. We continued like this until the end of the record. Then he lay down on the carpet and pulled me down too. His legs were sleek after bathing and, as I held my hand near his skin, I could sense the humidity in the air as he dried. His feet had high insteps and he shivered when I traced my finger over the soles.

'You know what I really want,' he whispered, following the line of my jaw with his finger, kissing the base of my neck, taking my face carefully in his hands. 'I want you to fuck me.'

I looked at him as he lowered his eyes.

'It's the only precious thing I can give you,' he said.

I didn't reply but unfurled his towel, pushed him gently back, and began to explore his body with my lips.

'I mean it,' he told me.

'I know you mean it.'

'Well . . . '

'We'll think about it maybe some other time,' I said. 'I don't have any condoms.'

'I didn't mean you to use a condom,' he said. 'I can't get on with condoms. I gave it up completely instead.'

I stopped kissing him and sat up.

'Except that you want to be fucked by me.'

'This situation is different. You're an exception. You are my saviour,' he laughed. 'Besides, I know you're safe. You told me I was the only one in years, except for Andreas.'

'That's not really the point. I might have been lying – and Andreas might not be safe.'

'Rick,' he sighed. 'This doesn't matter to me. I wanted to do something special, that's all, to show you that this is different for me, too.'

'Don't be dim,' I said. 'You don't need to do special things. You don't need to make grand gestures.'

Oliver lay back and closed his eyes.

The next day I booked a flight to Salonika and paid for it, in cash, so that when I told Andreas about it he couldn't talk me out of it. I borrowed the cash from David against the money that I was due for the sherry ad. I agreed to return after seven nights – it was the only booking available.

'Go for it,' David said. 'It's time you settled for yourself what you want to do – whether you want to go out there, I mean. If you're in any doubt, that is.'

'Why should I be in doubt?'

'Because of Oliver?'

'I need to top myself up,' I said. 'I need to immerse myself in Andreas' presence, for a while at least. It's extraordinary how absence rubs the edges off memories of even the most vivid experiences. I need to know what it feels like to brush my teeth beside him, to watch him drink his coffee, comb his hair, shave, dress. I need to remind myself what he smells like. I don't need to remind myself that I love him – I need to remind myself of other more mundane things.'

TWENTY

June 14th

Dear Andreas,

Maybe it is worth thinking about teaching English. I'm certainly prepared to give it a go until we can get some idea of what I can and can't do, jobwise, once with you. I wish now that I'd forced you to teach me Greek. Your reticence was understandable, but just think how useful it would be now? Maybe I could trade English lessons for Greek lessons with some impoverished student?

I've got the strangest young man staying with me at the moment. I think you'd hate him on sight. I've rescued him from the streets and he's staying until he can find somewhere to go. How's that for philanthropy?

He's sweet enough and not demanding, and he keeps me company, which is more valuable than anything else. I don't know how long he's staying. Not long I should think. We don't really have much in common. Isn't life strange?

love Rick

PS I've booked a flight to Salonika for 26th June – arrives Salonika 3.00 a.m. Sorry it's such an inconvenient time, but at short notice it was all I could get at a reasonable price.

PPS I can afford it.

TWENTY ONE

Of course, the flight was delayed. It was a cheap charter flight, after all. But I'd checked in my luggage before I discovered that there was a delay. My address book was in my case, with all my phone numbers in it, including Cosmas', so there was no way I could contact Andreas to warn him I'd be three hours late.

I slept badly for a while on the lounge seats, bought many coffees, flicked through many magazines. I found myself wondering if this was how Andreas had felt – travelling alone when we had come to associate this journey with being together.

The flight was uneventful. I managed to get at least a little sleep, and we arrived shortly after dawn, heat devils already rising from the runway, at 07.00 Greek time.

There was no sign of Andreas as I came through passport control, or as I waited for my case. I came out into the brilliance of a Mediterranean morning, and looked around. There were tour operators, relations and friends – and all my bleary travel colleagues. But no Andreas.

I went into the shabby cafeteria to look for a call box, then had to buy a can of Coke with one of my 5000 drachma notes, causing considerable annoyance to the cashier who had trouble finding change. I then had coins for the phone.

`Nai?' came Andreas' sluggish voice after the seventh ring.

`Kalimera Andreas, it's Rick.'

`Rick! Where are you?'

`At the airport.'

`We were there at three,' he told me. `Ria and I. We waited for ninety minutes, but you didn't show, so we came back because we both have to work today.'

`That's okay,' I said. `Just tell me how to get to you.'

'Don't take a taxi,' he said, 'they're too expensive. Take an airport bus. They run regularly. Get off where the bus terminates at the airline offices. I'll meet you.'

'Okay.'

'Right, bye,' he said, 'and thank God you're here.'

I went out to the dull-grey bus stop and waited for a quarter of an hour until the bus arrived. The fare was absurdly cheap, and I settled into a doze as we moved off towards the city. Here I am, I thought.

There had been such a taboo surrounding my coming down that I almost felt I was breaking the rules. We had both realised that money was likely to be scarce for a while and so had steeled ourselves for the six months apart. Now I was here, I felt as though I had strayed from school bounds. Maybe I should have stayed at home and sent Andreas a cheque...

The bus passed down streets pale with dust, and later, shop-lined thoroughfares and block after block of flats – all seven stories high; all with balconies and awnings. I slipped in and out of a doze, leaning my head against the window. I'd only had two hours sleep and felt rough.

I didn't know Thessalonika. It had always been merely the starting point of our journey to Kavala, where Andreas' parents lived. Now, I looked out for the offices where I would meet Andreas. But I never saw them. Instead, the bus terminated on the wide earthy forecourt of the railway station.

Fishing for a coin, I went to phone Cosmas' flat. When I found there was no one there, I had a choice. Either I could take a taxi to the relevant offices, or I could go to the flat. The flat seemed a better bet. Andreas was bound to return there eventually, and besides, I didn't know how to tell a Greek taxi driver Andreas' instructions. The flat was the only place I knew how to find.

When I hailed a taxi, I showed the driver the address I had for Cosmas: Aghias Theodoras 3.

'Andaxi,' said the driver. 'You Engleesh?'

'Yes.'

'You visit fren's?'

`Friends, yes.'

`Good, good. Ver' good. I been Lon'n, yes. Tower of Lon'n,' he grinned. `Beeg Ben! Preencess Diana! Ha, ha.'

`Ha, ha,' I said.

I began to sweat. I was wearing clothes for an English evening in early summer – a light jacket, warm shirt, jeans, comfortable shoes and ribbed cotton socks. I could feel sweat trickling down my thighs as the sun glared from car windows. A drop fell from my armpit and trickled down my ribs.

`Here Aghias Sophia,' the man said, turning seawards by a round terracotta-tiled church. `Ees church – Byzantine, yes? Aghias Theodoras down here.'

He stopped after a hundred metres or so and I paid him, tipping him well and wondering if that was correct. I picked up my case and set off up Aghias Theodoras; a short pedestrianised street. At number three I rang Cosmas' intercom button. There was no reply. I sat on my case and continued to sweat. There were several expensive looking boutiques that flanked the street, and curious people began to glance in my direction. I moved my case to a short bench in the shade of a tree and settled down to wait. It was now 9.20 a.m. I took out a novel that I'd started the previous evening and fell asleep before getting to the bottom of the page.

`Rick!' Andreas was shaking me, `Rick, how did you get here?'

I jumped, shocked by the sudden interruption, and looked up.

`Come up to the flat,' he said, kissing me on both cheeks, taking some keys from his pocket and picking up my case. `You look dreadful. How long have you been here?'

`Half an hour,' I said, checking my watch.

We took the lift to the fifth floor and went into Cosmas' cool, pale, bright apartment.

`When did you last have something to drink?' he asked.

'I had a cup of tea on the plane and a Coke at the airport.'

'You're dehydrated. I'll get you a litre of iced water.'

'Sounds good.'

'So where were you?' he shouted from the kitchen. 'I waited for over an hour at Olympic.'

'I took a bus and it went to the railway station.'

Andreas groaned and came through, carrying a jug of water.

'You took a bus. What kind?'

'An ordinary bus. You know, they're everywhere. A bus bus.'

'Not a coach?'

'No.'

'I meant for you to take one of the Olympic Airways coaches,' he said. 'They run passengers in and out of Thessalonika from their head office just round the corner. I didn't mean for you to take ordinary public transport . . . '

'I didn't know,' I sighed.

'Drink this,' he said, 'have a shower, make yourself at home. Get some sleep. You can tell my bedroom – it's the messy one. If I dash now, I might just make it to the clinic before I blow my second appointment.'

He picked up a briefcase.

'Where's your ring?' he asked suddenly, noticing my bare finger.

'Don't know,' I shrugged. 'Down the side of the bath, probably. I'll have a proper look when I get back. There's a panel that's got a gap at the top – I've already lost a sliver of soap down there.'

Andreas looked down at his bare fingers and sighed.

'Well,' he said, 'they've both gone then. Maybe we should buy another pair?'

'Rings are only important if you let them be.'

'True. We can buy more when we're properly together, maybe . . . Look, it's great to see you, but I must go. I'll be back here at one. Bye.'

I drank the whole litre of water, then poured myself another one. I remembered when we'd gone to Istanbul together several years before and bought our rings in the Grand Bazaar. It did seem a meaningful punctuation mark in our lives that they were both lost. Perhaps if we replaced them when I finally arrived in Greece for good it would be a suitable gesture.

My God, I thought, *gestures*, I'm beginning to think like Oliver.

I took a brief, cold shower, then wandered round the flat, looking in all the rooms. There was a long, thin reception room with a dining area partitioned off, a barely functional kitchen, two bedrooms, a large hallway, a dressing room, study and walk-in cupboard. There were balconies front and back, and a slight breath of air that circulated from the open windows. There were no carpets, only well polished parquet – and white walls, with one or two hangings. Sleek chrome and leather furniture was placed discreetly here and there. It all looked very Italian-chic and expensive. I knew that Andreas would have hated it from the moment he walked into the place.

I was right. His room smacked of rebellion. It contained a straw mat, posters, books, and had a kind of brash dishevelment that offset the clinical tidiness of the rest of the place. I liked this room best, and settled down there. But as so often when overtired, I couldn't sleep.

I dozed from 10.30 to maybe 11.15 and then gave up. I got up, dressed in a pale yellow polo shirt, white shorts and espadrilles, then set out to find open water and somewhere to sit down in the shade overlooking the seafront.

Aghias Theodoras was only a couple of blocks from the sea. I turned down Aghias Sophia and walked down to the water's edge. Here were souvenir shops, cafés with fake leather seats, and incessant traffic. A few streets along, towards the docks, there was Platia Aristotelous – open, airy, looking out over the water, cafés bristling with bright sunshades and round, white tables. I sat here and ordered an orangeade and looked out over the square. There was a statue of Aristotle to one side, and an extraordinary glass structure in the centre, catching the light and looking like some controversial artwork from the Tate in London.

Here, although I tried not to, I fell asleep propped up on my elbows for an hour or so, and had to rush back, late, to the apartment to meet Andreas. He was already there when I arrived back.

'Rick,' he groaned, 'don't do this to me. I thought you'd gone and got lost again.'

'I dozed off.'

'You look better though. Come on outside, there's a Greek salad on the balcony.' He grasped the ends of my fingers and pulled me to him, then we hugged and kissed. 'It's good to see you,' he whispered.

The balcony had been soaked in order to cool the air a little, but in spite of the shade, it was hot.

'33 degrees,' Andreas told me, 'and rising. They say it'll hit 40 by the weekend. It's not usually this hot in June. There's fruit juice here, and plenty of ice in the ice bucket.'

He took off his shirt and draped it over the back of the wooden balcony chair, slipped his shoes off and rubbed an ice cube across his chest. I pulled my polo shirt over my head.

'You're brown,' he said.

'You're not,' I said. 'At least no browner than your residual colouring.'

'No time. Anyway, you wouldn't believe it but the weather's been lousy until this week.' He sighed and looked out over the balcony at the dazzling white of the block of flats opposite. 'When I'm down here it's difficult to imagine it ever being sunny in England, because English sun is so much less intense than down here.'

'You know Brighton. The South Coast . . . '

Andreas laughed.

'I do miss it,' he said. 'But not the practice. I'm glad I'll never have to set eyes on Ian Carlisle again.'

'Homophobia is never easy,' I said, 'especially in an employer. At least here you're your own boss.'

'Except that Cosmas doesn't know I'm gay. After the disaster of telling Ian, I'm being rather more circumspect. But I hate the secrecy already. It was difficult to explain why it was so important to take this afternoon off just to say hello to a friend.'

He lay back in his chair and stretched his neck.

'How is everything? How's the crumbling West Pier?'

'Still crumbling.'

'And all those pebbles and the groynes, and the sea that we always used to complain was so polluted. You should look at the water down here . . . Oh, I miss the wind, Rick, and the quiet conversation, and talking in English. And friends. David, how's David?'

'Pleased that I've come down here to see you.'

'Good, good.'

He leant over and began to serve us both some salad.

'Now,' he said, 'eat.'

I hadn't eaten those plump Greek tomatoes for over a year, nor the rich olive oil and feta cheese, and wide leafed Mediterranean parsley.

'By the way,' Andreas said, 'I have to warn you that Cosmas and Marina are real sticklers for appearances. There's no shorts or bare chests when they're around. We'll have to perspire in silence I'm afraid.'

'Okay.'

'There's no problem at Ria's, of course. I haven't seen her nearly as much as I've wanted to. We're dining with her tomorrow, by the way.'

And so I felt at home, at once, in Andreas' company. I slipped into his presence so smoothly and so comfortably that I wondered at the slight anxiety I'd felt, the worry that there may have been some tension caused by our separation. Oliver suddenly seemed insignificant. Andreas and I understood each other so well that conversation became a pleasure, not an obstacle course. And there was the weight of our shared experience, too. All that we'd done, been, seen together. It was all there behind our smiles. And I'd risked all this to spend some time with Oliver.

Oliver. I wondered briefly what he was doing now – now that I'd given him the run of my flat for the week. Would he still be there when I got home? It didn't really matter in the end.

Andreas ate, and smiled at me, his cheeks slightly plumping as he did so. His forehead was more deeply lined, I thought, than when I'd seen him last. But his dark eyes were the same, shimmering with intelligence and humour. His squared-off broad nose flared as he drank; his small ears looked compacted against his head; sleek and streamlined. He had a broadness to his smile that still held an air of optimism which was more attractive to me than anything else – and he was attractive, with his tight musculature and insistent energy. He had that half-caste in-between beauty that appeals to so many – the result of an English mother and Greek/Turkish father. The mixture was refreshingly, unspecifically placed, though definitely Mediterranean.

When we'd finished eating, I noticed a creeping shadow on Andreas' lip as though his face was creating its own shadow.

`Watch out,' I said, `you're getting a nosebleed.'

Andreas touched his finger to his nose and smeared a streak across his lip.

`Shit,' he said, `it's the first one I've had since I came down here.'

Watching Andreas, I was reminded of Oliver's nosebleed – but the circumstance of Andreas' bleeding was utterly different. This was part of our life together and nothing thus far had been so completely familiar. He lay on the balcony for a few minutes whilst I massaged his back and we talked. Then, when the bleeding had stopped, we ate some fruit and drank iced coffee.

`Come on,' he told me, getting up. `Let's have a siesta. Cosmas and Marina aren't back until this evening, so we won't be disturbed.'

And so, with cotton wool bungs in his nostrils, he led me through to his room where we lay on his mattress and made love with the luxury of familiarity, of knowledge and easy communication.

TWENTY TWO

On that first evening we dined out with Cosmas and Marina in a taverna down by the docks. We ate outside from red and white plastic gingham clipped to insubstantial tables. Orange trees grew in large tubs and live Greek music wailed at us from inside the restaurant. The water by the seafront had been sluggish that evening as we'd walked there, slow waves lazing beneath a transparent tar-coloured smog; the distant big-wheel of a fairground revolving behind an impersonal drape of pollution.

'Only Greeks come to this restaurant,' Andreas told me. 'It's too seedy for your average tourist. The food, of course, is nostimo – delicious.'

I ate deep fried courgettes in batter, aubergines with chili sauce, chips and Greek salad.

'I do not understand this,' said Cosmas, 'you not eat meat. We have these, here,' he opened his mouth and pointed.

'Molars?'

'No, these teeth here.' He tapped his canines. 'They are for meat. We must eat meat. Is good.'

'We are geared, physically, to eat meat,' Marina said. 'It is part of our evolution.'

'Evolution, yes,' Cosmas agreed.

'So was rape and pillage part of our evolution,' I said, 'but we've given that up.'

'Pillage?' Cosmas asked. 'Rape I understand.'

Andreas said something quickly in Greek and Cosmas laughed.

'This is different,' he said. 'This thing, this pillage, we had to do it in times of – what do you say – no food . . .'

'Famine.'

'Yes. It was to stay alive.'

'And we ate meat to stay alive too,' I told him, 'which

we no longer need to do.'

Cosmas shrugged and chewed his barbecued octopus.

`I don't know why we're discussing this,' I said. `I don't object to you eating meat.'

`The Greeks,' smiled Andreas, `are macho about these things.'

Cosmas lit two cigarettes and passed one to Marina. They looked as though they'd stepped from a glossy Italian magazine. Young Fashionable Couple Dine in Seedy Splendour at Dockland Diner. They weren't my type at all – nor Andreas', though he hadn't said anything yet. They were too wrapped up in being perfect on the outside. The kind of energy it takes to do that leaves so little for other more important things.

Cosmas was dark, with permanent five o'clock shadow. He was around our age, or maybe a year or two younger. He had a thickness to his waist, and a droop to his cheeks that suggested a growing sedentariness. He would end up with middle-aged obesity and a glamorous sylph-like wife. I briefly wondered if Marina realised this, but she was too intelligent not to. By then, Cosmas would be rich and that would have its own compensations for a woman like Marina. She glinted gold everywhere – on her fingers, wrists, ears, neck . . . She wore an outré gold ankle bracelet – her token safe outrage.

Well, I thought, if she wants to recede behind her man, who am I to say she shouldn't?

Andreas and I caused raised eyebrows later when we said goodnight.

`There is a bed,' Cosmas said, `in here. You must unfold it. I will show you.'

`No,' Andreas told him, `he's staying in my room. There's plenty of space.'

I saw the flash of recognition in Marina's eyes; understood the reason for her mild disdain when we'd met – she'd guessed that Andreas and I were lovers. We slipped into Andreas' room and kissed.

`Do you think I've blown it?' Andreas asked.

`Cosmas hasn't got a clue,' I replied. `Marina knows.'

'Why do you say that?'
'That's why she hates you.'
'You can't know that. You've only just met.'
'It shows.'
'Yes, okay. I wouldn't go so far as to call it hate. I assumed that it was because she didn't want a long-term house guest.'
'Especially a long-term gay house guest.'
'Maybe these things aren't so easy to hide in the end,' Andreas sighed.
'Not when you drag a boyfriend into your bedroom in front of your hosts.'
'You have a point,' Andreas laughed. 'Now, let's get some sleep.'

In the morning he left me dozing. I had the day ahead with no prospect of seeing him until early evening.
'What do you expect?' he asked. 'I took the afternoon off yesterday. I have to make up for it today.'
'But you've only just started this business,' I protested. 'I'd have thought you'd be sitting round, bored as hell, waiting for customers to show up.'
'You aren't used to the Greek way of doing things,' he told me. 'You've also forgotten my father. He's drumming up enough business to fill our books on his own.'
'Looks like I'll be coming down in August then,' I said. 'I don't think this venture is likely to fail.'
'It's not likely,' Andreas agreed, and left.
'Unless,' I said aloud to the closed door, 'Cosmas causes trouble.'

I wandered along to the White Tower and browsed the antiquities; took a boat trip round the harbour. Bought myself some sunglasses and a wide-brimmed hat. All the usual tourist stuff. I lunched in the old town, ate ice cream in a croissanterie and generally absorbed the atmosphere.
Andreas was right about the sea. It was a morbid looking green, except where sewage outlets pumped a brown, untreated sludge into the harbour. The stench was a

mélange of foulness. I stood on the quay and watched a cuttle fish flail weakly on the slick surface as it succumbed to the filth.

The wide curve of the city gleamed in the brilliance of the sun. The temperature was rising, as Andreas had predicted, and I had to walk everywhere in slow motion for fear of sweating. As it was I seemed to be permanently exuding.

A cool shower at five helped, then I drank iced coffee on the balcony and read until Andreas' return at six.

`Come on,' he said, `let's get straight off to Ria's. We'll go in shorts, but we'll need trousers for when we get there. There's going to be other people there for drinks. To meet you really. Prospective students of yours, mostly . . . '

I set off with a sinking feeling, not wanting the constraint of good behaviour. I'd looked forward to relaxing with Ria, now I steeled myself to be formal. We took the bus and arrived ten minutes later outside a glamorous apartment building – older than most, but splendidly repainted in pastel colours. Andreas buzzed apartment 8.

`Hi, it's the wild boys,' he shouted into the intercom, and the door clicked open in welcome.

The apartment was extraordinary. Marble floors, stucco walls mostly obscured by lush drapes, discreetly lit stained-glass panelled alcoves. It was overwhelming. Ria stood amongst all this wearing a slim, low-waisted Twenties style dress. She had a fine black headband with a feather trailing from a diamanté brooch.

`Ria,' I said, `I didn't know you'd become a millionairess.'

`I borrowed the flat for the evening, darling,' she murmured. `Achilles, the owner, has gone to Halkidiki to be very brazen with an English waiter. How are you?'

`Better,' I said.

`Have a drink. Come through. You're the first. There are four or five people coming over for a while, then we're dining *à-trois* on the balcony.'

I sat with a gin and tonic, enveloped in the luxury of

deep liberty-print cushions that were scattered abundantly across the settee. I bathed in Ria's throaty drawl, shivering luxuriously at the grated consonants that stuck in her throat.

`I think they know,' Andreas told Ria, by way of continuing a previous conversation.

`About you and Rick? I should hope so. What did Cosmas say?'

`Oh we haven't actually talked about it. But I suppose that will come.'

`Good,' said Ria.

The door buzzed.

`Don't move,' she told me. `Your future is waiting on my doorstep. Be languorously aristocratic, mention Lawrence Durrell and say how Cavafy never survives translation – then you can double your prices.'

She answered the intercom, then smiled at me.

`Good, it's Sophie, I didn't think she'd turn up. She's rich.'

`Is this how one is supposed to look for students?'

`It's better if you can allow yourself to be seduced by them,' she laughed. `But I suppose in your case that's out of the question?'

`Rick would make a terrible Gigolo,' Andreas said, raising his eyebrows in mock horror. `He's far too intense to be casual about sex.'

`Oh, well . . . ' Ria sighed as someone knocked at the door.

`Kalispera,' came a woman's voice as Ria opened the door. Then came a torrent of Greek, a man's voice, and laughter.

`Chrisanthos,' said Ria.

She brought them over and introduced them.

`I no spik Eenglish ver' well,' Sophie said simply and shook my hand.

`I, on the other hand,' said Chrisanthos, `speak it excellently. I hear you're looking for pupils.'

`Yes,' I said.

`Then grab Sophie quick. She needs it. Don't you darling?'

Sophie hadn't understood our exchange and was helping herself to a handful of pickled olives.

'Drinks,' said Ria. 'I'll get the gin.'

She mixed cocktails for Sophie and Chrisanthos, then for Thomi and Theamandis, when they arrived. I was introduced, but very little more. Ria was showing me off – presenting me as a possibility. Conversation, however, was in Greek.

I've always felt uncomfortable listening to Andreas speaking Greek. It's because I am so familiar with him and the way he thinks that to hear him speaking unintelligible sounds makes me feel excluded. As background noise, though, it was restful and I found myself drifting off in the warmth.

'Were you terribly bored?' Ria asked when they had gone.

'Not terribly,' I said.

'Come through and help me carry the food from the fridge.'

We ate rice with a range of cold, cooked vegetables and drank icy Italian wine.

'Tch, tch,' she said, shaking her head at me as we started on a pudding of orange flavoured halvas. 'Andreas tells me you have been fraternizing with another man.'

I looked at Andreas, but he was helping himself to more halvas. I felt a brief chill as I contemplated blurting that I'd made love to Oliver. It was like one of those what-if feelings I sometimes get as I look over a cliff edge, or a high bridge, and I think "What if I jump?"

'Oh,' I said nonchalantly. 'You mean my waif. My stray.'

Andreas looked at me as I said this. He looked interested, but not suspicious. I'm expecting him to doubt me, I thought. I'm feeling guilty and I'm worried that it shows.

'How did you meet?' he asked.

'I was stood up by Gary one evening,' I told them. 'I was supposed to meet him in the Cross-Keys for a drink, but he got stuck looking after Max. Oliver is a barman there.'

Andreas glowered suddenly, as though thinking of

something unconnected with the conversation.

'Oliver,' he said. 'Stupid name.'

'What's he like?' Ria asked.

'Sweet,' I said. 'But very young for his age. He needed somewhere to stay for a while to sort himself out. I met him in such a coincidental way – he needed somewhere to stay, I had the space. It was meant to happen, I suppose. I believe in that kind of chance.'

'Is he beautiful?' she wanted to know.

'You want to cause trouble,' I smiled. 'You want to make Andreas jealous.'

'Maybe. But you haven't answered my question.'

'I suppose in a certain sort of way he is beautiful, yes.'

'And you haven't been tempted by him?'

I shrugged.

Ria laughed. Andreas looked annoyed. When Ria went out to get another bottle of wine, he flashed me a glance so black it made me catch my breath.

'What are you doing?' he hissed, and for a moment he looked startled or guilty.

'Forget it,' I said, 'it's just Ria winding us up.'

He looked as though he was about to say something specific, but he didn't. Ria, arriving in our silence, caught our mood, and poured us all another glass of wine.

'Sweethearts,' she said, 'I was only teasing. I didn't mean to make you sad.'

'I couldn't bear it, that's all,' Andreas said, half choking on his words. 'I couldn't bear it if Rick left me for someone else.'

'I won't leave you,' I assured him. 'I'll come down in August, or whenever it's right, and we'll be together.'

'But,' said Ria, 'you'd better clear it up with Cosmas first.'

'Yes,' Andreas agreed. 'I'll talk to him tomorrow. This has all got to come out into the open.'

Later, in Andreas' bedroom, he clutched me and said, 'I love you and I've missed you, and I'll never be so crass as to take relationships for granted again,' and he cried a little, which made me cry too. We sat up in bed, gripping each other, and crying and laughing – talking in heavy whispers interspersed with giggles. It's funny, isn't it, you can go so long and know people so well, but still they surprise you. I'd never heard Andreas giggle before. He went "hee-hee-hee" and showed all his teeth. The first time he did it, it made me scream with laughter and he had to shove a pillow in my face to muffle the noise.

`Sssss!' he hissed, `you'll wake Cosmas and Marina.'
`I don't care.'
`You're drunk.'
`Yes, but I wouldn't care even if I was sober.'
`Is that true?'
`Of course.'
`Well then, let's get some sleep.'
`Okay.'
`Goodnight.'
`Goodnight.'
`Hee-hee-hee.'

TWENTY THREE

The following evening, Friday, Cosmas and Andreas arrived home together. I'd heard footsteps coming from the lift and went to open the door, hoping to surprise Andreas with a kiss. Instead I saw Cosmas, bristling and furious, with Andreas slightly behind. I froze in the doorway, not sure if I was supposed to be seeing this anger. Cosmas hesitated when he saw me, then stopped dead. When I didn't move, he sidled past me, pausing only briefly to spit in my face.

'*Thiestramenos!*' he whispered – pervert – and turned his back.

Andreas raced after him and there came an explosion of argument from the sitting room. I didn't need to be able to speak Greek to know what they were saying – passionate accusations were flying with uninhibited fervour.

So Andreas has told him, I thought.

I stood in the open doorway and felt a certain pride that he'd done it. I'd privately thought he might not have the nerve, but there was no doubting the aggressive righteousness with which Andreas was defending himself against Cosmas' disgust. Hearing this conflict, hearing what Andreas had put on the line for the sake of our openness made me feel strong.

I closed the door and walked into the sitting room; light from the balcony warmly backlighting the vitriol.

'Whatever you might think of us,' I told Cosmas, 'we are still human beings and deserve your respect for that at least.'

'Pah!' Cosmas spat, and continued his discourse in Greek.

'What are you doing,' he seemed to be sneering at Andreas, 'how could you do this to me, my wife – our honour?'

'For God's sake, Cosmas,' I said, 'you're acting like a child. What's the big deal if Andreas is gay? It doesn't affect you.'

'No?' he said. 'No? I have to see this man, this *o-vlakas*, this *thiestramenos* every day. This disgusting thing is not right in my profession. It is for those bars in Athens where men dress as women and go with other men for money.'

'I think you are suffering from a lack of decent information,' I told him. 'Your prejudice comes from ignorance, that's all. The fact that he's homosexual doesn't alter the fact that Andreas is an excellent physiotherapist.'

'It makes him not fit for his profession,' said Cosmas. 'It makes him not fit to work with me.'

'If you only stopped for a moment to listen to what you're saying,' I told him, 'then you'd realise that it's a pile of shit.'

'Rick,' whispered Andreas, touching my elbow, 'this isn't helping.'

'This thing that you have done in my house,' Cosmas hissed at me, 'to make love like an animal, in my house. This I cannot forgive.'

'I couldn't give a fuck, literally, what you think,' I replied.Cosmas swivelled on his heel, took out his car keys and threw them at me. They caught my cheek, just below my eye, then ricochetted from the air conditioner, span across the parquet, and stopped at Andreas' feet. Cosmas turned and ran from the flat like some unhappy child who has just been overwhelmed by fear.

Andreas picked up the keys and came over to me.

'Are you hurt?' he asked.

'No.'

He touched my cheek with his finger.

'Am I bleeding?'

'A scratch, that's all.'

'Sorry,' I said. 'I should have been a little more circumspect in what I said.'

'Don't worry. What you said was true.' He bounced the keys in his hand a couple of times, then smiled ruefully at me. 'Looks like it's Ria's floor for us tonight. Let's go and get our things into Cosmas' car.'

The strangeness of driving across Thessalonika in Cosmas' smart BMW surrounded by Andreas' few belongings, made me feel dislocated and homeless.

'Was it worth it?' I asked as Andreas stared ahead without expression.

'You can't seriously ask that question,' Andreas told me. 'You can't. If you don't think I should have done it, then I have no basis from which to fight. The whole point is that we're unanimous.'

'Of course we are,' I told him. 'I feel that. I wondered if you felt it.'

He turned to me with a sigh. 'Why do people like him spend so much time shitting on people like us? I thought it was bad in England, but the sodding Greek macho culture makes me sick. Even the women are macho here.'

'Luckily,' I reminded him as we pulled up outside Ria's apartment building, 'there are always exceptions to the rule.'

Ria's flat was shabby. Unlike the marbled splendour of our last meeting, here we had only ourselves as decoration. I preferred it this way.

'So,' she said when we'd explained, 'you can't have expected anything else.'

'No,' Andreas conceded. 'Cosmas' reaction was so utterly as I'd expected that it was almost a surprise . . . He didn't react at the clinic – bad for business. It was in the car on the way home that he let rip. Marina's been whispering nasty things to him, it seems. Rick saw her hostility immediately.'

'What now?' I asked, 'business-wise.'

'Business as usual,' Andreas grinned. 'He knows I'm the better physio, that's why he made the original offer of a partnership. He also knows we get a lot of clients referred by my father. If I go, then he's in real trouble . . . '

'So, you'll both grin and bear it.'

'Yes,' Andreas nodded. 'Later, maybe, I can set up on my own; but right now I can't. Sixty per cent of the money was Cosmas'. I can't afford to leave.'

'What if he tries to smear your name?' Ria asked.

'That's always possible, but I think he's too greedy to jeopardise the business. And it wouldn't be the end of my career, unless there was some nasty scandal. Apart from the fact that we've both got dicks, there's nothing scandalous about me and Rick.'

'As if that wasn't enough?' Ria sighed.

But Andreas' grin lasted only as long as the adrenalin from his earlier argument. Later, he became morose as the three of us prepared food in the kitchen – me chopping vegetables, Andreas stir-frying them, and Ria plying us with wine and, at the dinner table, dope.

'Where did you get this?' Andreas asked.

'I always keep some aside for emergencies,' she said.

I hadn't taken dope for years, but now I was pleased to accept some. It helped make today's events seem pre-ordained and positive. Andreas had stood up for himself, he had been honest about me. We were taking a step forward to being able to live together here without lies.

'Here,' Ria said as we sat down to eat, 'a toast. To us, to our homosexuality, and to our future happiness.'

'Hear, hear.' I drank.

'Now eat up,' she said.

So we ate, and I felt that in eating we were sealing some kind of bond. We were going through something important together, the three of us.

'What's happening about your father's apartment?' Ria asked Andreas. 'When are you going to be able to move in?'

'Don't know,' Andreas replied. 'As far as my father's concerned, there's no hurry.'

'There still isn't particularly,' Ria told him. 'You can stay here as long as you like. Both of you. But it won't be so comfortable. You'll have to sleep in the corner of the sitting room.'

'Comfort,' I said, 'is relative. Physical comfort at Cosmas' would be infinitely less pleasurable than discomfort with you.'

'You know,' Ria said to Andreas, 'I like Rick.'

Andreas took my hand and pressed it to his cheek.
'We'll sort this out,' he said, 'don't worry.'
'I'm not worried,' I said.

We ended up dancing in the one gay bar in the city, βΑΝΑΓ. It was dark, like a late-Seventies bar at home, with blood red walls, photos of drag artists, a tiny stage-cum-dancefloor. The people there looked either depressed or as though they were seriously posing. The music was loud and varied, though nostalgia ruled the turntables.
 Ria greeted several of the people there with hugs and smiles.
 'I am a mother to them all,' she told me, 'though God knows why, I'm not much older than they are, and I'm the most screwed up person here. Why they come to me with their problems I'll never know.'
 'It's because you make people feel important,' I told her. 'It's a great gift, to be able to make another person feel important.'
 She kissed me.
 'I deserve a dance for that.'
 We climbed the three shallow steps to the dancefloor. I loosely placed my hand in the small of her back and we danced, alone together on the stage, a single spotlight trained on us, catching some of Ria's stray hairs and turning them from black to bronze. I was forcefully reminded of Oliver again, and I realised that I couldn't get rid of him as easily as all that. By getting on a plane I'd rid myself of his presence, but it was harder to get away from other things – things we'd shared.
 He's been with me all the time, I thought, waiting to jump into my mind at any moment.
 I looked down and saw Andreas talking with one of the people Ria had greeted so warmly. He looked happy, smiling broadly.
 'Who's that?' I asked Ria.
 'Oh Rick,' she smiled, 'I detect a glint of jealousy.'
 'Curiosity,' I assured her. 'Jealousy's not my thing at the moment.'

'Good.' She clasped my hand and we danced some more. 'He's a painter friend of mine. Andreas and I want to commission him to paint something for us. A portrait, maybe. But neither of us have the money.'
'Yet.'
'Exactly.'
'He seems quite smitten with Andreas.'
'Smitten, no, I wouldn't say so. Intense, yes, but he's intense with everyone. Sexually he's worth avoiding. He has a martyrdom complex to which all his lovers are sacrificed. His penis is twenty-one-and-a-half centimetres long, incidentally. I only know that because he tells everyone. He showed me once, though I was not exactly his most appreciative audience. He is a man of fixation and obsession. That's why he's such a good painter.'
'Fixation and obsession,' I said. 'Well, I can understand that in a way. We all need to find ways of making the world a more intense place; otherwise it becomes tedious.'
'I know you must be finding it difficult,' she said, 'living in Brighton and waiting to come down here.'
'Yes,' I said. 'But there's something else.'
Ria leaned over and grasped my elbow. She whispered in my ear: 'Your young man. You are having a love affair with him.'
I felt an internal jolt of shock and froze at the neutral way in which she said it.
'Is it that obvious?' I asked.
'Only to me,' she said. 'Call it intuition if you like. Andreas has no idea. Does this young man make you happy?'
'Happy?' I replied. 'He's been so timely, in a way. Perhaps I've been a bit obsessive about him, I don't know. He just appeared in my life like a *fait-accompli* – he was all-encompassing from the start. It's curious. But happy? I don't know.'
'Listen, Rick, you must know what is going on for yourself, but let me tell you – come down and make a life here. Love this person if you like, but leave him when you have to. That's the way it has to be.'

'I've deliberately not thought about it,' I said, 'but you're right of course.'

'Of course. But let him down gently, Rick. Love has a power all its own. It can be beautiful but destructive. It can leave you with regrets if you handle it badly.'

I sipped my drink and looked across at Andreas talking animatedly at the next table.

'Just enjoy yourself,' she said. 'God knows we all deserve that at least.'

I smiled and she kissed me, and that was all that was said.

Later, at Ria's, we sat out on the balcony and talked of other things.

'It's hot,' I said. 'It's three thirty in the morning and it's hot.'

'That's Greece,' said Ria. 'We all melt for months at a time.'

'Unless you've got air-conditioning, like Cosmas,' Andreas pointed out.

'Cosmas,' said Ria, 'is so protected from his environment that he's virtually a different species.'

'He'd say the same about you,' I said, 'about being a different species.'

'But then,' she whispered with a smile, 'perhaps I am.'

TWENTY FOUR

I flew home assured that Greece would be at least an adventure. Ria's established life in Thessalonika would provide some kind of starting point, socially, from which Andreas and I could expand.

As the plane began the descent over Gatwick I felt a flutter of anticipation. I would leave Brighton, I would give up my modelling. But my feeling of anticipation did not result from my decision to follow Andreas down to Greece. It came from knowing that I would be seeing Oliver.

Back in Brighton, I let myself into the flat without ringing the bell. It was four-thirty in the afternoon. The place was tidy but smelled of dope. Music filtered through from the front room.

Oliver was in there with Lulu. They were lying on the carpet smoking what I presumed to be dope, though judging by Guillaume's expression, he was also on something stronger. A sleeping bag lay rolled out on the couch.

'Hi,' Oliver drawled, 'I thought you were back tomorrow.'

'No,' I told him, 'it was always going to be today.'

'I would have tidied up.'

'It's not untidy.'

'But I would have tidied Guillaume away, out of sight, out on the streets where he belongs.'

'Hello Guillaume,' I said. 'You don't have to go.'

'Rick,' Guillaume said.

'Tea?' I asked. 'Is there any milk?'

'Yes,' Oliver told me, 'there's fresh. And I bought some Earl Grey, it's by the tomato sauce.'

He followed me down to the kitchen. The work-surface was set with cut and chopped vegetables, diminutive piles of herbs and spices; a packet of basmati rice.

'See,' he said, 'I did know you were coming back. This is a curry, or will be. I'll chuck it all together and boil it for an hour. I'm stoned Rick, don't worry about me. I'll start the food off while you make us tea.'

He hummed a little as he scraped the ingredients into a pan.

'Lulu's so weird when he gets stoned. I go kind of inside out and happy, but he goes blank.'

He picked up a large pinch of dark green-brown powder.

'Freshly ground dope,' he said and threw it into the pan. 'You don't disapprove?'

'No,' I said.

'Oh, I was hoping you might.'

I poured boiling water into the pot.

'I can see you've made up your mind,' Oliver said. 'You've come back here with the look of an undertaker. You've come back to England to nail down the last of your life, to pack it all into some exotic coffin so that you can bury yourself down by the indefinable Aegean.'

'What else did you expect?'

'A miracle maybe.'

'Look,' I said, 'I really have made up my mind that I want to live in Thessalonika. I don't know what the best arrangement is, but maybe we should cool off with each other.'

'You've forgotten,' said Oliver, 'that I knew this about you all along. Why should we cool off?'

'Because things will get too complicated.'

'They already are complicated, Rick. But am I making demands? Am I?'

'Not consciously, perhaps,' I said. Then he kissed me.

It was frightening how familiar his mouth was, how well my tongue remembered the regularity of his teeth. I still regarded him as a stranger in so many ways; still knew so little about his ornamented and concealed personality. But his body connected with mine, and we didn't need to know each other to be able to wallow.

'Mmm,' said Oliver breaking away and grabbing the tea

pot. `Up we go. Let's be olde worlde shall we and drink from tea cups? I found some at the back of the cupboard.'

`They came with the flat,' I said. `I've never used them.'

`There's always a first time. Let's take some crumpets up.'

`Aren't you going to toast them?'

`I'm too hungry.' He crammed one into his mouth whole. `I'm sorry, Rick,' he mumbled, `I'm too stoned to talk seriously about the future. Later. We'll talk about it later, much later.'

I followed him to the living room, carrying the tray of tea. When we got there Guillaume/Lulu was virtually asleep. Oliver seemed to be slowing down too, like a dying battery. He poured us tea but sat on the floor for several minutes in silence before he drank. I lay on the carpet too, looking up at the ceiling. I didn't need dope to feel relaxed. There's something about being with people who are feeling displaced. It rubs off somehow.

Here I am, I thought, home. But it doesn't feel like home. It feels like this is Oliver's home and I'm a visitor.

We ate the curry with Oliver's impromptu home-made chapattis – doughy pancakes, burnt on the outside and uncooked in the middle. But I was hungry and the dope made me mellow and spontaneous. Lulu only managed a few mouthfuls before falling asleep. Oliver was more awake, but we didn't speak much.

`By the way,' he said as I finished eating, `there's a message for you from Max. He said to call him as soon as you got back. He seemed to think it was important.'

`Why didn't you tell me when I got in?' I asked.

`I forgot.'

I left the table and phoned Max.

`Hello,' I said. `I'm back. Are you okay?'

`Fine,' he said, `but where's Gary? He hasn't been answering his phone for the last four days. I'm worried.'

`Did he say anything about going away?'

`No, that's what's worrying me. You don't have a key to his flat do you?'

`No,' I said, `but I'll go down and bash on his door.'

There was no sign of Gary downstairs. I phoned Max back and we worried together.

'Maybe he's sick,' said Max, 'or dead.'

'Surely not. If he was sick he'd have contacted someone.'

'What if he's fallen or something?'

There was no answer to that.

'Okay,' I said, 'I'll phone the Helpline to see if I can get hold of Paul. I don't have his home number.'

The Centre was closed and I got the answerphone.

'Hi,' I told the machine, 'it's Rick Bailey here. I'm trying to get in touch with Paul Wells or Piers. Could someone phone me back when the lines open. Thanks.'

That wasn't much good and I felt inadequate. Gary had Aids, but I had never thought ahead to a moment when he might be sick. I had never thought how I might react or how I might help him.

'If he was sick,' Oliver said later, 'he'd have called a doctor, or an ambulance, not Max. He might be in hospital.'

I called the Aids ward at the hospital. I knew the nurse slightly from having visited other people there in the past. Gary, he assured me, wasn't there.

I sat down with Oliver to talk about what to do. Was it my place to try and interfere? Gary might be perfectly okay and resent people running after him. But on the other hand . . .

The phone rang just after eight.

'Hello Rick,' a young male voice said, 'it's Phil. Piers isn't here, but Paul's going to be in a bit later. Shall I get him to call you?'

'Thanks.'

Oliver was of little help.

'Relax,' he told me, 'Gary wouldn't want you to be worrying about him like this. It's a waste of energy.'

I knew this was true, but the knowledge wasn't helpful. You can't cease to be concerned about a friend just because it's not constructive. However, I tried to ignore the wringing in my stomach and lay back, tired. Oliver knelt at my feet and unzipped my jeans.

It's as if I've never been to Greece, I thought as he took

my penis in his mouth, it's as if Andreas has no reality. Yesterday he was my reality. Today Oliver is.

The phone rang.

'Don't answer,' Oliver whispered.

'It might be about Gary,' I hissed.

'Let the answerphone take it.'

I was close to coming, so I closed my eyes and grasped Oliver's hair. After the requisite four rings, the machine switched on to relay its message – then came a voice: 'Hi, Rick, it's Paul here . . . '

I lunged for the phone.

'Hi, Paul,' I gasped, 'it's Rick here. Have you seen Gary?'

'No,' he said. 'Do you think there's a problem?'

I leaned back on my chair and took a deep breath.

'There may be a problem,' I said. 'He hasn't answered his phone for four days.'

Oliver was removing his trousers, tugging at his erection with vigour. I had gone limp.

'I'll be over in about ten minutes,' Paul said. 'I've got a spare key. Will you come down with me, in case?'

I agreed and hung up. Oliver, now naked, stood in front of me pressing his cock against my closed lips. I opened my mouth. He leaned down and deftly rolled my foreskin back and forth.

'God,' I said, pulling away, 'we've only got a few minutes.'

'That's enough,' he replied. He pushed me back on the settee and pressed himself against me, taking both our cocks in his fist and slowly pumping. He kept a steady rhythm and made small noises as we rocked.

'I'm in a storm,' he whispered. 'Steel . . . and salt, and pain . . . and love, and fullness . . . this. This . . . '

I rolled my hips against him and came. He was biting me and saying words against my neck, then he came too. When I leaned back again I felt the slipperiness of our semen on my stomach. It stretched between us like albumen on an undercooked egg.

'I love you Rick,' he whispered. 'Life goes on and it

starts here. Hello life.'

He held me loosely round my neck and smiled up at the ceiling. Lulu, inert against a cushion in the corner, hadn't stirred.

'Are you stoned?' he asked.

'A little,' I said. 'Are you?'

'Yes. It's the best way,' he said. 'I want to do it again almost immediately.'

'Can't,' I told him. 'Paul's coming over in a couple of minutes.'

'Time,' Oliver sighed. 'It slays us with its impertinence and drags us into sanity.'

I pushed him gently from me and started to dress.

'Come here,' Oliver whispered, 'and let me wipe you clean.'

He took a dirty rag from the floor beside the settee – already crisp with what appeared to be dried blood – and wiped me first and then himself.

I've done this thing, I thought, maybe I shouldn't have done it but I've left my mark. I've put myself behind his eyes. In future this will always count.

'There's another message,' Oliver told me as he dressed. 'Fotofit phoned. You've got a job next week. I've put it in your diary. It's a Japanese pop-video or something.'

Gary, I thought, where are you?

I was dressed and peculiarly calm when the doorbell rang. I let Paul in. His eyes narrowed slightly when he saw Oliver, but his face remained inscrutable. He glanced over at Lulu.

'You look pale,' I said.

'Rick,' Oliver said, 'black people can't look pale.'

'Of course they can,' I said.

'I am tired,' Paul told me with a worried laugh. 'Let's go.'

'Okay.'

Oliver stayed upstairs whilst Paul and I went down to the basement. There were no lights on. No sound. We rang the bell and waited, then Paul unlocked the door and let us in. The flat was deserted. There was no sign of Gary, no note, no clue as to where he might be.

'Okay,' said Paul, 'it looks like he's just gone off. Thank Christ. I wasn't ready to find him sick, or worse.'

We let ourselves out again and locked the door.

'Thanks for phoning,' Paul said. 'When I next see Gary I'll talk to him about maybe leaving you a spare key. Get him to phone me when he gets back. I've got to go.'

'Come up for a drink, now you're here.'

'No, I was in a meeting on Aids issues for black people. If I go now, I'll be able to get back before it ends.'

He leaned forward, secretively, though there was no one around who could hear us.

'What are you doing, Rick? Having a fling with Oliver? I've known him for years and I can tell you right off to watch out.'

'Why?'

'I can't tell you here, but just get rid of him, that's all.'

'You can't say that and then not tell me why.'

'Just tell him to sod off,' said Paul. 'Look, I've got to go.'

He gave me a curt half-salute and walked off up to Seven Dials. I stood and looked down at Gary's door feeling annoyed with Paul for being so cryptic.

I've made love to Oliver, I thought. Why am I so free? Why is Gary ill?

'Hey,' said Oliver when I got back upstairs, 'come on Rick, Gary's okay. Of course he is.'

I had a brief vision of Gary lying dead in a ditch beneath a clear sky.

'I'm doing what I used to hate my mother for,' I said.

'So, stop worrying,' said Oliver. 'If Gary's in trouble, then that's his responsibility.'

We sat for a time in silence.

'I didn't know that you knew Paul,' I said.

'I didn't know that you knew him either.'

'How come you met him?'

'We fought over a lover,' he said. 'It wasn't pleasant and really I don't want to talk about it.'

'He didn't seem to have much warm feeling towards you.'

'No, well I'm not surprised. I like him, though. What

happened wasn't his fault. It wasn't my fault either. But that's the way it is. Someone always ends up taking the blame.'

We went to bed and Oliver seemed distant, as though some sadness had caught him unawares.

`I want everyone to be happy,' I said. `I want to make a world in which there's no pain or illness or death. I want a world where there'll be you and Andreas in it at the same time and it won't just spell trouble.'

`You can't,' said Oliver. `It's not a perfect world. It never was and never will be. The world's a shit-heap. We have to find our happiness and throw it in the face of life – we have to grab our happiness when life's not looking, because as soon as it sees, it'll take it away.'

TWENTY FIVE

4th July

Dear Andreas,

It's Gary's birthday in three days and he's completely disappeared. I know you never met him, so you can't really know how worrying it is. I hope he isn't ill.

I saw David today. He says you've done me the world of good. He misses you and has agreed to be our first guest when we're settled in Thessalonika. Life has become so confusingly unfocused for me here in Brighton. It only seemed clear when I was with you in Thessalonika, and I hate that. I just want this period to be over.

Don't let Cosmas get you down. Be strong for a while and then we can face him together. We could always move down to Athens if things become too awful?

I'm working next week and again the week after that, so I'll be able to pay my flight down and so on. David's agreed to put a lot of our stuff up in his attic until we decide what to do with it. I've bought some books about teaching English, so it looks as though I've become resigned to that. Who knows, I might even enjoy it.

Life here seems like an extended farewell – like the last term of school. I feel as though I'm going to graduate, or something.

As for Oliver, I expect he'll take on the flat when I leave. He's no trouble and is actually quite helpful in some ways – he keeps me company for a start, and it keeps me motivated to have someone around the place, even if he does work odd hours. He's paying some rent too, so I can't complain.

Write soon.

love Rick

PS Enclosed as promised: photo of Royal Pavilion (farmhouse in drag, as Oliver calls it) for Ria.

TWENTY SIX

July 2nd

Dear Rick,

You've only just left and I feel wretched. I don't think you'll ever know how much I need you, nor how grateful I am that you broke our rule and came down to see me.

There's good and bad news. First; dad's tenants have moved out, so we can have the flat. The bad news: they've wrecked the place. Apparently they haven't been paying rent for some time and dad had them thrown out. They've pissed off to Italy or somewhere so he can't touch them. It'll take a while to fix the place up – I mean really. They ripped out the plumbing, wiring, cupboards, smashed the toilet and the bath, ruined the floors . . . I couldn't believe it when I saw it. It makes dad much more inclined to let me live there, even rent free, rather than trying to find trustworthy tenants. He's pleased, by the way, that you're moving in, though he doesn't suspect what we'll be getting up to. After Cosmas' mania I'm inclined not to tell anyone else, ever – but that's something we'll have to discuss.

Cosmas has been awful. Why are straight men such fucking CHILDREN when it comes to sex and honour and all that shit? He won't talk to me at the clinic. Marina doesn't conceal her dislike, and the other nurse avoids me. I'd really hate it if it wasn't for the customers. Quite a lot specifically ask to be seen by me – which makes Cosmas virtually explode with anger. I think he feels contaminated by my presence. But how does he think I feel? I think I'd have gone nuts if it wasn't for Ria. Her flat is comfortable, by the way, and we both enjoy each other's company. I don't see why I shouldn't stay here until dad's place is ready – it'll be fine as long as Ria's single. She's having an indiscretion with a Spanish diplomat's wife, who fortunately doesn't want to move in, or else I'd be packing my bags.

It hurts too much to be without you.

Andreas

PS The flat should be ready by September.

TWENTY SEVEN

'I'm in love!'
'What, with the same person you were in love with last time?'
'Rick, your cynicism does you no credit,' David told me, his voice crackling with happiness over the phone.
'Sorry. Who is he?'
'Come over and meet him. He's coming round in a few minutes. You know I always want my special friends to meet you.'
'How long have you known him?'
'A week. I met him while you were in Greece.'
'Okay,' I said, 'I'll come over in about an hour, after Oliver's gone to work.'
'Make it two,' David sighed. 'I guess we'll want to be intimate first. I haven't seen him for sixteen hours . . . '
I put the phone down with the familiar here-we-go-again feeling I usually get when David falls in love. Who would it be this time? One of his nascent window cleaners whose voices had only just broken? An absurdly overweight teenage football supporter? A beautiful but shy trainee landscape gardener? These were some of the people that he'd fallen for in the last year or two.
The problem was that he always fell out with them – unless they fell out with him first. There was never more than a brief flirtation with relationships.
I phoned Max.
'Still no word from Gary?' I asked.
'I was going to ask you that question.'
'It's his birthday tomorrow.'
'Yes.'
'Do you still want me to come round and get you up early?'
'Yes. If Gary isn't around we'll go out somewhere in the

ambulance. If he wants to go off, that's up to him. I'm not going to hang around waiting.'

Maybe that was the right attitude to have. Maybe I should have said to myself, fuck you Gary, if you want to disappear, that's your business – don't expect me to rush around looking for you.

`Hello love,' said David opening his front door and kissing me. He held my hand for a fraction longer than usual and smiled his beautiful, nervous smile.

`Come through.'

We walked into the sitting room.

`Hello Rick,' said Paul, getting up.

`You know each other!' David exclaimed.

`Yes,' I said, surprised, `Paul's a friend from the Helpline. He does the telephones and, amongst other things, looks after Gary.'

`Of course,' said David, `I should have guessed you'd know each other. So you've known Paul and never thought to introduced me?'

`Why, should I have?'

`You know how I feel about black men.'

`Yes, and it's a good reason not to introduce you to them.'

Paul laughed.

`I didn't know you knew Gary,' David said to Paul. `I don't suppose you've seen him?'

`No.'

`I would do that,' David told us, sitting on the settee and leaning against Paul. `I mean, I would get up and go off somewhere if things were getting me down. Why not? Solitude is sometimes the only way to get your perspectives and priorities in order.'

`Maybe,' I said. `But I wish he'd left a note.'

David slipped out to make coffee. Paul smiled shyly at me.

`David mentioned a Rick and I thought it might be you,' he said. He leaned back and looked up. He must have been in his mid-twenties. And David was thirty-nine. I got up and followed David into the kitchen.

'A bit old for you I'd have thought,' I whispered into his ear. 'I thought you preferred them in shorts.'

'He's twenty-four,' David whispered back. 'Now, go back and talk to him.'

Paul was slender with a slowness to his movements that suggested extreme confidence. His hair was cut so short that it was possible to see the skin of his scalp. There was a fine line shaved where a parting might have been if his hair had been longer. I smiled at him.

'I didn't expect this,' I said. 'David's been so at sea lately, emotionally. He spent the first part of the summer clutching at straws. I'm glad he's met you. Is it serious?'

'I don't know,' Paul replied. 'Maybe. There are too many important things to be done for me to want to waste time being casual. I'd much rather invest time where it's worth investing.'

'I suppose that's why you joined the Helpline.'

He shrugged. 'Motivation is always a complicated thing.'

'And you?' Paul asked. 'How are you getting on with Oliver? Would you describe yourself as going out with him?'

'I don't think I'd better answer that question,' I said. 'I don't think I know the answer.'

'Rick,' David said, coming in with the coffee, 'how can you say that? You're going out with Andreas and that's that. Oliver is nothing.'

'Not nothing,' I said, 'but, yes, you're right. Andreas, as you know, is my boyfriend. Oliver is . . . '

'A mistake by the sound of it,' said David.

'I have to agree with David,' said Paul.

'Why? What was this fight you had with Oliver?'

'Didn't he tell you?'

'No.'

'Maybe I shouldn't say anything, then.'

'You can't give ominous warnings and then not explain yourself.'

'Okay,' Paul shrugged. 'But it's all a bit facile in the end.'

David put his arm round Paul's shoulder and they leaned together.

`I was going out with a guy called Lewis last year,' said Paul. `He was one of the dancers at The Arches, so obviously he knew Oliver. They ended up having a thing together whilst Lewis was with me, even though Oliver knew we were together. Okay, so that's no big deal in itself because it was as much Lewis' fault as Oliver's; but I thought it was pretty shabby.

`What I really hated Oliver for was that when it all came out and I talked to Lewis about it, I found that Oliver had been telling lies about me. He'd told Lewis that I'd been sleeping around. He even pretended that he'd slept with me himself – which he hadn't.

`Once, I left a note at The Arches asking Lewis to meet me. He never turned up. I later found out that Oliver had prevented the note from getting to him. I went to The Arches in person, though I hate the place. Oliver was there and told me that Lewis refused to come out to talk to me. That was a lie, too – Lewis wasn't even there. Oliver had organised the whole thing so that Lewis would think I'd dropped him.'

Paul sighed with annoyance.

`The only good thing about the whole business was that Lewis left Oliver almost immediately afterwards, so his schemes were fruitless.'

`Sounds like a pretty devious young man to me,' said David. `I think you're mad to even think of having an affair with him. Even if it is only a discreet fling.'

Oliver had already gone to work when I got back, so I settled down with a glass of wine to try and read. I felt pleased for David about Paul, though that pleasure was inevitably tinged with sadness at what Paul had told me. But regardless of Paul's fracas with Oliver, it was good to see David serious about someone again. Paul wasn't an airhead, he didn't fall into the category of strangely shallow young men that had pressed themselves through David's life recently. And David hadn't once mentioned the size of his penis.

The doorbell rang just after midnight and I went to answer it with a sinking feeling. Midnight callers are usually bringers of bad news. It was Gary. He stood there, casually, half-smiling, as though sharing a private joke with me. I lurched inside with pleasure and concern and, taking his elbow, pulled him in.

`At last!' I said. `Come in. You look well.'

`Thanks. I feel well. Why? Did you think I might not be?'

`When people disappear,' I said, `friends always fear the worst.'

`I'm sorry, Rick,' he said, `I didn't think to tell anyone. It was such a spur of the moment thing.'

`Where have you been?'

`Morocco.'

`Morocco!'

`A friend of mine in London was going and at the last minute his boyfriend had to cancel. He asked me if I wanted to go instead – I only had a few hours notice. I chucked some stuff into a bag, organised a few things to do with money, and jumped on a train to Heathrow. I sent you a postcard but it won't have arrived yet.'

`Thank God you're okay. Sit down,' I said, then glanced at my watch. `And happy birthday.'

`Thanks,' he said sitting and pausing for a moment to ponder. `I've always wanted to see Morocco and that was my last chance I suppose.'

`Well . . . ' We looked at each other briefly and smiled. `Coffee?'

`Please.'

I called from the kitchen to tell him how worried Max had been.

`I'll phone him in the morning,' Gary assured me.

When I came back with the coffee, Gary continued to talk about Morocco.

`I had to stay out of the sun,' he told me, `because of my AZT, but that wasn't a problem as it was so hot. We sat in the shade on the hotel terrace with iced drinks, and swam in the sea after sunset. I even made love,' he smiled, `once, after I'd sent your postcard. It was lovely.'

He looked at me with a new kind of calmness. I realised then that he was tired. The superficial glow of health was cosmetic. Underneath he was exhausted.

`I wanted to go off the beaten track, out to some of the villages in the desert, but it might have been dangerous for me. We did hire a car one day and drove to the edge of the desert. I could have stayed there forever. I could imagine dying there. I mean dying happily.'

He was gesturing expansively as he talked, and I suddenly noticed that his fingers were bare.

`Your ring?' I whispered.

`I had to pay for the trip somehow,' he replied. `And, besides, it had started to drop off, my fingers are getting so thin.'

TWENTY EIGHT

We went to the Seven Sisters the following day for a picnic. There wasn't enough time to arrange a proper party. Gary drove the ambulance. Paul, Oliver and I went with David. It had been somewhat problematic persuading Paul to come along, seeing as Oliver was going to be there. But, in the end, he did it for Gary who had specifically invited both of them. I'd offered to drive the ambulance, but Gary had insisted on doing it himself. It was obvious he wanted to be alone with Max, which was fair enough.

I had never been to the Seven Sisters and was unprepared to find them so meadow-like. We'd parked by a farmhouse and made our way across the flower-strewn landscape to the cliffs. Oliver, Gary, Paul and David went ahead, whilst I toiled behind with Max. Oliver walked with Gary; Paul and David went together each carrying a handle of the hamper. There was a difficult atmosphere. Paul and Oliver hadn't spoken, and it was obvious that David thought I was being tactless in bringing Oliver along at all. At the cliff, David turned and looked over his shoulder, uncharacteristic irritation clear in his expression as he began spreading a blanket on the grass. `Come on,' he shouted.

`Have you ever tried pushing a wheelchair through grass?' I shouted back.

`Ignore him,' Max said, `take as long as you like.'

The sun, less warm than of late, was shining and the hiss of the waves could be heard from the beach a couple of hundred feet below. From where we sat I could see, on my right, a couple of ridges making up the first two of the Seven Sisters. We were on the third. The last four reached eastwards, with Beachy Head visible beyond. It was all open, windswept, and wild in a municipal country-park sort of way. The breeze kept catching my hair and blowing my fringe down into my eyes. Everyone else's hair, except Oliver's, was too short to be windswept. Oliver had walked the few yards necessary to be able to see the sea. He stood silhouetted like the central figure in some apocalyptic painting. I still felt ambivalent about him; unable to fully believe Paul, despite his obvious honesty.

There's so much gossip about, I thought, the only thing to do is take things as they come and make up my own mind through observation – and, anyway, people change . . .

Oliver had been so attentive to me, so careful in our relationship that I couldn't see him as devious. And as there was so much hostility towards him from Paul and David, my instinct was to defend him, regardless of my own suspicions.

`So that's Oliver,' Max whispered to me cryptically.

David, his back to the cliff edge, was unpacking the picnic: Paté de foi gras (from Max), home-baked rye bread (from Max's mother), Japanese pickled seaweed, tinned raspberries, olives, pastrami, anchovies, fresh strawberries. There were poppy seed rolls, prawn and melon salad, wild rice compote, aubergine paté, white wine, champagne and a large box of Belgian chocolates.

`Happy birthday Gary,' said David when he'd laid it all out. He handed Gary a china plate and a wine glass.

`Not bad,' Gary murmured, looking at the picnic, then out at the expanse of sea.

Oliver joined us and we ate in a desultory way, sampling everything (except meat, for me). Oliver was calm, seemingly happy in his cut-off way. I'd been afraid that David was going to be cold towards him, but in the end he was too smitten with Paul to be anything but charming.

`This is the kind of place I'd come to have a nervous breakdown,' said Oliver. `You could lose your mind here and never find it again.'

`I think it's peaceful,' said Max.

`Pleasantly undulatory,' I said.

`It gives me vertigo,' said David.

Gary smiled.

David leaned against Paul. Oliver, sensing hostility

towards him, surreptitiously took my hand and held it. Gary knelt by Max's wheelchair and fed him morsels from the picnic. It was like an allegorical vignette – 'Revellers on the Edge of Doom'. I think it was Gary's intention to make us all feel this.

Later, when everyone else had gone home and Oliver was working, Gary and I sat together in his flat. We continued our conversation of the previous night.

'You know,' he said, 'Morocco was a shock to me in a way. I always thought that I could get away from my illness, that I could get on a plane and leave all that stuff behind – at least for a while. But of course I can't. I can never get away from being ill. Not when I've got a bleeper that goes off every six hours to tell me to take my AZT. It's like a message machine that goes off throughout the day, saying "You've got Aids, you've got Aids." It even wakes me up in the night to tell me I'm ill . . . '

'But you're not ill at the moment,' I told him.

'No, but I have an illness.'

He peered at his naked fingers and sighed.

'Let's talk about something else.'

'Okay. Tell me about your sexual encounter, then. If you want to.'

Gary smiled.

'Alright.'

He rubbed his hands against the denim of his jeans as if trying to conjure up the memory.

'Ralph, the guy I flew out there with, was going to Morocco for the sex. He might as well have gone to Amsterdam or somewhere, because he's not into Arab boys particularly. It was his boyfriend who was more interested – ironically, seeing as he was the one who couldn't go.

'The hotel was pretty well exclusively gay, but had that ubiquitously non-specific international feel to it. I had a lot of time to kill whilst Ralph went off to amuse himself. I met a guy in the hotel who, as it happened, also had Aids – KS. I recognised a small lesion on his neck. It put me off him a bit. I know that's a terrible thing to say, but when I was in hospital I realised that just because two people share the same disease, it doesn't mean they'll like each other. And there's nothing I hate more than sitting around talking symptoms, therapeutic though that is for a lot of people.

`This guy recognised me straight away as a colleague, as-it-were. I think my weight loss has reached the recognisable stage.'

`You don't look any different from when I first met you,' I objected.

`That's because I've been losing weight so slowly that you haven't noticed. The first two stone dropped off before we met. The rest seems to be slowly evaporating. Have you noticed how my energy levels seem to be tailing off even more?'

`No.'

`Come on, Rick, it won't hurt me if you admit that you've noticed it.'

`I can't see you as being ill,' I said. `I can't do it.'

`Denial. I can understand that,' he said. `It was good to meet another person out there who had got through the denial stage.'

`Was he ill?'

`He was bursting with energy. It was kind of infectious. Infectious, ha, ha. We met by the pool and he asked me in a round about way if I had Aids, so I said "yes, but I don't want to talk about it" and he said "good, neither do I". It didn't occur to me that we would end up making love. Sex is so complicated when you're dealing with someone who doesn't know you're ill. But that was never an issue.'

`Are you going to see him again?'

`We didn't exchange addresses,' Gary said. `He lives in America.'

TWENTY NINE

I had forgotten that I'd agreed to go with David to a fancy dress party. I'd spent a long, fraught afternoon organising the phone rota at the Helpline, and then gone on to a protracted discussion at GAF about renaming the group to include the word lesbian. No suitable name had been thought up – GLAF we thought sounded too forced – so we'd adjourned again to think about it.

It was only when I heard the taxi's horn that I remembered David and I had agreed on a just-like-old-times evening.

`Hello love!' cried David, skittering across the pavement on heels as dangerous as knives. `Ready?' He adjusted his leatherette bobby cap, then heaved his arm across my shoulder.

`Come up,' I said, relieving him of his voluminous drag bag and turning to go inside as the taxi drove off.

`I'm just a girl who can't say no . . . ' David sang to the street and staggered into the hall, up the stairs and into the flat.

`A glass of wine, with ice,' he gasped, sinking onto the settee. `And what's up with you? You're not dressed yet.'

`I've only just got in,' I said. `I don't think I can face a party. I'm shattered.'

`Oh, love, don't say that,' he wailed. `I can't go on my own. Not like this.'

I looked down at his beige, sparkling one-piece dress, pinched at the waist with a six-inch-wide gold plastic belt. His look of distress was so comic, and so sincere, that I laughed in spite of myself.

`You know how I feel about wearing dresses,' I said. `I just don't feel right.'

`But men love wearing dresses, if only they'd admit it.'

`You mean *you* do.' I handed him his wine and he

gulped it down.

'Just look at my goodies,' he told me, ripping open his bag and pulling out a vest-dress with flamenco frills. 'No? Well, what about this – black taffeta embroidered with gold leaves?'

'Nice try,' I said, 'but not me. Here, I'll help you with your make up.'

'Yes,' he said, 'I'd better get my lips right. I left a kiss on the cabby's fiver.'

Later, I succumbed slightly when, dressed in white, David draped a white shawl over me.

'Very you,' he said. 'The angel in white. Here, I think I've got just the thing. Most appropriate!'

He took a white nylon turban from his bag and pulled it onto my head.

'Oh, love,' he said. 'A bit of slap and you'll be gorgeous.'

When we finally left to get another taxi I had been worked over and, feeling self-conscious – even after several rapid glasses of wine – I followed David. He'd given me black-rimmed eyes and darkened eyebrows and, although I didn't look as though I was in drag, I felt like I'd stepped out of some tacky pantomime. He'd attached plastic oranges, apples and bananas to my turban – very Carmen Miranda – and we both looked a sight.

The taxi driver, when he stopped, laughed.

'Oh my God,' he said. 'Get in.'

'Waterloo Street, driver,' David said, then turning to me he added, 'isn't he a cutie?'

'Mmm,' I replied non-committally, still not absolutely comfortable with either my clothes or David's outré persona – a campery he took out every now and again, dusted down, and wore like his outrageously unfashionable outfit.

'What's your name?' David asked the driver.

'Guy.'

'Doing anything later, Guy? Wanna come to a pard-ee!'

'Thanks,' he said, 'I'm going home to the missus.'

'Me and my friend Charlene could show you a real good time,' he told Guy. 'What's your missus got that we ain't?'

'A cunt?' the driver said.

'Okay, okay,' David drawled. 'No need to get personal.'

The driver didn't reply. I clutched David's hand and banged it against the central arm rest.

'Shh!' I whispered, thinking that Guy, beautiful though he may be, could stop and throw us out. I didn't mention my dislike of being called by a woman's name. David knew well enough and was doing it out of mischief. I refused to rise to his bait.

When the taxi pulled up at our destination, David handed the driver a note.

'You can keep the change, love,' he said, 'but only if you give me a kiss.'

Guy leaned over to kiss David on the cheek, but David grabbed his face and crushed his red-greased lips against Guy's. There was a horrific tableau as David seemed to be inflating the driver. And he just let it happen. He sat there allowing his head to be waggled from side to side. At last, with a gasp, David let him go and jumped from the car.

'Thanks, gorgeous,' he called to Guy. 'Come on Charlene,' he said to me, 'we haven't got all night.'

As we walked to the flat, David laughed.

'I got my tongue right in,' he told me, 'to the hilt. I know these Taxi drivers. They'll do anything for a couple of quid.'

The door was opened by Gavin, a vague acquaintance of mine – a close friend of David's. He was dressed as a medieval pauper in tights and ripped white shirt. A small axe was protruding from his back amidst an ooze of gore.

'Hiya, David,' he said. 'Stephen isn't it?' he asked me.

'Charlene,' David said, pulling me inside. We walked through to the kitchen. David had told me that it was a drag party – but it was only fancy dress. He was the only one in drag.

'I feel like a tart,' I whispered.

'But y'are Blanche,' David yelled, 'y'are.' He thrust a glass of wine into my hand and pulled me through to the next room. Here there was music; a couple of people were dancing.

`Just like the old-days,' he purred, putting our glasses on the mantelpiece and draping his arms round my neck.

`No,' I said, `this isn't like old times. We've changed.'

`I told you you were going middle-aged,' he sighed.

We danced for a while. It was enjoyable, but I felt that I was trying to be a previous self – one long since consigned to a past in which superficiality had to be adhered to as a fashion accessory. A plastic banana banged against my ear and I felt old.

`If Oliver could see you,' David laughed, `he'd never believe it. You know, you're too straight sometimes.'

`Well, Oliver isn't going to see me.'

`Are you getting on okay with him?' David asked, stopping short at the curtness in my voice.

`I don't know,' I said. `I keep on thinking what Paul said about him; it's made me kind of cautious. And Oliver has picked up on that, which has made him moody. It's ridiculous, David, all this stupid conjecturing. The fact is that Oliver has been fine with me, so there's no reason to take notice of anything else.'

`Except that it's a good idea to keep him at arms length. He shouldn't be living with you, Rick. He should have a place of his own so that if you ask him to leave, he's got somewhere to go.'

`I know,' I said, `I know. But I can't see that far ahead right now.'

`It's up to you, and I've told you too often to be careful to have any intention of telling you again. But I'm here for you, Rick. Remember that at least.'

He smiled at me, and without thought I found myself smiling back.

`Anyway,' he said, `enough of that for this evening. Stop worrying. Have fun.'

Sod it, I thought. He's right.

Several hours later I let myself into the flat. It was ten to two and I felt calm. I went into the bathroom and looked at my smeared make up, my clammy forehead, my damp shirt. I had danced with David until we'd collapsed together in the corner. There's nothing like physical tiredness to make me feel close to someone.

David was always so good at giving affection. I have to be feeling relaxed before I can be tactile. But we'd talked, laughed, cuddled (always a strange experience when David was in drag) and joked our way through the evening. Now I wanted to sleep.

Oliver would be home in half an hour or so, but I couldn't face him. I didn't want to defuse the glowing happiness of the evening by confronting him. It wasn't really any of my business what he'd got up to in previous relationships. But I was shocked by the thought of his vindictiveness against Paul and couldn't understand what could motivate such unpleasant behaviour. I don't think I worried for myself; because I could walk away from Oliver if I wanted to. I just worried, period.

Damn Paul, I thought, I don't need this.

When Oliver got in, I was in bed, but I hadn't been able to sleep. He came to bed and nestled against me.

`Are you okay?' he whispered when I didn't respond.

`Shh,' I said, `get to sleep.'

He lay looking up, then clicked the light on.

`It's not like you to sulk,' he said. `I've had a think this evening and I've realised what's caused your moodiness. You've been talking to Paul . . . Of course, once I worked it out I realised it was inevitable.'

`I see Paul all the time. Of course I talk to him.'

`And?'

`And what?'

`You believed him?'

`You mean he was lying?'

Oliver stayed silent, stroking his shoulder for a while.

`Don't you want to hear my side of it?' he asked.

I turned to face him.

`Would it help?'

`You obviously don't think so.'

`Tell me, then,' I said.

`You believed him, didn't you?' said Oliver. `I knew you

would.' He lay on his back again, breathing steadily.

'Okay, tell me what happened between you and this Lewis guy, then,' I said.

'Would it help?' he asked with cutting sarcasm. 'You've obviously made up your mind already.'

'Come on Oliver, just tell me. Then we can get some sleep.'

'You want me to tell you so you can get some sleep! How nice that you're so concerned about my feelings.'

'Tell me, alright. I've asked you to tell me, so either tell me or go to sleep.'

Oliver looked at me, then suddenly his face seemed to crumple; to deflate. The brightness of his anger dulled and his voice came out only slightly louder than a whisper.

'It was all a game of Lewis',' he said. 'He likes to make people jealous, and Paul wasn't the only one he did it to. I worked with him, so I knew what he was like.

'He pretended that he'd slept with me, even though it wasn't true, to try and make Paul jealous. And he succeeded. Once, when Paul came round and delivered a note to the club asking to meet him, Lewis pretended he hadn't got it, even though he had. Another evening when Paul came round to speak to Lewis, he sent me out to tell Paul to go away – then pretended he knew nothing about it. I was just an errand boy. I didn't realise what Lewis had been saying about me to Paul – that I'd lied to him and all that. It wasn't until I was frozen out by Paul a few months later at a friend's house that the story came out. Oh, not from Paul, of course, we're not on speaking terms. It was a friend of his who reminded me what it was I was supposed to have done.'

'I see,' I said.

'I hope you do,' Oliver said, 'because life is not always as straightforward as you think. Paul believes I lied and cheated on him. I can see why he thinks that, but he's wrong. He had one story from Lewis and one from me. I can't blame him for believing Lewis . . . You can believe me or disbelieve me, but that's how it was.'

I remembered the tone of conviction in Paul's voice, and

the distaste with which he'd spoken of Oliver.

`This guy Lewis sounds like a pretty messed up individual,' I murmured.

`You've said it,' Oliver agreed.

I reached out my left arm and Oliver moved to me, laying his head on my chest.

`Who gives a toss about the past anyway,' I said. `It's the present that matters.'

`And the future,' whispered Oliver.

The pressure of his head was reassuring and as I looked down I could see a single grey hair growing from the centre of the swirl of growth at his crown. I flattened it against his scalp with my fingers, feeling as I did so an indentation at the top of his cranium.

`I fell off a gate when I was three,' he said, noticing that my fingers had paused. `If I ever go bald I'll look deformed.'

I felt the stirrings of an erection as his breath drifted against my ribs.

THIRTY

'Rick, good,' said Marti as I walked into the Fotofit office, 'the car has arrived to take you to your assignment. We're just waiting for Julia now.'

'I thought it was a cast-of-thousands pop video.'

'No, it's a cast-of-two pop video. Julia and you.'

She leafed through her papers.

'It's Japanese. You're supposed to be a mid-forties crippled Mafia boss . . . And don't blame me,' she interrupted as I began to protest. 'They wanted you. It's work.'

'I thought Godfathers were supposed to be fat and foreign-looking.'

Marti shrugged.

'To the Japanese, anyone who's not Japanese is foreign-looking. It's for their home market – a video compilation of oldies-but-goldies. You're doing . . . *A Whiter Shade of Pale*, by Procol Harem.'

I sat on a leather-chrome seat and waited. The office was decrepit-chic – battered floorboards under expensive furniture. White painted brickwork hung with signed art photos. There was a time when this sort of place seemed to spell my future, but now I was happy that I would be giving up. There was something ultimately suffocating about my modelling. Perhaps it was because I am not, and never have been, a performer, an actor. It wasn't a thrill in itself to stand in front of a camera and try to be alluring, aloof, available, unavailable, straight, zany – a businessman, a bank clerk, a father of two or, even, a mid-forties crippled Mafiosi . . .

Roll on September, I thought, as Julia walked through the door.

'Julia, this is Rick. Rick – Julia,' said Marti. 'Are you ready to go? The car's waiting.'

We threw our bags into the back of the rusty Toyota Estate.

'Fucking parking,' said Julia. 'It took me twenty minutes to find a space.'

As we moved off, the driver gave us a few words of warning.

'I don't know if you've ever worked with the Japanese,' he said, 'but they expect a little more from their actors than the British do.'

'What does that mean?' Julia asked.

'Let's just say that if a Japanese director was to ask a Japanese actor to jump from a moving vehicle, the actor would do it.'

'We're not going to have to jump out of a car are we?' Julia asked, suspiciously.

'I don't know what you're doing today,' he told us. 'All I'll say is that yesterday's actors refused to do what they were asked.'

'And what was that?'

'I'm not at liberty to say.'

We were driven to Richmond park where a camera crew and make-up artist were waiting. I was given a dark suit, cashmere coat, cream silk scarf, wide brimmed trilby and dark glasses. 'Oh, and this,' said the interpreter handing me a walking stick.

'Is this for real?' Julia smirked.

After make-up we were asked to get into a limousine. We sat in the vehicle with the chauffeur, a lighting man, an assistant lying at our feet and the cameraman.

'Okay,' the interpreter told us through the window as the director gave instructions. 'You married. Julia, you are young wife. You are going for drive in park with husband.'

'Right,' said Julia. 'Am I in love with him? Are we happy or sad? What emotion should we play?'

'Do as you feel,' the interpreter said. Julia laughed.

'So?' I asked, 'are we in love?'

'Might as well be,' she said, and smiled.

The car moved off and I tried to look rich, crippled and in love.

'Fotofit always get the weird shoots,' she said as the car swung out into the road and the opening bars of *A Whiter Shade of Pale* sounded from a stereo on the floor.

'This is mood music?' I whispered.

'I wonder where the limousine fits in?' she replied. 'It's not in the song.'

'Nor is a middle-aged crippled Mafiosi.'

Julia snorted. Deer gazed at us with innocent eyes as the limousine crawled past. I gazed back, thinking: this is not me. I am not sitting in a limousine pretending to be rich and in love. I am someone else, and I want to be somewhere else.

'Okay,' said the interpreter, 'this is where you get shot.'

'I get shot!' Julia exclaimed.

'No, not you. Rick.'

There was a buzz of conversation with the director.

'Julia, you hate Rick. You want to kill him for his money. You have hired a hit-man who is going to assassinate him.'

'But I was in love with him in the limousine.'

'You looked as if you were in love with him, but you weren't.'

'Ah.'

'Rick, you walk through trees with your wife. You walk slowly because you have bad leg. When director claps his hand, that means you been shot.'

'Look,' I said, 'I can limp no problem, but I don't know about being shot . . .'

There was another brief consultation with the director, who came forward, tugged my sleeve, and pointed at his chest.

'He show you,' said the interpreter.

The director – short, expressive, energetic – hobbled forward a few metres, stopped suddenly, threw his head back, clutched his hands to his heart, fell slowly to his knees, let his hands fall, inert, to his sides then crumpled forwards, rolling over a couple of times for good measure.

Julia and I laughed.

'You can't do that,' she whispered.

'Why not?' I shrugged. 'It's money. If it looks stupid on camera, it's their fault for not hiring a stuntman.'

We waited as they aligned the equipment and got a smoke machine to waft mist across the scene, then the clapperboard clapped and we began to walk – or in my case, hobble – towards the camera. After a dozen paces or so the director clapped his hands. I lurched backwards, flinging my face towards the sky, dark glasses flying off into the grass. I sank slowly to my knees, arms slightly raised at my sides, eyes closed, then toppled slowly forwards, my face contacting with the wet earth in a long smear as it was pushed forward by the weight of my body. Because of the angle, I couldn't roll over, so I lay as still as I could, an unhealthy taste of mud in my mouth. There was a brief silence.

'Cut,' shouted the director.

Julia looked down at me as I turned onto my back, her lips trembling from the effort of not laughing. There was a polite spatter of applause from the camera crew.

THIRTY ONE

A couple of days later I took a call from David.

'It's Gary again,' said David. 'We'd better go and see what we can do.'

'What's happened?'

'He's chained himself to the railings outside the Health Authority headquarters.'

'It must be part of the hospice protest,' I said. 'I didn't know he was involved in that.'

'Obviously he is. Let's go.'

Gary was not alone, though he was one of only two that had actually chained themselves up. The other one was Nigel, a member of GAF, who greeted me with a smile. I stopped between them.

'Well done,' I told them as a policeman ushered me on.

There were several other GAF members who greeted me, but I was surprised to see Max there, with a helper I'd never met. Paul was there too, carrying a placard with the old faithful slogan: LIVING WITH AIDS – DYING FOR MONEY. He greeted me with a smile, David with a kiss. The police began talking earnestly to Gary and his companion.

'How's it going?' I asked Paul.

'People keep saying they're doing all they can to get a hospice here – everything, that is, except putting up money. It's sick, and pointless.'

I heard Nigel saying loudly: 'If they can afford to burn wheelchairs, they can afford to pay towards a hospice.'

'Burning wheelchairs?' David asked.

'Didn't you hear about that?' I told him. 'The Health Authority were going to burn all wheelchairs that had been used by people with Aids.'

'Surely not.'

Paul shrugged. 'Nothing surprises me these days.

Popular ignorance is bad enough, but when the Health Authority joins in . . . ' He turned back to the small demonstration. 'We were hoping for the press, but it seems they've decided to ignore us. Joey from the Aids Centre brought his camera to record what goes on, but I'd hoped for the *Argus* at least.

'Incidentally,' he added, 'have you heard that the Family Conference has been banned from coming back to Brighton?'

'No,' I said, 'when did that happen?'

'Yesterday. It just shows how a few angry people really can make things change.'

A police officer appeared carrying a pair of heavy duty wire cutters. The dozen or so protestors jeered. I joined in. There was a gathering crowd of onlookers. I suppose it's not every day you get the chance to see two people with Aids being cut from the railings in front of the Health Authority headquarters.

'Have they been arrested?' I asked after Gary and his fellow chainee had been taken away in a police car.

'I should think so,' said Paul, 'though whether the Health Authority press charges is another matter. If they did it would only give us more publicity. I'll get straight down to the station with Andy and Joey and see what we can find out.'

'Need any help?' I asked.

'No, but thanks.' He left with a wave and went to talk to the other demonstrators who were beginning to disperse.

Max nodded us over.

'Fancy a drink?' he asked.

'Okay. David?'

'No thanks, I've got work to do.'

We went to The Exeter; me, Max and Philip, his silent helper. Philip was slow, careful, neatly dressed in well-worn clothes. He neither smiled nor frowned and, once I was used to his eeriness, it was easy to imagine that Max and I were alone.

'Gary looks strained,' Max said.

'So would you if you'd chained yourself to some

railings.'

'I don't mean today particularly. He looked better today, with all that fight in him. I meant generally. Especially since he went to Morocco.'

'Yes, I know what you mean.'

'And he's sold his ring. I can't believe he did that. If he'd asked me, I'd have paid for him to go. I may not have all that much money, but I could have paid for that at least.'

There was nothing I could say.

'He's been spending more and more time with me, which I like. But it worries me all the same. I think he's beginning to give up, Rick. I've asked him if there's anything wrong – if he's got any symptoms, but he won't talk about it.'

'There's nothing we can do,' I said. 'I learned that when he disappeared. It's his life, and these are his decisions . . . '

'There are so many things I want to do with him. That's the thing. I know you took me to the Crayford, and that was wonderful, but I want to do more of that kind of thing. I want to do things like that with Gary; I want to *experience* things with him.'

'If you call being beaten up a worthwhile experience,' I muttered.

'Of course it is, in the right circumstances,' he said. 'I can see you still think the whole thing's daft.'

'No I don't.'

'Of course you do. You think it's all stupid, or a silly game,' he said. 'I know you do. I can understand that. But look at it from my point of view. When I was seventeen I used to hang around down by the West Pier waiting to be picked up for sex. It was easy. Sometimes I'd get money out of it, but I did it for fun mostly. I could go down there and have the thrill of wondering what was going to happen, who was going to turn up.

'And then I had the accident. Long before I grew up; before I really understood what sex was, before I'd ever tried looking for a relationship. Well okay, that was twenty years ago. But there's still anger there, Rick. Sometimes I'm so angry I can hardly breathe. I am so stuck inside this body. Did you know I've never had a love affair? As an adult, I've never got up and gone off by myself. I've never cooked myself a meal. I've never been up a ladder, mowed a lawn, run for a bus, climbed a mountain, rowed a boat, driven a car. I've never had anyone lean over and whisper that they love me. I've never lived with anyone. But I still feel desire. I still have sexual feelings. They just don't get as far as my cock. But I feel them up here. I still want to have sex. But I can't. And I know, from the past, what it is possible to do with your body. I know what it feels like – or used to. I dream about it sometimes, but that only makes it worse.'

I sat and looked at Max sitting there flushed, immobile.

`I'm sorry Max, I didn't realise.'

`Of course you didn't. Why should you? You're not quadriplegic. But that's why I wanted to see some seedy bar brawl,' he said. `I wanted to see some anger, some aggression. I've kept mine shut up for so long I've forgotten how to express it. And it's all got so much worse lately.'

`Why?'

`Because of all the unbelievable things that might have happened to me, of all the unexpected things – the most incredible has happened. For the first time in my life I've fallen in love. With Gary. And do you know what,' he added, lowering his voice. `He's said he wants to sleep with me.'

`That's wonderful,' I said.

`Is it?'

`But is it possible?' I asked. `I mean, logistically.'

`Mmm,' said Max, `maybe with a little imagination . . . But, as you know, it's a single bed.'

`A pretty big single bed.'

`But there are all those gadgets . . . and we couldn't do anything.'

`I don't think he wants to sleep with you for sex,' I told him. `I can understand wanting to share a bed with someone you care for.'

`But what would the nurses say at seven-thirty when

they came in to give me my morning enema?'

'Have a laugh, probably.'

'I don't know,' he sighed. 'I've been quadriplegic for twenty years and no one's ever asked to sleep with me before.'

'All the more reason to give it a go.'

Max nodded. 'And there's not much time to sit around wondering whether to say yes, is there? Gary might not be around much longer. I'm only trying to be realistic.'

I shrugged.

'I feel so sorry for him,' he sighed. 'I know I've got problems, but at least they're relatively stable. I've had time to get used to being quadriplegic. By the time Gary's got used to what's happening to him, it's all changed.'

'He seems to be taking it well,' I said. 'He's always sounded so objective when he's mentioned his illness to me.'

'If I was him,' Max whispered, 'I think I'd consider suicide.'

'I can't imagine you ever thinking of suicide,' I said. 'You're born to survive.'

'I wanted to commit suicide when I first broke my neck.'

'Then why didn't you?'

'What could I do?' Max retorted. 'How could I have killed myself?'

'Lots of things. An overdose . . . ?'

'Fine. How would I manage that? I can't move my arms. I wouldn't be able to take the pills, even if they were by my bed. And I could hardly say, "I'll have all sixty of my tablets tonight please nurse". People don't realise that quadriplegics *can't* kill themselves. We don't have the physical ability to kill ourselves. And you can go to prison if you help someone to commit suicide, so it's more complicated than just finding someone to administer an overdose. There's hunger-striking, I suppose, but that's a pretty drawn-out affair, and it's by no means certain that you wouldn't get force-fed if you tried it.'

I'd never thought of it, but it was true. There really was no way that Max could kill himself. He couldn't overdose without implicating the person who fed him the pills, he couldn't drown himself in the sea, stick his head in the oven, shoot himself, throw himself under a bus . . . he was doomed to live on, whether he liked it or not.

I mused about the problems of quadriplegia as I walked home. When I got back, Gary's postcard had arrived by second post:

Dear Rick,
80° here and beautiful. The management are more optimistic than me and have left two condoms in my room. I've hidden them to fool them.
Gary

THIRTY TWO

'Right,' said Oliver, throwing a towel in my face, 'it's nine-thirty, it's hot and we're going for a swim.'
'What, in Brighton's murky waters?'
'No. Littlehampton's. I've had enough of pebbles. I fancy seeing some sand.'
He'd prepared a breakfast of croissants with butter and apricot jam, and a jug of real coffee.
'There's a letter from Greece,' Oliver said as I sat down at the breakfast table. He handed it over with a cross between a smirk and a frown.

July 14th

Dear Rick,
I've told my sister about us. She came up from Athens for a few days and I told her. I was surprised to discover that she already knew – or at least that she'd already guessed from seeing us together in the past. She's convinced that in spite of her knowledge about us, mum and dad have no idea that we are lovers, and she tried to swear me to secrecy on that score, saying that it would probably kill dad if he knew. As for mum, who knows? She seems to have an infinite capacity for seeing the world as she wants to see it, rather than as it is. I told Effie that it wasn't only my decision and that I'd have to talk to you, but she threatened never to speak to me again if I do tell.
Isn't it amazing that she can accept my homosexuality for herself, so long as it is a secret – so long as she doesn't have to admit to anyone that she knows. It's because she finds it shameful, even though she can see by looking at me that there is no shame.
I feel stronger than ever now that it's all out in the open with Cosmas. I have Ria's support and a new business that looks set to thrive. If we decide to tell my parents, and I'm inclined to in spite

of Effie's dark warnings, then I know we are strong enough to survive — and who knows, through our love and commitment to each other, we may get them to accept us . . .

Things are changing throughout Europe, Rick. The Greeks are desperate to become more and more Western, no matter what the cost. Even if it means accepting homosexuality . . . At least, that's what I hope for, and it would be wonderful to be a part of it all. The future seems so much brighter all of a sudden, and I think only of how short a time it will be before you are here to share it with me.

I never want to be apart for so long again.
All my love
Andreas

Oliver was watching me as I read. Did he guess what Andreas had written? I don't know. I handed it over.

`Why are you showing this to me?' he said as he read it.

`Because this is the situation that I am in,' I told him. `You might as well know about it.'

Oliver licked his forefinger and pressed it down on some croissant crumbs, then lifted them thoughtfully to his tongue.

`There's only one thing that puzzles me,' he said.

`What?'

`If you're so sure it's what you want, why aren't you down in Greece now?'

`I can't be there,' I said. `I'm contracted to stay here.'

`But that isn't the reason, you see,' said Oliver. `It wouldn't have cost you much to stay down there with Andreas whilst waiting for your shoot. Your agency wouldn't strike you off because you'd gone away for a while — so long as you came back whenever it is that you've got to be available.'

`Except that Andreas would have had to support me, and all our money went into the business.'

`That's crap,' he said. `He's staying with your lesbian friend now, isn't he? You could be staying on her floor for nothing. The only thing you'd have to buy is food, and how expensive is that?'

'You don't understand,' I said, dismissively, thinking privately that he had a point. For as long as Andreas had been with Cosmas, living with him had seemed impractical. At Ria's, there was no reason why I should have taken the plane back to England before my shoot in August.

'No,' Oliver whispered into his coffee, 'you don't understand.'

'Are you trying to tell me something?' I sneered, feeling suddenly guilty for sounding so hateful.

We took the train and arrived at Littlehampton just after eleven, then made our way across to the dunes. The breeze was light but warm and desiccating. I was wearing a pair of espadrilles I'd worn in Greece and was enjoying the gritty feeling of having sand in my shoes. After twenty minutes or so, we arrived. Men were already sunbathing nude, and Oliver found a suitable indentation in one of the dunes to spread our blanket. All around there were tussocks of scratchy grass with sand between. From where we were we could look down over the sand to the shingle of the upper beach and the flat shoreline beyond.

We lay on our blanket, oiled ourselves, then gradually started to bake. I have a limited ability to cope with heat and needed to take frequent dips in the sea. In order to swim I had to wade out a long way because the shallow incline of the beach made it impossible to run down and take a plunge.

On returning from my third swim, I discovered Oliver talking to a tall man of around my own age. I could see them laughing together as I approached, then Oliver turned towards me and abruptly stopped speaking. I waved and walked up to them. I noticed several things then, the first being that they had a caught-in-the-act look about them, the second being that they were both slightly tumescent.

'Hi,' I tried to sound cheerful.

'Rick, this is Clive.'

We exchanged nods, but Clive didn't stop to talk further,

just wandered off with a `see ya' to talk to someone else.
'Who was that?' I asked. 'Did you know him?'
'No, why?'
'No reason.'
I dried myself briskly with my towel, then reapplied my lotion.
'Did you fancy him?' I asked as I lay down again.
'Yes,' he said. 'You should be flattered. He looks quite like you.'
I didn't say anything. I closed my eyes and let the sun glow red through my eyelids.
'He's asked me to see him later.'
'And will you?'
'I suppose that depends on you.'
'On me?'
Oliver turned over abruptly and glared at me.
'After all we've been through,' he said, 'I thought you might be a bit more concerned.'
'Look, Oliver, if you want to have sex with this man, that's okay.'
'How about a threesome. He suggested that too.'
'No thanks.'
'Why not? After all, you seem to have no qualms about casual sex.'
'By saying I don't mind you having casual sex with that guy, it doesn't imply that I want to have casual sex myself.'
'I didn't mean that,' Oliver told me. 'I meant that you've been having casual sex with me. I'm just a useful orgasm machine.'
'If you can't tell the difference between a quick blow-job and making love,' I told him, 'then we might as well give up now. We don't have to swear undying love and fidelity to mean something to each other.'
'But for you there's meaning and meaning.' He turned onto his stomach, facing away from me. I closed my eyes again but was unable to drift off. I moved my toes in a rhythm, the sand scratching pleasantly between them.
'You don't know what I want,' said Oliver suddenly, still facing the thick grass beyond our hollow.

`Tell me,' I said, `and I'll see what I can do.'

I could see Oliver taking a couple of deep breaths, could see the expansion of his diaphragm – the brief outline of his ribs. He turned to me again.

`I want to have a threesome with Clive.'

Clive came back an hour later, on his rounds. He stopped to talk.

`It's hot,' he said, looking at me. `Have you been for another swim?'

`Yes.'

`Sit down,' Oliver offered. Clive looked intensely at Oliver for a moment, then joined us on the blanket. He leaned back and looked up at the sky. It was a languorous movement designed to show off the musculature of his shoulders and the base of his neck. `I love it here, don't you?'

`It's the first time I've been,' I said.

`Hmm,' Clive murmured, looking to me. His eyes traversed the length of my body with such obviousness that I found myself smirking. Clive laughed, then turned to Oliver.

`I like your friend,' he said.

`Do you?' Oliver replied.

I looked at the gentle brown of Clive's skin, the sun-burnished hairs on his forearms, the play of muscle below the skin of his thigh as he turned to face Oliver.

`I don't suppose you've got any spare sun oil?' he asked, turning onto his stomach and curling up in a sinewy movement, `I need some on my back.'

Oliver took some oil in the crucible of his palm and spread it gently over Clive's back, then down, over his buttocks, to linger in the crack, idly running his hand up and down, as though tracing his fingers through water. All the time that Oliver was massaging, he looked directly at me.

`Mmm,' whispered Clive, raising his arse and slightly spreading his legs.

We looked at each other as Oliver tended to Clive's legs.

I glanced at Clive once, then back to Oliver. I shrugged. Oliver shrugged back. Clive turned slightly onto his side so that he discreetly showed me his erection – a characterless penis that looked functional and a little curved. Clive was obviously proud of it, and he touched the end briefly, pulling a gelling strand of moisture from the tip to indicate his arousal.

`Well,' Clive breathed, `are you two interested in coming back to my place for a coffee?'

Oliver looked down at him for a moment.

`Thanks, but no,' he said, `Rick and I don't really do that sort of thing. Do we?'

`No,' I said, `I'm afraid we don't.'

`Well,' I said after Clive had gone and we were packing up to go, `that was a bit pointless.'

`Why?' Oliver was busying himself rolling up the blanket.

`Calling my bluff like that.'

`Oh, that's what I was doing was it?' He got up and began to walk. I walked beside him.

`I wanted,' he said, then stopped again. `I just wanted you to see what casual sex is all about.'

`But I know that what I've got with you isn't casual, Oliver. You didn't have to be a prick-tease with Clive to prove it. I already knew.'

`I've realised a few things recently, that's all,' he said. `I've realised that for you the purpose of our relationship is to stop you getting dangerously frustrated, sexually, before you go and live with Andreas. You want an attractive de-spunking machine who won't cause trouble for you – who will defuse your libido and prevent you from making stupid sexual mistakes.'

`I suppose you're partly right,' I told him, `in that I thought we'd got an uncomplicated sexual relationship. But that doesn't make you a de-spunking machine.'

`That's what you told David you wanted before you ever met me.'

`Wait,' I hissed, grabbing him by the elbow and stopping

him again. 'What has David got to do with all this? How do you know what we talked about?'

'Don't be naive, Rick,' he said. 'I've seen quite a lot of David since you and I started going out together. He took me aside a while ago and gave me a few words of warning.'

'Oh,' I groaned, 'David. I might have guessed.'

Damn him, I thought, meddling.

'As far as I can remember,' I told him, 'the conversation went along the lines of this: David warned me that I would become frustrated without Andreas, and that I should consider having an affair. I thought he was being tacky and told him so. That was it. He has a meddlesome streak, I know. You shouldn't listen to him.'

'Nevertheless,' said Oliver, 'I did listen to him. And it hurt.'

'Oh God,' I said, 'come here.' I hugged him and felt suddenly old – too old for this kind of situation. I kissed him carefully on the lips.

'Let's go and get our train,' I told him.

Right, David, I thought.

On the train Oliver seemed more cheerful.

'Didn't you feel jealous when you came back from the sea to find Clive making a pass at me?'

'Should I have?'

'Probably.'

'I was curious,' I said. 'I'm afraid I don't seem to be the possessive type. If Andreas wrote to say he'd been screwing around a bit, I wouldn't mind.'

'You think that because it would make you feel less of a hypocrite,' Oliver told me. 'You think that because you know it won't happen.'

I shrugged and looked out of the window.

'So why are you looking so cheerful?' I asked him.

'It's kind of funny, really. I'm a walking disaster, emotionally. I walk straight from one disaster into another. First there's Duncan and then you. And there were others before Duncan. I should at least pick rich, generous people to have my disasters with, then at least I'd get something out of it.'

`And that's making you cheerful?'

`I can't be unhappy for long. I've decided not to think about you going. You will go. I can't stop you – I don't want to stop you because it would do no good even if you stayed. I've decided to accept your flat. I might get Lulu in to share with me, though maybe ex-lovers are a bad idea. Maybe ex-lovers are worth avoiding . . . '

THIRTY THREE

When we got in, there were three telephone messages. They were all from Gary. 'Rick, it's Gary. I was wondering if you could do me a favour. No, don't worry, I'll get someone else if you're not in. All the best. Bye . . . *Beep, beep.* Rick, it's Gary again, I'm a bit stuck. Could you call as soon as you get in . . . *Beep, beep.* It's Gary. Where is everybody when you need them? Call me, okay . . . '

'He doesn't sound well,' Oliver said as I dialled Gary's number. Gary answered almost immediately.

'Come down,' he said quietly, 'I'm sick and I need your help.'

I put the phone down slowly. I wasn't ready for this. I'd known for some time that I was the most practical person to contact if Gary was ill, because I was so close. I knew this, but still hadn't prepared myself. I didn't know what to do. What if he needed a doctor? Should I call an ambulance; try and find someone with a car?

'What is it?' Oliver asked.

'He's ill. Wait here.'

I went down to the basement and rang the bell. There was no reply. I rang a second time and when there was no answer, I knelt on the step and looked through the letter-box.

'Gary,' I called. 'Are you there?'

Again there was no reply. The hall light was on, but there was no sign of him. Then I became aware of a sound coming from one of the rooms.

'Is that you Gary?' I called. The sound came again. I couldn't catch any words, but there was a clear sense of urgency. I swore at myself for not talking to Paul about getting a spare key.

The door yielded immediately when I shoved it with my shoulder. Judging by the doorframe round the lock, it had been forced more than once in the past. I closed the door as best I could and went straight to Gary's bedroom.

He was under his duvet looking pale, glazed with sweat, and alarmed. His cordless phone was on the pillow beside him. He had deep, dark rings under his eyes.

'Sorry to bother you,' he croaked. 'I couldn't even come to answer the door.'

'Don't worry,' I said. 'What do you want me to do?'

'Call Dr Everley. He wasn't in when I phoned before. The number's there. If he's not in this time, we'd better call the hospital. I talked to them earlier and they said to phone back if I felt it was urgent.'

'Do you want to drink something?' I said. 'You look dehydrated.'

'Later,' he said. 'Call first.'

Gary lay back and closed his eyes as I phoned. I got Dr Everley's answerphone, then hung up and dialled the hospital.

'How serious is it?' they asked. 'Do you have a car?'

'No I don't have a car,' I said. 'It looks pretty serious to me.'

Gary opened his eyes and reached for the phone. I gave it to him.

'Who is this?' he whispered. 'Caroline? Hi, it's Gary. Look, I feel awful. Much worse than earlier. I've been on my own all day with no food or liquid. I haven't taken my temperature – I'm scared to.'

He listened for a while, then dropped the phone to the bed.

'What now?' I asked. He didn't reply immediately, just lay there breathing shallowly.

'Liquid,' he whispered. 'I have some there.'

I poured him a glass of orange drink and held it for him, thinking how familiar a movement it was – how often I'd done this for Max.

'They'll send someone over soon if they can. If not we'll have to get an ambulance.'

I sat and watched as he panted, grasping at each breath, eyes half closed. He drank half the drink, then gave up. I took his hand out from under the duvet and held it loosely in mine. He looked suddenly ill, really ill. Dog tired, and it was easy to believe that he could die. Soon. Now.

I wasn't ready for death. I wasn't ready to face it. As an abstract concept it was innocuous – as an intimate detail, a macabre bedfellow, it was appalling. Only Gary's breathing gave any animation to the situation. His face had the sunken appearance of a corpse.

So quick, I thought, only a couple of days ago he was out on the streets getting arrested, arguing, haranguing...

I was about to try and persuade him to drink some more, when Paul and David arrived.

'I'm here,' Paul said, coming in from the hall, going over to Gary's bed and taking his hand from mine. 'I got your message.' Gary opened his eyes and smiled. Paul patted the hand briefly and then became brisk. He opened the drawer of Gary's bedside table, removed the electronic thermometer and placed it gently in Gary's mouth.

'Go and get a flannel from the bathroom,' he told me, 'soak it in cold water, wring it out, and bring it here.'

I left and David followed me.

'Have you been here long?' he asked.

'Ten minutes,' I told him. 'I don't know how bad it is, but it's scary.'

David put his arms round my waist as I squeezed the flannel.

'It's okay Rick, he's not going to die.'

'How do you know?'

'Believe me,' he said. 'I've seen this enough to know when it's the end.'

I returned with the cool flannel and Paul wiped Gary's forehead as he looked at the thermometer.

'Haven't you seen one of the nurses from the centre?' he asked Gary.

'Yes, after lunch, but I wasn't too bad then. And I always play things down. You know me.'

'Yes,' he said. 'David, you bring the duvet up to the car. Rick, phone Caroline at the hospital to say we're on our way.'

'How high was the temperature?' Gary asked.

'Too high,' Paul told him. 'Now get ready, I'm going to carry you up to David's car.'

'Shall I come?' I asked.

'No. Phone the hospital. Then you can try and do something to make the front door a bit more secure. Come on after that if you want.'

He picked Gary up in one deft movement, folding him with ease so that his head could rest against a solid shoulder.

I found some general-purpose glue in a cupboard in the kitchen and set about repairing the splintered doorframe. Oliver came down with some coffee and, later, a vegetarian pizza. It was warm in the shady beginnings of dusk and I couldn't quite believe that Gary could be ill on a day like this. My skin still prickled from the sun at Littlehampton, my muscles still felt invigorated from my swimming. And Gary was in hospital. Oliver found some G-clamps and we left the frame glued and under pressure.

Before I went over to see Gary, I phoned Max to tell him the news. 'Ring me from the hospital,' he told me. 'Tell me what's going on.'

Oliver said: 'do you want me to come? I'm supposed to be working tonight, but it would be easy to cancel.'

'Don't,' I told him.

'I'll cancel the club, then,' he said. 'I don't feel like dancing.'

'No,' I said, 'do it. There's no point you coming to the hospital later. He'll be asleep and I'll be at home.'

'Come and sit down outside,' David told me when I got to the Aids ward. 'He's asleep.'

'Where's Paul?'

'He only stayed a few minutes. He had a meeting.'

'Is Gary okay?'

David shrugged.

'So-so. They've put him on an antibiotic drip, saline, and he's getting two units of blood. He was dangerously anaemic and dehydrated. And it looks like PCP again.'

I took a breath but failed utterly to feel calm, then looked around the sitting area. It was coldly clinical, with institutional comfy-chairs and a token plant – a money tree, requiring minimum attention for survival.

`He's got so many tubes sticking out of him that he looks like something from an SF movie,' said David.

Caroline came through. I recognised her from previous visits to other friends.

`Hi,' she said, `I've been in to see Gary and he seems stable. He's asleep so I don't think there's any point staying.'

`Thanks,' said David. `We'll come back tomorrow.'

Caroline kissed us briefly, smiled, then returned to the ward. David watched her go, nodded briefly to himself, then looked at me.

`Let's go and get pissed,' he said.

I nodded agreement and we left, walking down the five flights of stairs rather than wait for the rickety lift.

`Where shall we go?' he asked as we got into his car, `the Cross-Keys?'

`No, I'd rather not.'

David gave a slight smile of disguised triumph and tapped the wheel as he started the car.

`The Great Western?'

`Okay.'

I wasn't going to discuss Oliver right now. Much better to wait until I'd had a couple of drinks, then I'd have more chance of an unguarded response. Besides, Gary was far too preoccupying for me to feel like having a confrontation with David. It would seem petty in the shadow of Gary's suffering. I imagined Oliver pulling pints at the Cross-Keys and wondered what he was thinking now.

We parked a couple of blocks away and walked to the pub. `So that I can leave it there overnight and take a taxi home,' David said.

In the bar I ordered a pilsner, then broke the eerie silence that had descended between us.

`No matter how much you know about illness,' I said, `you always imagine that the case you're involved with might be different. You hope for the best and fear the worst; which is human nature.'

`Of course. And meanwhile, life goes on.'

`For us.'

I took several gulps of cold beer.

`But how do you feel about Gary?' I asked David. `I mean, you slept with him.'

`That's ancient history. We didn't ever have a relationship. I think we did a repeat performance the following day and that was it. Later, you think what might have happened, I mean regarding relationships, when you discover how nice they are as people. Sex should bring people together, but how many people have slipped through my fingers? It doesn't bear thinking about.'

`But doesn't it scare you that you slept with someone who you now discover has Aids?'

`No,' David told me, `why should it? I know he didn't give it to me. There are lots of things about this that are difficult to cope with, but for me anxiety about infection isn't one of them.'

He drained his glass and ordered another double.

`It's Paul I don't understand,' he went on. `He's young enough to have always known about Aids. His whole sexual life has been informed by fear. Even before he lost his virginity he had the information with which to avoid infection, and he used it. Yet he's out there, doing so much. I don't know why he feels so affected by it.'

`He must have friends who are infected. He must be personally involved as a gay man. It's impossible not to be.'

`Yes, but do you know how many friends of his have died? Friends he met outside the context of the Helpline, I mean.'

`No.'

`One. Do you know how many Aids funerals I've been invited to since my first one in May 1984?'

`No.'

`Forty-three.'

`David,' I said, `none of us can know what that feels like

unless we've experienced it. I can't know that. I just can't. It must make you so . . . '

'Weary,' said David. 'Sometimes I can't think of anything else but Aids. It becomes my entire horizon. It's worming itself into my psyche, colouring my future.'

I put my arm round his shoulder and we lapsed into silence for a while.

'How is it with Paul, by the way?'

He looked at me, sighed, sat up a little straighter, then smiled.

'It's funny,' he said, 'you think you've seen most things, done most things, felt most things – and then someone comes along who makes you feel different. If there's one thing that gives me strength, it's that.'

THIRTY FOUR

David and I ended up in The Dolphin. It was loud, brash and crowded. I was drunk and felt sentimental, which had not been my intention. How could I be angry with David for going behind my back? How could I talk about Oliver?

David, thoroughly drunk, had cheered up considerably after his initial despondency at the hospital. Somehow, being greeted by so any people here had made him aware of life existing in addition to illness. He'd become physically demonstrative too, which I always find irresistible. We'd hugged each other, kissed, and now were leaning against each other, faces poised only inches apart.

'Come home with me,' David whispered. 'Paul's not going to be around, so there'll be no trouble.'

'No,' I told him with a laugh, 'but thanks for the offer.'

'Just to cuddle,' he said. 'We're too pissed for sex, so what's the problem?'

'I promised I'd be back to tell Oliver the news about Gary.'

'Oliver,' he sighed. 'I know what he wants. He wants to stop you going down to Greece.'

'No he doesn't,' I said.

'Of course, I don't expect you to see it.'

'You're such a schemer,' I said. 'You've been talking to him.'

'I was telling him the truth – that you wanted a casual affair until it was time for you to go back to Andreas.'

'Why,' I groaned, 'why did I ever let this happen? I should have subscribed to a mountain of porno magazines and wanked myself silly every night. Either that, or I should have tried celibacy.'

'Impossible.'

'Difficult, maybe, but surely not impossible?'

'Anyway, there's no point trying it now, is there?'

David took a taxi home at 11.20. I walked along the seafront to The Arches. Gus was on the door again and he waved me through with a smile into the thunderous interior of the club. I bought myself a can of lager and sauntered across to lean against a far wall.

`Rick?' a voice called. I turned to see Andy, an air steward acquaintance – more a friend of Andreas' than mine.

`Hi,' I said, `how's things?'

`Haven't seen you for ages. How is business in Thessalonika?'

`Fine,' I told him. `I'm off down there, sometime next month I think.'

`For a holiday?'

`No, to live.'

`Oh,' he said. `I heard that you two had split up. Someone told me that you'd got a new boyfriend.'

`Andreas and I are still together,' I said. `I'm going to go down and live with him. Nothing's changed.'

`Okay, okay,' he said, smirking at the irritation in my voice.

I drifted away wondering how many of our mutual acquaintances suspected that I was having an affair.

God, I thought, I'm turning into the kind of deceitful person I hate. But I'm learning something about truth whilst I'm at it. I'm learning that truth is different for different people – even for the same person at different times. To sit at home and want to be unfaithful yet not to be unfaithful; is that being true?

Life with Andreas remained, no longer unquestioned or untested, but surely more certain? By unsettling myself, I realised how important my previous stability had been.

And the price, I thought, is that in finding out how much I need him, I might have ruined everything.

When Oliver came on to dance I saw him in a completely different way. The first time, he had been less familiar – the glimpses of flesh had been erotically inviting. But now that I knew what was underneath, was familiar with all of his flesh, he ceased to be erotic – became sensual instead. I could focus on the way he moved, the way he seemed to scoop up the air around him and rhythmically pull it this way and that.

His clothes were of that secret kind – the sort that you might buy, keep to one side, and never have the courage to wear in public. He had bum-hugging lycra shorts, a thick leather belt with a huge eagle buckle and a white top made from some quilted material that was low-cut and narrow-waisted. Whilst he wore the jacket, the sleek indent between his pectoral muscles looked like the beginning of a bust, or the valley left by overdevelopment of muscle, but when he took it off to reveal his chest, the unshadowed musculature receded into a taut flatness filigreed with gentle hairs. I don't want to labour the point by going on about his looks, because another person with different tastes wouldn't find him special. It's just that, for me, there was a combination of looks and demeanour with Oliver that overwhelmed all rationality and made me want to ravish him.

He saw me towards the end of his stint and smiled across with a half-frown of questioning concern. I shrugged back. There was no simple way that I could communicate how Gary was. Instead, I sipped my lager and watched as he danced mesmerically before this typically capacity audience.

When he'd finished and left, dripping, to shower and change, I went to the bar.

`Can I go through to see Oliver?' I yelled to the barman.

Recognising me, he lifted the counter and steered me through to the doorway at the back. Inside there was a stock room and a bare concrete square with a toilet and newly installed shower, euphemistically called a changing room by the management. Oliver was changing here, wearing only his jock, and talking to the dancer who was preparing to go on next.

He came over to me and we embraced.

`How is he?'

`Asleep,' I said. `I'll go over and see him in the morning.'

`Do you want to talk about it?'

'No. I'm pissed. David and I went out.'

Oliver nodded. I sagged against him.

'Wait here while I take a shower,' he said, 'then we can go home and I'll make us coffee. I've got some dope, too.'

'I want to sleep,' I said. 'I want to go to bed and sleep.'

'Let's go now, then. You can sleep as long as you want to.'

'I've got to drive Max up to London in the morning, and I want to see Gary first.'

'Okay. I'll have a wash at home.'

He dressed quickly and we left.

'It's good to get drunk sometimes,' he said. 'We should do it together one of these days. There are some bars we could go to, aside from the usual gay ones.'

I nodded but said nothing. The cool air had made me feel unsteady and I grasped his arm. I knew as I walked that it wasn't just Gary that had made me feel so uneasy this evening. It was my whole situation – the continuing absence of Andreas, the continuing presence of Oliver, the unfaced intimacy that I felt for David, and the betrayal I felt when I'd realised that he was trying to scupper my relationship with Oliver.

If only I could jump on a plane tomorrow, I thought.

Oliver coaxed me into his bath when we got back. The water was amniotic in the constricting womb of the tub. I held myself pressed against him, memorising all his surfaces whilst he washed. Afterwards, he rolled a joint and we went to bed, making love slowly, hazily. I felt desultorily attached to him in that precious goodbye way.

Tomorrow, I thought, I'll start wrapping this life up. I'll make my plans to take the trip to the other side. I'll wait until I get a date for the Profile Two shoot and then book my ticket to the future.

'I feel lighter,' Oliver whispered as sleep submerged me. 'Don't you feel you could become a beam to slowly illuminate the bigger darkness inside? It's the darkness of the present that gets between people, somehow, and we forget that we have the power to light the spaces.'

THIRTY FIVE

The next morning it was Oliver's turn to get a letter that would effect us both. He opened it, unconcerned. I was curious, in spite of my dull head, because I wondered who he might have given his address to. He read it twice.

'Shit.'

'What?'

'Duncan. He's finally found out where I'm living.'

'And he's threatening you?'

'No, worse, he's suing me. He lent me some money, and now he wants it back.'

'And he's taking you to court?'

'I signed something to the effect that I would pay it back. I thought he'd forget it.'

'How much was it?'

'Only a couple of thousand.'

'A couple of thousand!'

'But it looks as if he wants interest.' Oliver laughed. 'Of course, I won't pay.'

'If you signed something, he could have you done.'

'Another new experience,' said Oliver.

'You don't know what you're saying,' I told him, annoyed that he wasn't taking it seriously.

'I've got seven days to cough up. It might as well be seven months, as I haven't got the money. But I've learned not to worry about things I can't change. No, that's not true, I do worry about some things, but money isn't one of them.'

I drank coffee, followed by orange juice, followed by water, to try and deal with my hangover. Oliver was too cheerful.

'You've been in debt,' he said, responding to my irritation. 'You told me about it. You still haven't cleared your Visa card.'

'Nowhere near,' I said. 'But that's not the same thing. I'm not going to be taken to court.'

'Cheer up, Rick, it's my debt, it's my responsibility.'

'Look, I've got to leave for the hospital. If I go now I've got time to walk. Want to come?'

'What else could I do on a day like this?'

We set off in the gentle warmth of the late July morning. The sky was brightly overcast as we walked. Oliver hummed a tune from Cabaret. The sea was subdued as we turned to walk along the esplanade; the open air café was serving its first customers as seagulls called to each other across the still water.

The hospital had the sterile smell of death about it, the kind of smell that makes me imagine bodies swabbed with formaldehyde. Fortunately the Aids ward smelled of roses. Gary was in room four with his breakfast tray beside him. He had two drips in his arm, but he looked better. He smiled when we came in.

'You look pink,' I said.

'All this new blood they're pumping into me. Sorry about last night,' he said. 'I hope I didn't put you out or scare you too much.'

'It's okay,' I said, sitting on the edge of his bed. Oliver sat on the single chair.

'How are you feeling?' I asked.

'Chesty. I did some nasty coughing in the night, but I seem better today. This blood seems to be helping. They're giving me two units.'

I looked at the red bag attached to the second drip. The blood was dripping at the rate of about one drop every five seconds. I couldn't help watching for the next drop to fall. Gary noticed.

'This transfusion should give me some strength,' he said, 'then I can get home.'

'It's alright here,' said Oliver. 'More congenial than any of the other wards.'

'But it's still hospital. The trouble with being on an Aids ward is that you're surrounded by people with Aids. Actually, that's good in a way because people know what you're going through, but it's still distressing to see how much worse it's probably going to get . . . '

I took his hand again. 'Have they said how long you'll have to stay?'

'At least until they've checked out these antibiotics. I've been on so many different tablets over the last eighteen months I'm riddled with chemicals. This new drug is more experimental than most, which means there may be side effects. But if things go well I could be out in a week or so.'

'Not bad.'

'They'd be prepared to let me out sooner if they knew I was being looked after,' he said. 'It's a bit worrying at first going back to live on my own, though I'd rather that than stay here.'

'Come to us,' said Oliver. 'There's a spare room, and we're both around during the day. If you need somewhere to recuperate for a day or two, do it with us.'

Gary looked questioningly at me.

'Sounds like a good idea to me,' I said.

'I couldn't have brought myself to ask,' he said, 'at least not directly. It's such an imposition. If I was healthy I wouldn't be too pleased about putting someone else up.'

We talked for a short time about other things and I got up to leave.

'I'm taking Max up to London for the day,' I said, 'so I can't stay longer. Tell Caroline we'll put you up. I'll phone tomorrow to arrange it.'

'Okay, and tell Max there's wheelchair access to the ward,' Gary said. 'I'd love to see him.'

THIRTY SIX

Arriving at Max's, it made me smile to see that my bike had been hacksawed off Eddie Tavistock's railings. The rusting frame was by the basement door awaiting disposal, wheels buckled from the ritual kick I'd always given it as I passed. The D-lock, I noticed, was still attached to the railings, scarred by repeated attempts to hack-saw through it.

Max was pensive when I got him up. He was listening to Maria Callas, which always meant nostalgia – he'd met her once and was a major fan. He was always interested in people with strange or sad personal lives; was attracted to tragedy, I think.

As I drove, I told him about Gary and how much better he looked.

'Good. We want to try sleeping together again.'

'So you've already done it once?' I said with a smile. 'You kept that quiet. You should have told me.'

'I didn't say anything because it didn't work very well. He got into bed and lay beside me, but he couldn't get comfortable and slept badly. I think he was coming down with this fever, maybe, and that didn't help. He got up eventually at around seven to go home and had left by the time the nurses got in, so I didn't bother to mention it. We reckon that if we move my emergency button to the left, it'll give us both more room. I won't need it if Gary's there, I can always wake him up if something happens.'

'Sounds fun if you can work it out.'

'It was fun, actually,' he said, 'in spite of the discomfort for Gary. We kept on talking and talking long after we'd decided to try and sleep, and he had his mouth so close to mine that we could whisper away like schoolboys after lights-out. And it was strange too, because although I couldn't feel him holding me, I was aware of it all the same.'

Max was going to an afternoon recital of various summer pieces at the Queen Elizabeth Hall. He'd only been able to get two tickets – one disabled, and one attendant. He had a friend coming, so it meant I had two hours to kill whilst the concert was in progress.

I left the ambulance at the Hall and took a tube to Dave's Place, a gay café near Charing Cross. I settled down with coffee and a cake, and wrote to Andreas.

14th August

Dear Andreas,
I was interested that your sister has realised about us. I thought your family would always blindly assume that you were heterosexual. As far as I'm concerned, it would do her good to have to confront our relationship in a wider context than her own secret horror. As for your parents, I think they'll have to know eventually, though after your fracas with Cosmas you might want to wait a while. It's just that if we never tell them and they find out that we're lovers, then they'd say – rightly – "see, even they thought it was something to be hidden". We both know this. It's not a question of "do we tell them?" – it's a question of coming to terms with the fact that we might hurt them. Their inability to cope with your sexuality really is their problem, not yours. If they want to share that pain with us, then we can help. If they want to cut us off, then we'll have to cope.

I know you'll say that I've let myself in for this, and you'll be right in a way, but I've agreed to look after Gary at the flat whilst he's sick. At least I've got Oliver to give me a hand, and it won't delay my journey down to Greece. Either he'll get better and move out, or – even writing this seems like a bad omen – he'll die.

Max is off at some concert with an inebriated cellist friend. He's been so happy lately, though I can't help worrying about the future, given his attachment to Gary.

I hope you're keeping my potential English students interested. I'll need something to occupy me whilst you're busy with your manipulation. Give Ria a hug.
Lots of love
Rick

PS At last I can see a time when I'll be able to say I've survived our separation.

I folded the letter and pushed it into its envelope.
And I'd been hoping to book my flight today, I thought. How long is Gary going to be with us?
The Profile Two shoot would almost certainly be sometime in the next couple of weeks and I couldn't decide whether agreeing to stay behind to play host for Gary was helpful or incredibly obstructive. By playing host, I'd be prolonging my time in Brighton. Maybe I wanted to squeeze the last drops out of my life there before I left it forever.

I did the phones with Paul again the following evening. He was less talkative than usual, which made me feel formal with him. It was quiet, too, with only a couple of simple safe-sex enquiries and an internal message.
I hadn't noticed Paul's discomfort until towards the end of the evening, when I realised he wasn't looking at me directly when I talked to him.
`Look,' I said, `is there some kind of problem? You look stressed and upset.'
`It's nothing,' he said.
`It can't be nothing. Is there something wrong between you and David?'
`No, nothing like that,' he said, straightening the Aids Bulletins that he'd been flicking through. `Actually, it's about Oliver.'
`Oliver? What now?'
`I just didn't tell you everything about him. I reckoned it was all between you and him, but David says I ought to warn you about Oliver's stealing.'
`Stealing!' I laughed. `What's he supposed to have stolen?'
`He took clothes and cash from Duncan for a start; and there was some scandal at The Arches, though nothing was ever proved. He had a gold bracelet that he nicked from someone, who never had the heart to ask for it back. I still

can't believe that anyone could be so blatantly dishonest.'
He shook his head for a moment.
My ring! I thought.
`Just be careful,' he warned me, not for the first time. `Oliver seems so sweet and innocent, but don't leave any valuables lying around.'

THIRTY SEVEN

'At least I don't have KS,' Gary said as he reclined in the spare bed, sipping a mug of Horlicks. 'I've never regarded myself as a vain person, but I find I do have a horror of being disfigured by lesions. Especially on my face.'
'That's unlikely, though, isn't it, at this stage?'
'So they say.'
He smoothed the bedclothes with his fragile hands and looked out over the grass to the Regency façade beyond.
'I've missed having a view,' he said. 'Living in a basement you look out on mouldy bricks.'
He hummed a little to himself.
'Maybe it would have been better with KS,' he murmured. 'People with Kaposis live longer. Maybe it would have been good for me to get lesions on my face. I would have had to confront my illness then – try to come to terms with it. I wouldn't have been able to pretend it wasn't happening.'
'You've always struck me as being a realist,' I told him.
'A cynic, more like,' he sighed. 'I've always been a dreamer trapped in a cynic's body. I've always predicted the worst whilst hoping for the best, or even better than the best. I've always hoped for the impossible; wished that I could fly, or that I could visit outer space, or that I could fall in love forever. But strangely I've never wished away my illness. Probably because my other dream's were so impossible as to hold no fear of disappointment.'
'Possibly. But we're always so bad at knowing why we do or feel things. And it's at the times we're most sure that we're often most wrong.'
Gary had turned introspective. I suppose he had no energy to go anywhere except inwards. His face, sunken a couple of days before, had lost its skeletal look but had taken on a benign wastedness that made him look hauntingly angelic. It was our third or fourth conversation

of this kind in the day and a half he'd been here. He'd recovered in a way after his hospital treatment, but it was clear to us all that he wasn't going to get better. He'd never be able to dance again at The Arches, for instance, even if he did manage to get out and about for a while.

He had a profusion of visitors. David came, and Paul, who spent a long time talking through funeral arrangements and so on; all those seemingly morbid things that become perfectly normal so suddenly. Max came every day, sometimes with me as his helper, and had to have his wheelchair laboriously dragged up all those stairs. Oliver, to my surprise, was always popping in to say hello to Gary, to crack a joke or simply to flash a smile. I'd expected him to be more hushed – like I was – but if anything, Gary's presence made him more vibrantly alive and Gary obviously enjoyed being treated in this way.

Friends of Gary's that I didn't recognise called, and staff from the Aids Centre who had got to know him. I had to buy a catering tin of instant coffee.

`What do you do all day when you haven't got me to sit with?' Gary asked.

`As you know, I look after Max part-time. I also cook and eat and talk to friends and go out for walks. I sit at home waiting for my agent to phone, which is the boring part of it. Then I do some canvassing for GAF and my political stuff, and of course the Helpline, which stops me from feeling useless when I have no modelling work.'

`It sounds a full life.'

`I've got Oliver too, and Andreas to look forward to, and I've got you.'

`You could do worse,' he said, `than to stay here and get on with loving Oliver.'

`You've never met Andreas,' I said.

`But it'll be tough leaving Oliver.'

`I don't seem to have the conscious energy to think about that right now.'

`Savour these worries,' Gary told me. `They're part of life. To have worries about the future means that you have a future.'

On the fourth day Gary got worse. He'd been suffering from thrush in his mouth for some time, but now he presented a livid, extensive shingles rash across his chest and back. But he refused to go back to hospital. He was sometimes irrepressible in his anger at the thought of readmission and would shout at me through tears. These bouts of temper were usually accompanied by phases of confusion and memory loss, and it was agony to contemplate the onset of dementia.

District nurses came and monitored his drugs. The Homecare Team arrived from the Centre to care for him, turn him, run errands and retire for whispered conversations in the kitchen. Oliver and I cooked meals for three, though Gary ate so little we always threw food away. We couldn't bring ourselves to prepare food for him on a minute scale because of the admission that this would represent.

I had to rub cream onto his blisters several times a day. He bore it, mainly with anger – but sometimes with astonishing grace, smiling more than I would have thought possible. Max would sit alone with him for an hour or so every afternoon and whenever I passed the door I could hear them quietly talking as though making plans.

But Gary was becoming lethargic from the morphine which he took daily in syrup form. After six days the doctor stopped his antibiotics altogether. We all knew what that meant.

`I want to go home,' Gary told me on day seven, after the district nurse had been and he had refused a meal. `I want to die in my own bed.'

It wasn't difficult to arrange a rota to ensure that he was never left unattended. Oliver and I covered most daytimes. David, Paul and various other volunteers could cover the evenings. One of the Homecare Team stayed each night.

Oliver and I became more formal, drinking coffee together in Gary's kitchen whilst he slept, or going for long evening walks before making love in a less abandoned way than usual. Everything we did that affirmed life, reminded us of death. Gary's illness made me feel ashamed to feel pleasure. I knew this was crazy – that he would be upset if he knew, but still I felt suspended. Oliver did too and cancelled a couple of sessions at The Arches, sitting up late with me instead, getting drunk or stoned.

I had a casting on the Thursday and ran home from the station afterwards, angry to have been distracted. But when I got in, I found that Gary had been sleeping. I had missed nothing.

On Friday the doctor gave Gary a pump-injector. It fed into a vein and pumped drugs into him automatically every few minutes.

`I don't feel pain,' Gary whispered to me in a lucid moment, `though these fucking shingles blisters are annoying. When they burst, my pyjamas stick to me.'

I felt more and more sad as I rubbed cream into his skin and saw the beginnings of a pressure sore at the base of his spine. I could pull him forward with ease now to apply cream, he was so light.

`Thanks,' he said to me on the Saturday morning. `You've put in so much time and made it so much easier than I'd ever thought it would be.'

I didn't reply. There was no point – he sank straight back into sleep.

It was a quiet morning. I'd taken over from one of the Homecare Team at ten. Oliver was out shopping and due to join me at one. At around eleven, Gary, after waking briefly when I treated his skin, became immobile, perhaps comatose. His breathing slowed gradually and became more noisy, hesitating for awesome seconds after each breath.

I phoned the nurse whose number was pinned above the bed.

`It's terrible,' I said, `his breathing sounds so painful. What can I do?'

`Nothing,' she said. `Don't forget that he's in no pain. Listen, Rick, I hate to tell you this over the phone but he sounds like this because he's starting to die.'

`I know that,' I said. `You only have to listen for a moment to know that.'

'This is going to go on for some time,' she told me. 'Days probably. I can't come over straight away, but I'll drop in after lunch to see you. Just let him sleep undisturbed and be there if he wakes up. I know this is difficult for you.'

I phoned Paul next. There was no answer. Then David.

'It's Rick,' I told the answerphone. 'I'm with Gary and it looks bad. Give me a ring as soon as you get in.'

Then I went back to Gary. He looked completely absent. His body lay there breathing, with a curious movement, as though he had been rigged to an electric machine that worked his lungs for him. Nothing else seemed to be alive. I stood in the doorway for a while, watching him, then went back to the sitting room and the book I was reading. But I couldn't concentrate. The words became meaningless and I worried that he might say something important, so I went back to his room and sat carefully by him, taking his hand.

'It's okay, Gary,' I said, 'I'm here. It's Rick.'

And he stopped breathing. The silence that descended was eerily complete, totally unmenacing and indescribably sad.

THIRTY THREE

I was sitting with Gary's address book, systematically phoning his family and friends. To all of them the suddenness of his death was a surprise. For most he had been at least relatively well when they'd seen him last. I was strangely unemotional sitting there with the phone, telling people the news, listening to that pause before the reaction came – the choke, the cry, or the deadpan acceptance.

Paul and David were the first to get there, followed by the community nurse, three members of the Homecare Team, and Max with Philip. Gary's parents lived in Litchfield and wouldn't be down until the evening.

Paul was frighteningly efficient and knew exactly what to do, organising the undertaker and making us all hot drinks. With nine of us there, excluding Gary, it seemed almost festive. After some initial tears from others, we stood talking about Gary and smiling in the front room. In the kitchen I cried briefly in David's arms, but that was from the charge in the atmosphere and not yet for myself or for Gary.

When Oliver arrived, the body had already been removed. Only David, Paul and I were there, talking about the funeral arrangements.

'How long ago did it happen?' he asked as he hugged me.

'A couple of hours.'

'You've been here too long, then,' he said. 'Come with me. Have you eaten?'

'No.'

'I'll take you for lunch.'

He offered to take Paul and David too, but they declined.

'I'll stay by the phone,' Paul told us. 'Maybe you can take over when you get back.'

We agreed and left, kissing them in that meaningful way people have when they're feeling tragic. It struck me then that all we had talked about for the last two hours was the superficial – funny or touching anecdotes about Gary; arrangements for the flowers; which songs would be played at the funeral. No one had said "I'm going to miss him". No one had shed more than preliminary tears.

I know so little about death, I thought.

In the restaurant all I felt was tiredness for the time I'd spent sitting with, caring for, and looking at Gary as he died. And he'd died so quickly, that was what was so shocking.

'It was his ring,' Oliver said. 'You said it was his emblem, his symbol of implication – his symbol of life. When he gave it up, he gave up trying to live. Morocco was his last blast. After that, he wanted to die.'

I looked down at my ominously bare finger and then at Oliver.

'I don't know,' I said. 'Did he want to die?'

'Did he ever say that he didn't want to?'

'No,' I admitted, amazed at the concept that anyone could ever reconcile themselves to death; unconvinced that it was possible.

Max seemed to take it well. I was booked to look after him on the following Tuesday, the day of the funeral. I had never seen him dressed smartly until then. He wore a dinner jacket – perhaps not the most appropriate clothing, but striking. Oliver met us at the church and pushed Max's wheelchair. We hadn't bought wreaths. Instead, by request, all money for flowers was to be donated to the hospice fund. But there were flowers nevertheless.

'I would have spent thirty quid on flowers,' David whispered to us when I entered the church, 'so I gave thirty to the hospice fund and spent thirty on flowers. If Gary would disapprove of that, then fuck him.'

The small church was full. I recognised perhaps a third of the people there, not necessarily through Gary, but generally from the pubs. As I watched everyone take their seats it struck me that I had only known him a short time – just over four months. It was extraordinary. I'd met him in the spring, and the summer was not even over. Oliver sat beside me, his arm through mine, his head resting against my shoulder.

Gary's family sat in a huddle on the left of the pulpit. Mother, father, brother with wife, two teenagers. I had never heard him speak of them, though Paul had mentioned that they were estranged. They were so obviously uncomfortable here, among all these gay men. Their prejudices had lubricated their views so much that they had slipped beyond the reach of our sympathy.

The funeral itself was short, with two pieces of music by the Cocteau Twins. There was a short address, and a speech of thanks and remembrance from Paul.

`We all have our own feelings about Gary,' he said, `and I am not going to eulogise him here, because he was a human being like everyone else, and it would be foolish. For all of you who have come here today, there is nothing that I can say to help you with your grief. We all have to grieve in our own way and in our own time.

`Personally I feel angry, and I think it is right to feel angry. I am angry that Gary has died so young. I am also angry that whilst he was ill he was aware of the low priority that the government has attached to the treatment of his illness. He knew that potentially life-saving treatments were being denied him through lack of funds, that precious resources were being wasted by people who didn't understand the disease. With Gary's help, we have fought in Brighton for the best services for people with Aids outside London. We have demanded and received excellent nursing in what are, through lack of funding, inadequate treatment facilities. We have achieved a great deal through the constructive anger of people like Gary. And if there is one thing we can do to honour him, it is to carry on being angry and to use our anger to precipitate change.

`A lot of people here have been to many – too many – funerals. Gary, I know, was concerned that his shouldn't be just one more in a long line of funerals for people with Aids. He urged me to ask you today to think of him as a man, a friend, a colleague, a lover or acquaintance who has died. It is important to remember him for the person he was and not for the illness that killed him.

'I loved Gary. Thank you for coming here today.'

'Thank God there was no mention of God,' Max whispered to me as the proceedings came to a close.

I agreed.

'It seems to me,' he said when we got outside, 'that the church has spent too much time assiduously persecuting homosexuals. When we have lived out lives in spite of their disapproval and without their help, it strikes me as hypocrisy of the highest order that they should accept an invitation to become involved when we die. I wouldn't have been able to take it if Gary had succumbed to tradition. But I should have known he wouldn't.'

David invited the family to the reception afterwards at his house, but they declined, and we set off in our various vehicles, Oliver coming in the ambulance – sitting in the back holding Max's hand. The reception was lively, loud and brisk. Paul had brought Gary's collection of CDs and we danced to his music. I ate too much, drank moderately, and spent a lot of time feeling close to Oliver.

Perhaps the most surprising event of the whole day occurred after people had left the reception. Only Paul, David and I were left – Oliver had gone to work. Paul was tidying up in the kitchen. David and I were drinking coffee in the living room, sitting amongst bowls of crisps, half-empty platters of sandwiches, and the alien smell of cigarettes in this normally smoke-free house.

'Look,' David said, 'I'd better tell you now, so that I can get it over with. It's about Oliver.'

'What about him?'

'I haven't been kind about him.'

'There's no particular reason why you should like him,' I said. 'There's no reason why we should always like our friends' friends.'

'That's true, but I haven't been impartial. I tried to put Oliver off you – for your sake mostly, I thought. I want to apologise,' he said. 'I want to apologise on my own account because I've realised that it's your life and all these decisions are yours. I also got into trouble with Paul about it. He said that I was being selfish – that I was trying to oust Oliver because I was jealous of his place in your life. Maybe that's true as well, partly at least, but now that I've got Paul it's more or less irrelevant. I was also worried about Oliver being bad for you.'

He paused and looked suddenly so shy that I laughed.

'If you're going to apologise,' I said, 'then fine, I'll accept your apology. But I was so angry with you. I kept on waiting for the right time to bollock you, but it never came. By the time I got round to it I'd stopped being angry. I realised that Oliver is intelligent enough to come to his own conclusions, whatever you might say to him.'

'That's true,' David admitted. 'It's taken me a long time to realise that Oliver is not a bimbo. Whatever else he might be, he's not that.'

'Maybe he's grown up a bit,' I said. 'I think it was getting away from his protective relationship with Duncan that made him change.'

'How it has happened is immaterial,' said David. 'The fact is that Oliver is much, much more risky now that he's a little saner; risky because he's so much more appealing. But he's still dishonest, and that makes him dangerous too. I can tell that you're falling for him. Please, don't.'

'Is that what you think? God!' I said, 'I don't love Oliver. Not really.'

'So long as you're sure,' said David, unconvinced.

THIRTY NINE

August 16th

Dear Rick,

Things are more or less ready here. The flat has been replastered, rewired, refloored and looks fabulous. It should be ready by the beginning of September. I've got myself in order and dad's lending me 300,000 drachma now that he perceives the business to be succeeding. I'm sending you a banker's draft for £500 sterling which should cover the cost of your flight and any other arrangements you have to make.

I can't wait to move. It's okay sleeping on Ria's floor, but it isn't very satisfactory for her to have me around so much when she's been used to being on her own.

You can go ahead and book your flight, if you like, for September 1st or as close as you can to that date. You'll arrive for the best part of the summer that way – after this terrible heat has diminished. I'll phone you nearer the time to see how it's all going. I can't bear the idea of speaking to you now; I've survived so long without you that your voice would be torture. I want you to be here, that's all, not at the end of a phone line.

Looking forward to seeing you soon (how wonderful to be able to write this).
love
Andreas

FORTY

'I want to ask you a favour,' Max told me the next time I saw him. We were having an after-show drink at The Dolphin, having seen a production of Julius Caesar at the Theatre Royal. The Friday night crowd seemed more jovial than usual, though that was probably only because of our subdued mood.

'Ask,' I told him as I held the glass of red wine to his lips.

'It's quite something,' he said. 'I don't know how to start.'

'Just get on with it,' I advised him.

'Okay.'

He looked from side to side as though wanting to avoid being overheard.

'I was hoping you might be able to help me with an overdose of my tablets.'

I put his drink down, took a gulp of my pilsner, and stared at him.

'You want me to kill you?'

'No. I want you to help me commit suicide. And before you say anything,' he added quickly, rushing his words, 'you've already agreed about voluntary euthanasia. You've agreed with me in the past that people should have the opportunity to decide when to die. It so happens, as you know, that I don't have the choice. I'm dependent on others to do it for me.'

'Why, though?' I asked. 'I can't believe that you could want to. And anyway, my agreement about euthanasia was in principle only.'

'I've been thinking about it for a long time,' he said. 'Long before Gary died, though obviously that was the focal point for me – the final happening that convinced me that I was right to want to stop going on like this. That's what Gary and I spent a lot of time talking about in the afternoons when he was ill. At first he was dead against it, if you'll forgive the pun, but gradually he came to see it my way.

'Why should I go on? Why? In knowing Gary I found that I could share some kind of bond – the bond of our mutual disability. For him, his illness was terminal. Even you said that it was for the best when he died. That's how I saw it. There came a time when he was tired of being ill, a time when it was right for him to give up. Well, that time has come for me, too. I know Gary didn't commit suicide, but in the end he really didn't want to live, and that's what made me realise that it was within me to make this decision. I'm tired, Rick. Gary made me happy for a while, but now he's gone. It's not easy being quadriplegic, and although I've coped well and had some wonderful times over the last two decades, my big danger – and one thing I will never allow myself – is that I might become bitter.'

'It's grief that's clouding your judgement,' I told him. 'You don't want to go on without Gary. Give it some time and you'll feel differently.'

'No, now you're being condescending. It's taken twenty years for me to come to a conclusion about how I feel. Gary has of course informed how I feel, but I won't change my mind.'

As I sat there with him, I realised that this was true. Nothing about Max was in doubt. He had never been indecisive or unsure of himself.

'What do you want me to do?' I asked.

'Administer enough drugs to kill me,' he said. 'I know how many I'll need and of what sort.'

'I'll think about it,' I said.

'Fine. I didn't expect you to say yes straight away. There are a number of things I need to sort out, so it wouldn't be for another few days, at least.'

He smiled at me as he said this, a smile of sureness, a smile of happy decision.

'Don't do it,' Sarah told me. 'It's not worth it.'

Sarah was a lawyer friend of David's. He'd phoned her as soon as I'd told him of Max's request, and arranged a meeting at his place.

'It's alright for Max if you administer an overdose – he'll be dead, so it won't affect him. But you could be in trouble. You'll be an accomplice. Don't forget, if you've been looking after him for some time, then you'll be familiar with the dosages of his drugs. They'd never believe that you would administer an overdose without knowledge of what you were doing. At the very least, you'd get a suspended sentence. At worst, they could do you for manslaughter, or even murder, and put you away for years.'

'Never mind,' Max said when I told him. 'I didn't really think you would. I know how big a responsibility it is for the person who does it.'

'Are you going to ask anyone else?'

'No. If it came out that I'd been asking around for someone to bump me off, then it would implicate anyone who might be pretending they were doing it in all innocence.'

We were at an afternoon recital of Berlioz. The concert was in St Margaret's Church Hall in Hove, one of Max's more drunken afternoon entertainments.

'Good red wine always goes so well with classical music,' he grinned as I started him on his fifth glass. He always brought a whole bottle to the vestry buffet when he came here, especially when there were two intervals, as today. It always amused me to see him drunk, especially when I was driving and had to remain sober. I was pleased to see that he had regained his old sparkle after several days of gloom following the funeral.

'Isn't Berlioz pompous?' he remarked, 'though he knows how to get the heart pounding when he wants to. It's the nearest thing I can get to sex, so I like to make the most of it. And, unlike with sex, drink actually enhances the climax.'

We got back at around seven, both of us saturated by the music, me feeling impatient because I was meeting Oliver for a meal at Food For Friends at half past. Max was in one of his strange fantasy moods.

'You know,' he told me, 'I'd love to have enough money to afford a purpose-built house. I'd have a huge lounge, a guest bedroom; maybe even a toilet . . . '

'Are you sure you don't want me to get you a snack before I go?' I asked.

'No,' he said, 'I'm fine. Philip is coming over at half past to go through some correspondence with me, though I'm probably too drunk to concentrate. I'll get him to feed me something and then chuck me into bed. Just leave me within reach of my Possum alarm when you go.'

As I gave him his pills, it struck me how very easy it would be to give him an overdose. I gave him the usual – 1 Hiprex, 1 Maxolon, 2 Diazapam, 3 Heminevrin, 120 mg Amitriptylin, Fybogel, Stemetil to help with nausea from drinking too much, 2 soluble paracetamol for the same reason, and a Triazolam to get him off to sleep.

So many drugs. Surely no one would hold me responsible if I slipped him a few extra? It was tempting to imagine that I might say yes if he ever asked me again.

FORTY ONE

I arrived at Food For Friends, out of breath, at 7.35. Oliver was already there and had ordered me deep fried pancakes with leek and potato filling.

`Profile Two phoned,' he said, `the long range weather forecast is good. They reckon the 29th or 30th. How was it at the concert?'

`Apart from the fact that I hate Berlioz,' I said kissing him, `it was fine. It was great to see Max laughing again.'

`So he's cheering up? I'm sure I wouldn't be able to bounce back so quickly. I'd have carried on until someone relented and agreed to give me an overdose.'

`Don't joke,' I told him.

`I'm serious. I would do it if he asked me. Maybe I should offer.'

`But what if I had agreed straight away to help him?' I asked. `He'd be dead by now. But he's clearly feeling better. It frightens me to think how final suicide is, and how easy it is to make a judgement that seems rational at the time, but which is really only disguised spontaneity.'

`What about our right to individual self-determination? If Max wants to die, then who are we to play God and say he can't.'

`Judging by this afternoon, Max doesn't want to die.'

`But maybe he will again, and then the same questions will arise.'

`Okay,' I said, `point taken.'

I started on my food, then turned the conversation.

`And you?' I asked, `did you talk to Duncan today?'

`I went to see him, yes. I decided to see what he had to say. I thought maybe there was a way to get out of it without coughing up.'

`Such as?'

`I had a feeble idea that I might ask to see the paper I'd

signed, then grab it from him and rip it up. Either that or I thought I might try pleading. Or having sex with him. It might be a bit humiliating, but I wouldn't mind doing it for £2000 plus interest.'

'Did it work?'

'No. As usual I ended up humiliating myself for nothing.'

'So you slept with him?'

'Oh, Rick,' Oliver laughed, 'that's the first time you've showed jealousy. How sweet.'

'It wasn't jealousy, it was curiosity.'

Oliver smiled and shrugged.

'Whatever.'

'Did you?'

'I'm not telling you.'

It was my turn to shrug, but it annoyed me that he wouldn't say – and, of course, my irritation proved his point about the jealousy.

'No I didn't have sex with him,' Oliver murmured. 'But I'm seeing him again next week. To try and sort something out.'

After Oliver had left for the Cross-Keys I walked along the seafront to David's house. He was having one of his Saturday evening dinner parties and when I got there his guests were still seated at the table.

'Come and sit with us,' he said, drawing up a chair. 'Pour him some wine, Paul.'

I accepted the wine with a smile and sat down.

'We're playing a game,' David explained, indicating a flimsy paperback. 'I ask questions from this book, and you all answer them.'

'That's a game?'

'You'll get the hang of it.'

I looked round the table. There were four guests plus David, Paul and myself. I had met all of them before, but they were what I called David's beach-party set, people I had never wanted to mix with – the more well-heeled of Brighton's gay community who spent their time going to dinner parties, going abroad, being responsible citizens and keeping their hands clean when it came to gay politics. Gary, I knew, would have despised them.

'Have you ever stolen anything?' said David. 'If so, what?'

'You're asking me?'

'Yes, then we'll go on round the table.'

I thought for a moment.

'I stole my best-friend's action man when I was at school,' I said, 'plus a photo of his brother who I fancied like hell. I stole a coffee filter machine from my parents when they refused to give it to me, although they never used it. I've stolen plenty of things from the flats that I've rented. Cutlery, crockery, picture frames, bookshelves, rugs...'

'Prospective landlords beware,' laughed David. 'I think that's enough, Rick. You don't want to seem too much of a reprobate.'

'I don't mind,' I said with a smile.

'Nigel?'

'I used to steal tea and coffee from work, because I knew they wouldn't miss it...'

Paul glanced at me from across the table and raised his eyes to the ceiling, then grinned. I took his point immediately. The so-called confessions around the table, he was telling me, were going to be mundane to the point of tedium.

'You missed the one interesting question of the evening,' Paul told me, 'which was: how many lovers have you had, and can you remember all their names?'

'Yes,' said David, 'you did miss that. I think you should answer it now, Rick.'

'Okay,' I agreed, 'but only if you all tell me the answers you gave.'

'Right.'

'Well,' I thought aloud, 'there was Beth at school, though that probably doesn't count. I didn't ejaculate. I think I was too young to ejaculate, though maybe I didn't want to. Then there was Joe and Toby in the upper-sixth, Tim,

Michael and Bruno at University, Andreas and Oliver. That's eight, and yes, I can remember all their names.'

'Okay,' said David with a smile. 'Now, let's see if I can remember what the rest of you said. Nigel, you've slept with thirty-five or so and you can remember most of their names. James has had two hundred plus . . . '

'Three hundred, I reckon,' he said, 'I've been trying to work it out and I think I underestimated.'

'Jeff's had ninety. Pete a hundred and twenty. Paul sixteen – and he's the only one apart from you who can remember all the names.' He squeezed Paul's hand over the table.

'And you?' I asked him.

'Me? I reckoned something over a thousand, but more than that I'm not prepared to say.'

The next question went something like this: If you had a vaccination that would cure all illness in the world, but it would kill 5% of the people injected, would you make everyone have the injection?

I didn't answer. Everyone else except Paul said yes, of course.

'Much more than 5% of people die of illness as it is,' said Pete, 'so it would be worth it to make sure everyone that was left had good health.'

'Aids would be cured, too,' said Nigel.

'But that's not the point,' said Paul. 'It's typical of the book to ask that kind of leading question. It's designed so that we can say yes or no to really important questions and feel that we are, all of us, so wise underneath it all. But that's not the case. The fact is that all the questions are loaded to start with, and also, the correct answer is, surely, "I would give people the choice". We're far too happy to say we would do things for other people's good, without consulting them. It's fascist and I hate it. People sitting in Westminster are taking exactly this kind of decision, in ignorance, about gay people.'

'It's only a book,' David pointed out, 'and it was asking about vaccinations, not gay rights.'

Paul looked down at the table and drank some more wine.

'Right,' said David. 'Last question of the evening.' He flicked through the book, musing over questions. 'Here we are . . . Is there anything you regret not having done in your life? If you had five years, would you be able to put this right?'

'I regret,' said Jeff, 'that I didn't buy that house up by Seven Dials, now that's it's getting to be such a good area. I don't suppose I will get another chance.'

'I regret,' said James, 'that I didn't get off with Stephen Arnold at last year's staff party, and, yes, I hope to rectify that within the next five years.'

There was general laughter. Only Paul and I didn't join in.

'Rick?'

'I regret,' I said slowly, 'that I never told Gary that I loved him before he died. And I'll never be able to put that right.'

Silence swamped the table. David looked at me as though I had spoiled the fun.

'I'm sorry,' I said. 'I shouldn't have come round. I haven't been very congenial, have I?'

I got up. Nobody moved as I walked from the room. I picked my jacket up from the hall and let myself out of the house into the warm darkness. I hadn't expected to say what I'd said – hadn't even been aware that it was something I regretted. I walked down towards the sea, scuffing the paving stones and trying to think of nothing.

I've never told Oliver I care for him either, I thought. Am I expecting to leave for Greece without telling him that at least?

'Rick.' Paul's voice sounded behind me. He walked up and took my arm. 'Don't worry about that. It was a stupid idea of David's to play that game.'

'I should have kept quiet,' I said. 'There was nothing wrong with thinking it. I shouldn't have said it.'

'That's it, though,' said Paul, 'too many people don't say what they think. I'm pleased you said it. I feel the same.'

'Do you?'

'Yes. I never really talked to Gary about how I felt,

towards the end. We were too busy talking about funerals. I thought that if I ever mentioned that I was going to miss him, then he'd assume I thought it was the end. As it was, I always thought there would be time. I always thought I'd be there when he was really sick so that I could say goodbye properly. But it was you who was there when he died. I envy you really, in a way.'

'Don't,' I said. 'Apart from the advantage that no one had to break the news to me, it still didn't leave me feeling I'd sorted things out about how I felt, and about what I might have said to him.'

'Come back to the house,' he said, 'there's coffee and liqueurs to come.'

'No, it's okay, I don't want to interfere any more than I already have.'

'It was David's fault that this happened. Come back. We both want you to.'

David embraced me when I got to the house, and handed me a mug of coffee.

'Grand Marnier, Cointreau or Tia Maria?' he asked.

'Grand Marnier.'

I went through into the sitting room. There was a frisson of embarrassment as I came in which made Paul laugh. He sat down and made room on the settee. Talk was about drugs.

'I don't know anyone who takes poppers any more,' James was saying, 'in spite of the fact that they're no longer stigmatised regarding Aids. They've sort of become something that people used to use in the Eighties.'

Talk of drugs reminded me of Max and I wondered briefly if I should phone to see if he was alright. Sometimes, when he drank so much, he was sick later, which always caused trouble for whoever was looking after him. But then, he'd taken some Stemetil, so that should have helped. And I'd given him a sedative.

A sedative! I suddenly felt panicked that I'd left him on his own after taking a sedative . . .

'David,' I said, as he came in with my liqueur, 'can I use your phone?'

'Go ahead.'

I took my diary from my jacket, looked up Philip's number, then dialled. He took a long time to answer and sounded both sleepy and annoyed when he did so.

'Hi,' I said, 'sorry to phone you so late, but I wanted to check how Max was.'

'Max? Haven't seen him.'

'Weren't you putting him to bed this evening?'

'No, why? There's nothing wrong is there?'

I caught my breath as I realised what had happened.

'No,' I said, 'don't worry. Sorry to have bothered you.'

I replaced the receiver and went back into the front room.

'It's Max,' I said, 'I've got to go and see him. I'll phone for a taxi.'

'I'll drive you,' said David.

'No, you've drunk too much.'

'I'll come in the taxi, then.'

'You've got guests. Besides, I've been enough trouble as it is.'

I tapped my foot anxiously against David's pale Wilton carpet.

'What is it, anyway?' he asked.

'I don't know,' I lied. 'I'll phone you later.'

It was midnight as the taxi pulled up, and it took ten minutes to get across town. When I got to Max's place, I let myself into the house. The heating was off and, despite the warmth of the evening, it was cool inside. I quietly opened Max's door, half expecting him to be asleep in bed, but he was sitting in his wheelchair where I'd left him. I turned on his bedside light and crossed to him.

He wasn't dead, but he seemed either deeply asleep, or worse, in some hypothermic coma. His hands were icy and his breathing was so slow and so shallow as to be virtually undetectable. As I looked at him it was clear that I had a choice: either I could try to revive him, get him warm and put him to bed. Or I could leave him. By morning he would certainly be dead, of asphyxiation from sitting up so long, if nothing else.

I took his hand.

'Max,' I whispered. 'Max, can you hear me?'
But he didn't answer.
'What do you want me to do?' I asked him.

He sat impassively in his wheelchair, expressionless, immobile, and I knew I had to leave him. He had thought this out so carefully. He had worked it out so that no one else would be implicated, no one blamed for administering too many drugs. He had done it this way to spare me. I had no right to stop him. At any time before he'd lost consciousness, he could have pressed his alarm. It wasn't right for me to interfere.

I sat for a while, holding his hand, thinking of the laughter of the afternoon – thinking how absolutely he must have wanted to die in this way, quietly, painlessly.

'And it was so easy after all,' I whispered to him.

Death did not seem such an unwelcome stranger this time. With Gary, life seemed to have been ripped from him. With Max, it was a welcome friend. If I hadn't felt that so strongly, maybe I wouldn't have had the strength to leave him there and let myself out of the house.

This time I closed the front door quietly, looked around to see if there were any neighbours around to see me, then slipped down the hill to the taxi rank on the Old Steine.

It was half past one when I got in, but I phoned David anyway.

'It's okay,' I said to his answerphone, 'it's nothing to worry about. I'll talk to you in the morning.'

By the time Oliver got in from the club, I was asleep.

FORTY TWO

The phone rang at 8.10 a.m.

`Rick, it's Fiona here. I'm at Max's. According to the rota, you were looking after him last night.'

`No,' I said, `I did him from midday until 7.15. Someone else was supposed to take over at 7.30.'

`Do you know who?'

`Philip, I think. Why?'

`Look, there's been a terrible mix up at this end. I came over at 7.30 with one of the other nurses and found Max in his wheelchair. No one had put him to bed. He'd been dead for some time.'

`Where was his wheelchair?' I asked.

`At the table, by the fireplace.'

`That's where I left him,' I told her. `He told me Philip was coming later to put him to bed.'

`Poor Max,' Fiona choked, `sitting there like that until he died. And he must have done it deliberately, because you left him by his alarm. I just don't understand it. Mrs Ewart is beside herself about it. We keep telling her it wasn't her fault, but of course she's taken it badly.'

I explained what had happened to Oliver. He smiled and hugged me.

`I'm so proud of you,' he said. `I wouldn't have thought you had the guts to let him die.'

`Well I did.'

`Have you ever read a book by Albert Camus called *A Happy Death?*' he asked.

`No.'

`This, I think, is a happy death. Can you imagine, dying when you want to? In a way it's the most positive thing I can imagine.'

`Except that life must be bloody awful for you to want to

end it.'

'Life wasn't awful for Max,' Oliver said, 'you know that. It was difficult, restricted, uncomfortable . . . that's what he was tired of. At least he died whilst he could still get out to concerts and theatre, whilst he could still go out boozing – in the knowledge that he had friends.'

I phoned David on his mobile phone, and arranged to meet him for a drink at the Cross-Keys that evening.

'It was so simple in the end,' Oliver mused. 'No one's been arrested for what has happened.'

Nevertheless, I had a visit from the police at eleven.

'According to Mr Philip Newton,' the police officer told me, 'you phoned him at around 11.45 p.m. last night to ask after Mr Ewart. Can you tell me why you did so if you weren't concerned about Mr Ewart's welfare?'

'I was concerned,' I said. 'That's why I phoned Philip.'

'But when he told you that he hadn't put Mr Ewart to bed, you didn't try and find out who had put him to bed? You didn't go round to check on him?'

'I realised that it was none of my business. It was Max's responsibility to see that he was covered. I didn't want to interfere.'

'Did you have any idea that he'd been considering suicide?'

'He had mentioned it, yes.'

'And you still didn't check on him?'

'Like I said. It wasn't my place to interfere.'

'You're lucky the nurses corroborate that it was probably suicide,' the police officer said, 'otherwise we'd have to take this more seriously. Are you aware of the consequences of being an accessory to suicide?'

'Max asked me to overdose him some time ago,' I said. 'I refused.'

'As it is, we're only following up a complaint by Mr Newton. Apparently Mr Ewart was a life-member of the Voluntary Euthanasia Society. As far as we're concerned, circumstances are not suspicious.'

After the man had gone, I sighed with annoyance.

'Why did Philip tell the police?' I asked Oliver, irritated.

'Look at it from his point of view,' Oliver suggested. 'If you did help to kill Max, then you were doing Philip out of a job.'

There was such a finality about Max's death that it broke my spell. After all, he was my only regular source of income, as well as Philip's. It seemed to free me of my obligations and, for the second time that summer, I booked the first available flight to Thessalonika – only I booked a single ticket this time, for the 12.45 p.m. flight on September 2nd. Five days' time. I also phoned my landlord about the possibility of transferring the lease of my flat into Oliver's name. He seemed okay about it.

'Just give me plenty of warning,' he said, 'so that I can get the documents drawn up.'

I walked to the seafront, took my shirt off, and lay in the warm sun. There was a Fotofit shoot coming up for a credit company which looked set to be the last modelling job I would ever do for them. Then there was the Profile Two shoot, and that would be it.

But how do I tell Oliver? I thought.

The waves rustled through my thoughts and the sun's glare flared red across my eyelids. I felt the travel agent's receipt in my pocket and recognised it as the beginning of the end of my time in England.

I hadn't been able to tell Oliver about the ticket. I'd told him about September 1st being a provisional date, so he must have been aware that the time of my departure was approaching. But I hadn't discussed having the tenancy agreement on the flat transferred into his name, nor had I made any attempt to pack, organise my bank account, tell relevant people . . .

I could decide not to go, I thought, and it wouldn't be a problem. It would just be a question of not getting onto the plane.

Oliver joined me on the beach later, and as we lay together I let my hand drift across the delineation of his chest, realising as I did so that he had become something different from what I had at first assumed I was looking for. I had never defined him or labelled my purpose in sleeping with him. It had merely been chance that he had needed somewhere to live at the time when I was in a position to offer him a place to stay.

'I can't believe Max has gone,' said Oliver. 'I can't believe that I'll never pour him another glass of wine at the Cross-Keys or wink at him from the bar. After everything I said about being willing to give him an overdose, I still feel sad that he's gone. If only I believed in life after death I might be glad at the thought of him and Gary being together.'

He turned onto his stomach and looked across at me, his warm skin glowing with health.

'It's a bit too pat for me, this life after death business. It's been dreamed up for those of us who ruin our lives. Or have them ruined for us. It makes us feel we might get the chance to have another go.'

I looked up at the sky and stared at the lowering sun so that it imprinted luminous green splashes on my retina.

FORTY THREE

Having fulfilled my contract with Profile Two, the Fotofit ad was my last shoot ever, and it was not one that I was inclined to take seriously. It was a television ad for a multi-national credit company, and I was hired to be a harassed waiter carrying a tray of glasses across a busy restaurant. They'd hired the restaurant and catering facilities of a prestigious central London hotel, though the service they gave to the models and actors was shit. But it wasn't just the hotel that caused problems. The director was one of those people that sometimes have talent, but usually don't, who take out their insecurities on everyone around them. I was given my tray and told to practice walking around with a dozen empty glasses on it.

`Which will be full of champagne when we shoot,' the director told me.

There was no problem here until I was asked to hold the tray up on one hand. It looked good, maybe, but it was hardly safe. I tried to balance the precarious, and very heavy, silver tray, but it was a nightmare and made my wrist ache within minutes.

`Look,' I told the director after wandering around for a time, `can't you glue the glasses to the tray or something, so that they can't fall off?'

`Do you know how much those glasses cost?' he replied.

`Probably about a hundred thousandth of the cost of the advertisement, a thousandth of your salary for the job. A hundred per cent of mine.'

`They cost a fuck of a lot,' the director told me, `that's what. Hold your hand steady.'

He turned to his hoard of technicians dismissively. I put the tray alongside several other props – a plastic turkey, fake fruit, a board covered with plastic lumps of cheese. If I was going to have any chance of getting it right, I might as well rest my wrist. I retired to the wings where Karen from

Fotofit was overlooking the shoot.

'Can't you talk to someone about those glasses?' I asked her.

'I tackled the director about Tim's costume earlier,' she said. 'He wasn't helpful – he wasn't even polite. I don't think there's much chance of getting him to change anything.'

As is so often the case, we had been called for 8.30 a.m. though the set wasn't ready for shooting until after midday. Three or four hours of hanging around may be an occupational hazard, but it doesn't get any less tedious the more you do it.

Sometimes, like the previous day, modelling shoots go like a dream. After a day's delay because of the weather, I had been driven to Berkshire where, in a rural river-side setting, I had been Mr Married Bliss amongst harvest riches of apples, blackberries, home-baked bread and sick-makingly perfect children. Everyone had been polite; the director, whom I'd worked with on a number of occasions before, had been friendly; my 'wife' had been intelligent and talented. The whole shoot took just over five hours, including a two hour lunch break – and I'd earned several thousand pounds . . .

The credit advertisement was, unfortunately, not in the same league – in spite of a director who thought he was brilliant. When we did finally try the bustling restaurant scene, everyone had to be rehearsed and re-rehearsed. First the foreground diners' tables were too close, then the lighting was wrong. Then there was no room for the Maitre d' to make his entrance. For all these problems, we had to do a dry run so that the director could see the problem in context. My wrist was hurting after two dummy runs. After eleven, it was agony.

'Right,' the director said finally, 'let's go for a take.'

Three technicians rushed up to me and started filling my glasses with sparkling wine as I stood getting more and more anxious about the extra weight. I was in pain, a light sweat breaking out on my forehead.

'Are you alright?' whispered the Maitre d', who was

waiting to make his entrance behind me.

'No,' I said.

'Camera,' shouted the director.

'Rolling,' said the cameraman. 'At speed.'

'Action,' shouted the director.

We all started moving at once. I got to the middle of the set and felt the tray going. There was no way I could get out of shot before the glasses fell, so I stopped. In what seemed like slow motion the tray dipped, the glasses slipped in orderly fashion towards the edge and cascaded in magnificence to the floor. The tray clattered in the debris half a second later. I stood in a pool of effervescent liquid and shook my numb hand, trying to get some feeling back into it.

'Cut!' screamed the director. 'What's that idiot doing? Get more glasses, quick. What do you mean there aren't any? Find some!'

Technicians were frantically trying to clear up around me as I turned to the director, shrugging.

'It could have happened to anyone,' I told him.

'Like hell,' said the director, 'I knew you were trouble. Your lack of professionalism is awesome. Pull yourself together.'

'It's your lack of professionalism that's awesome,' I told him. With that I picked my way through the technicians to the main doors of the dining room, passing Karen.

'Fuck it,' I said to her, 'I don't want to be a model anyway.'

'Hi, Rick?'

'Andreas! How's things?'

'Okay. When are you coming?'

'The second. Two days. I get to Thessalonika at 5 p.m. your time.'

'Brilliant. The flat's all ready. I've got a car, too, an old one, so I can come and get you from the airport myself. Have you packed?'

'No.'

'You'd better hurry.'

`I know.'

`Are you okay?'

`Yes,' I said, `I just find it hard to believe that this is happening.'

`I know what you mean. I feel the same. We'll have a housewarming party at the flat on Saturday . . . the day after tomorrow. It's been too long. I've learned so much.'

`So have I.'

FORTY FOUR

Max's funeral was the day before my departure. I still hadn't told anyone – not even David – that I was going, and I had done no packing. I cooked a simple lunch for Oliver and myself and felt my secret as a tourniquet.

I'm learning how easy it is to lie, I thought, and how difficult it is to avoid the consequences.

Oliver came through from the bedroom as I served up soup and bread.

`What's this?' he asked, dropping the receipt for my ticket onto the table.

`It's a receipt for my flight to Thessalonika,' I said.

`I know. It's dated four days ago. Why didn't you tell me that you were flying tomorrow?'

`I didn't know how to.'

`You could have tried opening your mouth and saying, "Oliver, I'm flying to Thessalonika on the second of September".'

`I didn't know how to say it without . . . '

`Sounding like a shit. But you've failed utterly to avoid being shitty. What were you going to do – leave a note on the sitting room floor saying, "bye, bye, I've left my keys by the coffee machine."?'

`No.'

`What then?'

`I was going to tell you after the funeral.'

`Were you?' He pushed away the bowl of soup that I'd placed in front of him and got up.

`I'm going. I'll see you there.'

I watched as he left, then returned to my soup without enthusiasm.

The funeral was as well-attended as Gary's, with a largish contingent of nurses. The main difference between the two occasions was that today there were flowers everywhere.

David and Paul turned up looking more inseparable than ever and I thought privately how unlikely they looked as a couple. I sat with David. Oliver only turned up at the last minute and sat by himself at the back, looking pensive and pissed-off throughout the service.

We had to suffer dull prayers and turgid hymns, which was sad and felt wrong. I wondered briefly why Max hadn't thought to write an anti-religion clause into his will concerning his funeral – especially after what he'd said about Gary's – but he had always been too concerned with the act of living to have ever thought hard about what to do in the event of his death.

Afterwards, as the hearse slowly made its way to the cemetery and I followed in David's car, David came to the point immediately.

'So,' he asked, 'why did Oliver slink off like that at the end of the dedication? What's happened?'

I took a breath and looked over at Paul.

'I'm flying down to Greece tomorrow,' I said. 'I didn't tell anyone because I can't feel it as real.'

There was a silence then that lasted all the way to the cemetery, and on through the graveside ceremony. The three of us put in an appearance at the wake – a tired affair put together by an unconcerned brother who was obviously having a hard time consoling Max's mother – then went back to David's for a drink.

'It really does look like the end of an era for you,' Paul said, raising his glass of champagne. 'To Gary,' he said, 'and Max, and to Greece.'

'Thanks,' I said and raised my glass.

'Now,' said David, 'you're going to have to do something about Oliver.'

'I know,' I agreed, feeling suddenly tired at the prospect of a confrontation, 'but how am I going to do this without hurting him?'

'At least Oliver knows that you're going,' said Paul. 'He's known right from the start – so he can't hold that against you.'

'But I feel so *involved*,' I said. 'I don't even know exactly what I mean by that. But it seems strange to just go back and pull out a suitcase and say "Right, I'm off. Goodbye".'

'But why?' David asked. 'Why is that strange? Oliver's getting your flat out of it, so he's got no reason to complain. Just go home, pack your things and get off down to Greece. Andreas didn't deserve to have you faffing around here at the last minute.'

'Oliver was a mistake, Rick,' Paul told me. 'Realise that and you'll find it easier to leave.'

'I won't find it easy,' I said, with some anger, 'but I'll do it. I wish it could be over, that's all.'

'Think of Andreas,' said David.

'That's exactly what I have been doing,' I said, 'thinking of Andreas. Why does everyone always talk about Andreas as if he's perfect? That's all I've ever had since he left – a kind of hushed reverence. It's as though my affair with Oliver was the ultimate in bad taste; as though I've been wallowing in sin in Brighton whilst Saint Andreas bled on his cross in Greece. Well I'm not trying to defend what I've done by putting him down, but Andreas is not perfect. And neither am I.'

'But Andreas is someone really special,' said Paul. 'I took him as my role model when I first joined the Aids Centre. He seemed so purposeful, so controlled. He always knew what he was doing. He was my hero, really, and he never did anything to make me feel otherwise about him.'

'You were right to take Andreas as your role model,' I said. 'He was an excellent volunteer, but he was also a real, live person.'

'Okay, okay,' David sighed, 'don't take it out on us. We're not the ones who got you into this mess.'

'Is it a mess? Is that how you see it?' I looked at David, then Paul. 'A mess? When I think of Oliver, of how he supported me over Max, and how he reassured me when Gary died. When I think of how we've both changed for the better – and how much he's given me in the knowledge that I was going to get on a plane and leave . . . When I think of that I feel humble, grateful. Mess? I don't call that a mess at all.'

'Don't go, then,' said David with what amounted to a sneer. 'If you think so much of Oliver, then stay here with him if you owe him that much. You make it sound like Oliver and you are blameless, and Andreas is the one who's been cheating.'

'I can't believe you're saying this to me. I didn't come here for an argument.'

'Guilt does strange things,' said Paul. 'You feel guilty about Andreas and it's coming out as anger. You'll feel better once you've talked to Oliver.'

I walked home feeling depressed. I was flying down to Greece the next day and it felt like a burden. Of course, it is impossible to wrap up a whole life and cart it off with you intact. Life in Brighton was a tight mesh of friends, routines, possessions – and Oliver. To rip that fabric was bound to leave loose threads.

Just get on with it, I thought.

I fancied him too much. That was the problem. The charge of being in his presence had always made me want to extend that presence. Making love to him had seemed like such a tiny part of the pleasure we could share that I'd kept wanting to extend that point of knowledge endlessly. Even now I hadn't exhausted my imagination with regard to his body.

But when I got home Oliver had already left for the Cross-Keys. I had readied myself to talk to him, and now that tension burst, overwhelming me with a sense of anti-climax and lethargy. I lapsed onto the settee in the living room with a cup of coffee and stared into space. An empty suitcase waited next door, but I couldn't bring myself to start packing. I was inclined to leave with only my passport the next day – to start from scratch in Greece. It was a pleasing idea, though impractical.

The phone rang. It was David.

'Look,' he said, 'I love you, Rick. I'm sorry if I sounded hurtful, but I love both of you, you know, you *and* Andreas. You said you wanted me to be your first visitor in Greece, and I'd just like to say I want to take you up on the offer – if I can bring Paul with me.'

'Of course,' I said. 'And I know you love me, David. It's been obvious for years, but especially recently.'

'Good, I'm glad,' he said, 'now I've got to go. Good luck with Oliver.'

I lay there for an hour or so, my coffee going cold at my side. Finally, the phone rang again.

'Hello, darling,' came Ria's voice, 'how are you?'

In spite of her bland greeting, I knew from her tone that something was wrong.

'What is it Ria?' I said, 'what's happened?'

'I don't really know how to tell you this.'

'Just say it, Ria.'

'Andreas knows. About you and Oliver.'

'How?'

'I told him.'

I suddenly found it difficult to catch my breath. I paused for a moment.

'You told him! Why?'

'He knew, Rick. I wouldn't have just come out with it. He must have had his suspicions when you were down here. He eventually asked me straight out.'

'And you told him?'

'Look, I don't mind keeping quiet about things, but I'm not a liar, Rick. I haven't got it in me to lie. Andreas didn't have to get an answer out of me – he just asked the question and then looked at my face. I didn't say anything, but I couldn't hide it. That's how I am.'

'Okay, okay, it's not your fault. How did he take it?'

'Badly, I'm afraid.'

'Where is he?'

'In my bedroom.'

'Let me speak to him.'

'He won't come to the phone.'

'What am I going to do? I'm flying tomorrow. Does he still want me to come?'

'Of course he does, in spite of what he's saying at the moment. I'll talk some sense into him, don't worry. I just thought you ought to be warned, that's all.'

'Let me speak to him, please. Go and get him.'

I waited. I could hear a background murmur over the phone, but there was no emotional colour to it. I tried hard to catch my breath and think clearly, but my diaphragm seemed stuck and my mind was blank. Andreas eventually picked up the phone.

'Andreas?'

'Yes.' He sounded neutral.

'What do you want me to do?'

'I can't talk, Rick,' he said, 'it hurts too much.'

'We'll talk tomorrow,' I said.

'I don't think I want to see you right now,' he said.

'I can't cancel my flight,' I told him.

'You should have thought of that before. I'm going to go now.'

'I love you,' I said.

There was a brief pause as the phone was handed over.

'I'll talk to him,' Ria whispered. 'See you tomorrow. You might have to make your own way here. Bye.'

FORTY FIVE

Oliver returned at two-thirty. I was still sitting on the settee trying to work out what I was going to say to Andreas. I couldn't think of anything except `I'm sorry', but that was meaningless in the end. And was I sorry? Of course, I regretted hurting him, but did I regret Oliver? I couldn't answer that for myself. Now, I felt more sure of my needs. I felt more sure that going to Greece was the right decision for me. Inasmuch as Oliver had made me make up my mind, I couldn't regret him.

Oliver stood in the doorway waiting for me to speak. I looked across at him.

`Andreas knows,' I whispered.

Oliver dropped his keys onto the telephone table, but still didn't move.

`And?'

`And I don't know. I don't know what it means. He won't talk to me.'

Oliver walked into the centre of the room and looked at himself in the mirror above the fireplace. Then he began to laugh. At first it was a bright laugh, as though I'd told him a joke, but gradually it became more and more uncontrolled. He glanced at me in the mirror and laughed louder. It was like in a horror movie.

He's deranged, I thought, briefly. His behaviour was so strange it made me feel that he was capable of anything.

Eventually, he staggered from the room. I heard him fumbling in the bedroom, and then he came back. Deadpan. Silent. He tossed something light and metallic across the room at me which struck my knee with a clink and fell to the floor. I leaned forward and picked it up.

It was two gold rings, linked. On closer inspection I saw that one of them was mine – the one I'd lost so recently. Both rings were linked like part of a chain. I looked closer at the second ring which was similar to mine, only thicker.

Both were monogrammed on the inside. R B for Rick Bailey and A K for Andreas Karakantza.

'Yes,' said Oliver. 'It's his. I took them to a jeweller who sawed your one open, linked it with the other ring, then soldered it back together. He's done a good job. You can only see the join if you look closely in good light.'

'Where did you get Andreas' ring?'

He didn't reply but looked at me. I stared back and saw sadness fleet across his eyes, followed swiftly by a strange humour.

'I see,' I said. 'You slept with him.'

Oliver took an item from his pocket and handed it to me. It was a white piece of cotton, maybe a foot square, crusted with dried blood so old that it was dusty brown.

'He had a nose-bleed,' he told me. 'I kept the pillow case and cut the stain out. You know how I am about mementos; *significant* things. I took his ring, too, but that turned out to be less important.'

I looked at the blood, Andreas' blood, and a shiver stretched its way across my skin. There were other stains on the cloth, too. Oliver picked it up fondly.

'This is the cloth I used the day you came back from Thessalonika, do you remember? I used it to wipe us clean after we'd made love on the settee. It has my cum on it, your cum, and Andreas' blood. It's the most *right* acquisition I've ever made.'

'You're weird,' I whispered, shaking my head and trying to clear my mind; trying to work out the implications of what Oliver was saying. 'Did you know I was Andreas' boyfriend when you first met me?'

'Of course. I'd seen you about enough. On the beach. In the pubs.'

'Is that why you slept with me?'

'Yes and no. It seemed appropriate somehow, or else an odd coincidence. I fancied you too, which helped.'

I didn't know what to say, so I said nothing. Oliver sat beside me.

'I'm not a thief,' he said, 'not really. I do occasionally take things, but only when I feel I have the right. Paul and

Lewis and Duncan and the others could never understand that; that there are lots of kinds of honesty; that nothing is ever simple. I'm only honest to the spirit of love, and there's no greater integrity than that of being true to oneself. Everyone is an amalgam of their past. At least I retain something material in recognition that the past has embellished me.'

'But you don't need to take things to prove that.'

'One of the hardest things you can ever do is be honest with yourself. But that's what I've done. Always. That's what you tried to do, but guilt got in the way. Still, at least you tried.'

'Did I?' I asked, 'it seems so long ago now that I can't remember why I did anything.'

'You'll sort this out with Andreas,' he told me. 'He'll have to forgive you, seeing as you've only done something that he's done himself. Show him the rings and mention me. He'll forgive you eventually, but he'll be angry first. Angry with himself, though he won't realise it. That's the way guilt works, you see, I've seen it so many times. You give in to your curiosity and then it makes you pay. Over and over.'

He ran his fingers over the stained cloth that lay across my thigh.

'There are two ways of approaching infidelity,' he said. 'You can either do it honestly, like you did, in the hope that what you are doing might be right for the moment in which you do it; or you can do it dishonestly, knowing that what you're doing is wrong but not being able to stop yourself. That's what Andreas did. I saw it in him at the time and disliked him for it.'

He put his arm round my shoulder and I let it rest there.

'You never loved me,' he whispered. 'I would never have started with you if I hadn't known you'd go; even though I played with being in love for a time. In the end the only gratification you can get is for yourself, don't you see? You can use another person's love to help, but in the end you're only doing it to get back a little of what you give.'

I looked at him. His eyes were darkly personal; concerned. But I still felt empty.

'What's happened to you?' I said. 'When I last saw you you were angry with me for not telling you about the ticket.'

'I thought for a while,' he said. 'It's amazing how warped you can be when you get too subjective. I decided to let you go. Just like that. Without a fight.'

He threw his hands in the air as though releasing a bird.

'It's easy,' he sighed, 'when you get rid of all that longing for things that you can never have. My problem is that I chase and chase after things, even when my initial motivation was the knowledge that I could never possess them. It's a kind of fixation with me, an obsession. It took me a long walk on the seafront and a bit of sanity to realise that I could never have you. Okay, that's fine. It's the way I always knew it would be.'

'You're wrong in what you believe about relationships,' I told him. 'If you believe that you'll never find permanence, then you never will find it. You have to believe something is possible before you can achieve it.'

'Yes, yes, but you're spouting the stock phrases of the optimist. Everyone says these things as though they genuinely believe that life is fair. It's not Rick. At least I accept that and don't try to come up with twee concepts to make a meaningless life seem to have purpose.'

'This is ridiculous,' I said. 'You might as well kill yourself if you feel like that.'

'Which of us is happier?' he asked. 'Think about it, Rick. Let's just say I wouldn't swap places with you, in spite of the fact that I know you'll be okay with Andreas. I don't want life to be easy.'

'Nor do I.'

'Good.'

He smiled and stood up.

'Now,' he said, 'let me help you pack.'

I couldn't help smiling back as he helped me up and, taking me by the elbow, pulled me through to the bedroom.

'I still haven't drafted a letter to the landlord about you yet.'

'Don't worry,' he told me. 'I can do that.'

I began to pull various items of clothing out of my drawers and wardrobe.

'Look, I'm going to have to leave a lot of these clothes behind. You can have them if you like.'

Oliver parted the jackets and suits hanging in the wardrobe, smiling with either gratitude or amusement – I couldn't tell.

'Thanks, Rick,' he said, 'just what a go-go boy always wanted.'

I continued to pack whilst Oliver opened a bottle of wine.

'Blood red,' he said, 'I want to make love again, you know. We've got to do it.'

'No,' I said. 'I couldn't, even for the sake of symbolism. Don't ruin this, Oliver, not now.'

He laughed for a moment, then shrugged.

'Okay.'

I continued rummaging through my clothes.

'Tell me,' I said, 'how did you get off with Andreas?'

'You really want to know? Okay.' He crossed to where I was standing and, putting an arm round my waist, pulled me over to the bed. We sat down together. 'It was no big deal. I saw him on the seafront with you one time. You both looked wildly unapproachable and *attached*, which I suppose you were. But I felt challenged and decided to keep my eye out for an opportunity to seduce one or other of you.'

'Why, because we threatened you with our stability?'

'Maybe. But simple explanations never tell the truth – only part of it. I wanted to prove something to myself about relationships and people. I wanted to prove that no-one is unattainable if you try hard enough.'

'And you slept with both of us, so you've proved your point?'

'Unfortunately not,' he sighed. 'I proved nothing in the end. Every goal you set stands only until the moment you've achieved it, then it becomes obsolete and a new goal is set.'

'So I'm obsolete?'

'Perhaps you are. Who knows?'

I stood up and went over to do some more packing.

'And what is your next goal, or should I say who is your next goal?'

'I've given up on goals. Life always plays its dirty tricks one way or another. I've achieved all the people I set myself to sleep with except one. And, of course, that one is the only one that counts.'

'Who?'

'No,' he said, 'I won't say. I can't. It still hurts too much, and besides, you know him.'

I folded a shirt and placed it in my case. Suddenly I realised what he was talking about.

'Paul,' I said. 'You fell in love with Paul and never got him.'

There was a short silence so I turned to look at Oliver. His face was screwed up.

'Fucking Lewis,' he breathed. 'He knew how much I wanted Paul and deliberately destroyed our friendship so I would never get him.'

Oliver lay back on the bed, fists clenched, looking incredibly young and vulnerable.

'And you've spent all this time taking it out on other people!'

'You're pretty good with the amateur psychology, Rick. Well maybe you're right.'

He looked so anguished that I went over and hugged him. He sagged against me and let me stroke his head.

'You still haven't told me about Andreas,' I said eventually.

He looked at me, then away.

'Oh yes. Andreas. I met him at a Helpline party. I'd gone along with Paul and Lewis, but they pissed off quite early and I was left on my own. You were away in Ireland for a fortnight, apparently. I was quite pissed, very angry – and interested in Andreas. I chatted him up something rotten.

To give him credit he probably wouldn't have given in if he hadn't been drunk too, and lonely. But I persuaded him to come home with me in the end. I was pretty chuffed with that; attaining the unattainable. We slept together for the next three nights. I guess we had sex seven or eight times. I think he probably thought that having sex with me eight times was only slightly worse than sleeping with me once, so he might as well make the most of it. But he felt awful about it afterwards; really dreadful, and he pretended not to know me if we ever bumped into each other after that.'

`Why,' I said, `is life so complicated?'

`Because we make it complicated. We'd be bored rigid if we didn't.'

I looked at my watch. It was 3.30 a.m.

`Look,' I said, `if I don't get some sleep, I'm going to be shattered.'

I started to gather my important possessions – my passport, razor, a copy of *Le Grand Meaulnes* . . .

`God, this is impossible,' I told Oliver.

`Look, I'll get it all together and take it round to David's,' he told me. `Don't worry about it.'

There was so much stuff that I'd accumulated and I could only take a fraction of it with me the following day. I had a coffee table, a standard lamp, two rugs, piles of books, several ornamental pots, all my plants, bedding, modelling gear . . .

Then the phone rang. I let it ring three times so I could get over the shock of it, then picked up the receiver.

`Hello.'

`Rick, it's Andreas.'

`Andreas! What time is it with you?'

`Five thirty. Look, I'm sorry about earlier, I was irrational. I don't understand this and I don't like it, but come down tomorrow and I'll get you in the car and we can talk about it, okay? I just can't sleep, Rick, a voice keeps going on and on in my head saying that everything's been ruined by Oliver. I always knew something would happen because of him. Well, maybe it has, I don't know. Ria's been sitting up with me but she's gone to bed now. I just feel that my life has fallen apart. I know it hasn't, but that's how it feels.'

'I'm coming down tomorrow,' I said, 'nothing's changed.'

'Don't be naive. Of course things have changed. I just want to know in what way. I want to know where I stand.'

'I love you Andreas,' I said, 'that hasn't changed.'

'We're too old for this,' he said. 'Please come tomorrow. I hate myself for being so affected by this, but I need you.'

'Don't worry,' I said, 'it's alright. I'm coming.'

'I love you,' he whispered. 'Life is too short to waste time being uncertain.'

'Go to sleep,' I told him. 'I'll talk to you tomorrow. And don't worry.'

I said goodbye and replaced the receiver. Oliver was sitting cross-legged on the carpet looking suddenly happy and slightly smug, as though I was a wayward pupil who'd just learned an important lesson. He crossed to me and massaged my shoulders.

How is it, I thought, that I've found a crazy wisdom within deceit?

Also available from Millivres Books

On the Edge

Sebastian Beaumont

In this auspicious debut novel set in the north of England, nineteen year old Peter Ellis is on the edge of discovery – both about the artist father he never knew and whom his mother refuses to discuss and about the directions of his own life. Although he has had heterosexual relations with the teenaged Anna and the somewhat perverse Coll, it is with his life-long friend Martin, himself a painter of promise, that Peter seems happiest. *On the Edge* combines elements of a thriller – the mystery surrounding the life and sudden death of Peter's father – and passionate ambisextrous romance and provides an immensely readable narrative about late adolescence, sexuality and creativity.

ISBN 1-873741-00-6

`Mr Beaumont writes with assurance and perception . . . The writing is fluent and engaging and gently informative with regard to the complexities of a young man who is about to enter the world of adult men . . . '

Tom Wakefield, *Gay Times*

Summer Set

David Evans

When pop singer Ludo Morgan's elderly bulldog pursues animal portraitist Victor Burke – wearing womens' underwear beneath his leathers – to late night Hampstead Heath a whole sequence of events is set in train. Rescued by the scantily clad Nick Longingly, only son of his closest friend Kitty Llewellyn, Victor finds himself caught up in a web of emotional and physical intrigue which can only be resolved when the entire cast of this immensely diverting novel abandon London and head off for a weekend in Somerset.

`Quite simply the most delightful and appealing English gay work of fiction I've read all year . . . ' *Scene Out*
`A richly comic debut . . . ' *Capital Gay*
`Immensely entertaining . . . ' Patrick Gale, *Gay Times*

Unreal City

Neil Powell

One week in a hot August, towards the end of the Twentieth Century, the lives of four men overlap and entangle, leaving three of them permanently uprooted and changed. *Unreal City* is their story, told at different times and from their various points of view. Set partly in a London nourished by its cultural past but oppressed by its political present, and partly in coastal East Anglia, it is also the story of two older men – an elderly, long silent novelist and his retired publisher – whose past friendship and subsequent bitterness cast unexpected shadows over the four main characters. *Unreal City* is about love and loyalty, paranoia and violence, the tension of urban gay life in the century's last decade but it about much else too: the death of cities; the pubs of Suffolk; the streets of London, and the Underground – in more than one sense; Shakespeare's *Troilus and Cressida*; the consolations of music; the colour of tomatoes, and the North Sea. It is a richly allusive, intricately patterned, and at times very funny novel.

`Unreal City* is brilliant, understated, but powerful and should have a wide appeal.' *Time Out*
`Excellent. I suggest you buy it immediately.' *Gay Times*
`An excellent, extremely satisfying novel.' *The Pink Paper*